An Uncommon Folk Rhapsody

An Uncommon Folk Rhapsody

BY

C.J. HEIGELMANN

ISBN 978-0-9994898-7-1

Printed in the United States of America

Dedication

This book is dedicated to the innocent victims of violence and sexual assault who live around the world.

and

Bernice Victoria Heath

In Loving Memory

Susan Marie Jones Ebanks

Sept 9, 1968 - Dec 1, 2012

Linda Josephine Heigelmann

Sept 1, 1947 - April 18, 2013

Viventem in Sempiternum

Acknowledgements

Many thanks and much gratitude to Shaney Stewart and Geary Atkins. Their undying love, encouragement, and support helped tremendously in making this literary work come to fruition.

Foreword

Rarely does a manuscript cross my desk that is as moving and powerful as C.J. Heigelmann's *An Uncommon Folk Rhapsody*. From the onset, the reader is swept into a pulse-pounding sea voyage with the fate of a recently orphaned young Asian boy hanging in the balance, wearing a jade amulet once owned by his beloved mother, now the only link to his past. His unconventional bond with the ship's captain transforms this once timid young boy into an admirable young man and catapults him into life and death situations as he becomes a scout, fighting for the North during the height of the Civil War.

C.J. weaves an equally powerful parallel storyline as we follow a young girl ripped from her homeland in Africa and forced to endure the horrors and cruelty of a long journey aboard a slave ship set sail for the American shores. Upon arrival, she is sold into slavery and taken to a plantation in Alabama, where she must find the strength within herself to brave the new world and accept her plight in life. No longer a free child running through the plains of Africa, she is now considered livestock to do the constant bidding of her Master.

Although, the plantation owner seems kind at first, circumstances brought on during the Civil War harden his heart and the once fair man turns to cruelty and a harsh hand with his slaves.

By a chance of fate, the beautiful slave girl encounters the scout from the North and a forbidden romance is sparked. The two feel an immediate connection to one another, but the prospect of ever being together seems an impossible and dangerous dream to attain. The star-crossed lovers yearn to be with one another, but the dire circumstances of both of their situations continually prevent this from ever coming into fruition.

The dream keeps hope alive, until tragedy strikes. All hope seems lost… But through their love and their loss, hope springs eternal. The brilliantly woven canvas upon which C.J. tells his story is heartbreaking and triumphant in the same breath. Driven to tears one moment and crying out in joy the next, the reader will be forever touched by this eloquent story of love and survival amidst one of the darkest chapters in our nation's history.

I implore all of you to curl up on the couch with a warm cup of tea or a nice glass of wine, clear your mind, and escape into *An Uncommon Folk Rhapsody*.

Terrie M. Scott
Editor

Terrie M. Scott has been an Editor for over 30 years, with a MFA from the College Conservatory of Music, UC. In 2012, she produced the independent film, Through A Child's Eyes, *about domestic violence. Terrie is also a decorated United States Army veteran and an author herself.*

Preface

This literary work was inspired by true historical events and the people who participated in them during the American Civil War. While illuminating the lives of lesser known individuals and historical facts, it paints a unique and realistic picture of that tumultuous time in world history. Great care and effort was taken to ensure that every detail of speech, dialect and custom be replicated ethically and accurately. The reader is carried backward in time with each character, and into every situation which transpires, compelling them to share that character's intimate perspective of life.

Through dynamic content and multiple underwritten storylines, the reader is challenged to participate and experience the transformation of each individual. By achieving this, it provocatively invokes discussion about the noble heights and contemptible depths of humanity. It examines the human condition through the Art of Storytelling as it explores the paradigms of belief pertaining to morality, race, religion, social class, tradition, and spirituality. The reader is invited to pull back each layer and experience the full spectrum of romance, adventure, tragedy, mystery, suspense and realism. I offer this work as a positive contribution to the world.

My desire is that each reader might consider the reality that every person living in the world, regardless of ethnicity, sexual orientation, religious belief, or any other common difference, is of the same race, that being the human race. Furthermore, my hope is that we all might elevate from that understanding and become a human family. Without further delay, I humbly present to you the music of my words and the echoes of truth in *An Uncommon Folk Rhapsody*.

—C.J. Heigelmann

One

SUFFER THE LITTLE CHILDREN

In the northwest corner of the port city, on the second floor of a slum shanty, the strong winds and rain were relentless. The small boy and his mother lay beside each other, both exhausted. He was on his side with his arm across her stomach, his eyes open and staring at her. They were completely dry and his face was without notable emotion. His expression was peaceful; however, he was far from that. His previous tears had flowed in such a way, that it had washed the issue from his runny nose as he rested his head on a pillow made from an old sack. He had barely eaten any food over the last two days, save a portion of rice and fish, while his mother had not eaten in three days.

She was not long for this world and deathly ill. The exact sickness was unknown, as she had refused to call the doctors and healers, instead she slipped into a deep silence. Her condition was self-inflicted; the catalyst of her demise was caused by a broken heart. Her loss was so deep that it seemed the world had swallowed her up whole. She was sinking rapidly and had the sensation of her body being pulled down into the earth. With her last vestiges of strength, she stretched out her arms to the heavens, even to the fading light, and cried, *"Why?"*

Her husband had been everything in her life, but now he was gone. He was Chinese and employed as a *Coolie*. The Coolies were a type of indentured servant from throughout Asia; cheap labor, expendable assets, which were used along the merchant trade routes and beyond. Three months had passed since he started his journey to the island of Cuba, and the news had arrived of his death. A portion of her pain came from the constant thoughts of him. She dreamed of him, patiently awaiting his return, when in reality he had long been deceased. She was devastated. They both loved each other deeply and completely.

The moment she received word of his demise, she collapsed, in mind, body, and spirit. She wasn't previously disposed to indulge herself in spirits or herbs, but immediately immersed herself into the world of opium and alcohol. For many months, her son, Shu-Shay, sat in despair and confusion, while she became incoherent and totally neglectful in all her personal and parental responsibilities. There were other problems at hand. The landlord was owed past rent, and after confiscating all the items of value in their room, he still demanded payment. There was nothing left to give, save their sleeping mats and blankets.

Shu-Shay didn't know what else he could do, but knew crying wasn't helping, as he had already cried himself dry. He had never met any relatives, or known of their existence. The reality was that his mother had been disowned from her family and village. It was a grim repercussion of the times, dispatched by society. Her status as a Japanese woman living with and bearing a child from a Chinese man was looked down upon, and he being a *Coolie* was a social disgrace to many Japanese and Chinese alike. These mixed marriages were generally despised by the opposing cultures, with the exception being the wealthy, whose class and station imparted them such social pardons. Even Shu-Shay was affected, as he was constantly beaten and tormented by the local youths for being, in their eyes, a "half breed."

His mother lay beside him, burning with fever, quiet for hours. Suddenly she started breathing faster, but with shorter breaths as if she could not get enough air, moaning and grunting.

"Momma?" Shay called to her softly, in his native Cantonese. He lifted up his head, propping himself halfway up with his other arm.

"Momma! What to do, Momma?" he pleaded, hoping his mother would utter just one word, as he missed hearing her voice. The wind continued to bellow and howl as if speaking some primordial language of nature. The whole structure shook and vibrated from the power of the storm.

"Shu-Shay," she spoke in a barely audible tone.

"Momma…Momma, what to do?" his face crinkled up, about to sob.

"Take it," she mumbled.

"What, Momma?"

She brought her left hand slowly up to her waist, then to her stomach with great effort and difficulty. Her fingers clawed their way up her chest, toward her neck line.

Shu-Shay dropped on his knees and put his hand on top of hers while he reached under the neckline of her garment. There he found her jade amulet, which had been given to her by his father. He had forgotten that she still had it, assuming the slumlord had taken it long ago. He held it and stared at it momentarily. It was beautiful and majestic. After having it within his grasp, Shu-Shay briefly experienced a sense of fleeting hope for some inexplicable reason.

"Take," she said with her lungs full of fluid, trying to cough with no success.

He gently removed it from his mother's neck and put it on around his. He felt terrible, as if by accepting her last possession he was also taking her hope as well.

"Shu-Shay…so sorry," she uttered.

He was confused and perplexed by her words. Why was she sorry? Why? Shay had a sense of unwarranted guilt, even remorse. He saw himself as puny, small and weak. He could not help his mother in any way. He could not bring food and he could not heal her. He could not even protect her, nor could he protect himself.

"I'm sorry, Momma!" he said, with water welling up in his eyes.

She was trying to speak, but he could not hear her words. He put his ear close to her mouth. He heard her faintly.

"Water," she whispered, breathing rapidly. He looked around the room for the cup. Had the slumlord taken that, also? He wondered. He saw the wooden cup and knew he would have to leave the room to get the water, which he didn't want to, not even for a moment.

"Yes, Momma," he answered, and got himself up. He was dizzy as he stood up. His small frail bones were stiff from hours of lying next to her. His movements resembled that of an old frail man. He hobbled out of the room to fetch the water, and as he closed the door, he turned back to look at her. Her eyes were closed and her mouth was open. He shut the door, and walked to the top of the stairs, where he suddenly stopped. Wung, the landlord, was at the end of the hall, staring at him. How long had been standing there? What was he waiting for? Shu-Shay glanced at him for a moment and then walked down to the first floor, leaving out the back door to get water.

———————

"We are ten miles out from mainland China, at the Port of Canton, Captain," the First Mate, Mr. Higgins, reported.

"The storm looks to be about eight hours out sir, bearing the same and still heading inland. What are your orders Captain?"

Higgins asked as he stood at attention. They had sailed together for the past ten years, since the year 1842.

Captain Price sat back in his chair, relieving himself of his magnifying glass and manifest documents. He dug through his bushy beard with his fingers, until he reached the skin and that annoying itch, which evidently was caused by some godforsaken insect, origin and whereabouts unknown. Captain Price looked up at Higgins.

"Very well, Mr. Higgins, make all the arrangements which we discussed in great detail last evening, with one addition: inform the men that there will be no shore liberty today. We must deliver this cargo as expeditiously as possible. Again, we have six hours after setting anchor before we must depart and hope to God that we make thirty nautical miles southwest of this beast. If so, we can ride the outer rim of the storm and quicken our trip back to San Francisco."

"Aye, aye, Captain. And will you be finding the three men to supplement the crew?"

"Yes indeed. I intend to have two of the crew accompany me, lest on my last voyage I fall victim to ill fortune at the hands of thieves and murderers; the sort of scum who seem to grow and flourish in this part of the world. Yes, make ready and send two of our most capable. Have them fitted with sidearm and blade."

"Yes, Captain."

"Higgins, make no mistake about our predicament. We find ourselves in a dire straight and maybe in jeopardy of life, which is everything to *us,* if we do not depart this place within eight hours. If we stay at dock and try to endure this storm, the vessel will most likely suffer heavy damage, and the repairs, if even possible, will be time consuming and very costly. Perhaps even the mutiny of half the crew. We must leave on time. Whatever you need to do in order to motivate the crew to accomplish our turnaround, you must do! I will not be available for the duration due to this matter, and my usual presence will not be of assistance to you in providing the usual motivation this crew seems to require at times. In addition to the fact that port liberty will not be given, the ill temperament of some will no doubt permeate to the rest. Keep an open and watchful eye for agitators. Threaten a reduction in rations and half pay for our remaining voyage to 'Frisco at the first sign of even subtle discontent, as that should suffice."

"Aye, aye, Captain sir. The vessel *will* be ready as you have ordered."

"Very good, Higgins, make ready. That will be all." As Higgins left and closed the cabin door behind him, Captain Price let out a deep breath. He seemed troubled by the predicament he found himself in, but he was optimistic that they would meet the time, providing the storm did not increase in speed. He had been a seaman since twenty-two years of age, and through attrition and his estranged father's influence combined, he had attained the station of captain by age forty. He was now at fifty-five years of age, and ready to resign his commission.

His plan was to go back to Connecticut and settle near his childhood home. He wanted all of them to see how successful and prosperous he had become. He chuckled to himself as he thought about the chances and probabilities of a bastard son of a Jewish merchant becoming a captain. His mother was a common woman, a tailor by occupation and resided in East Haddam, Connecticut. Price did not know how they met each other, but he did know that Noah Samuel was his father. He was a wealthy Jewish merchant who was married and had two daughters. Notwithstanding those facts, he had great affection for the captain's mother, regardless of the discreet arrangements they had to make in order to continue their relationship, and despite how some folk in the community felt.

He considered them ill-willed, self-righteous bastards. They showed great amusement in illuminating any perceived flaw in one's character or circumstance. They were relentless with their gossip. It had also been rumored that Noah considered Caleb's mother to be his one and only *concubine*. His father evidently ascribed to the ancient practice indulged in by some of the biblical Jewish Patriarchs. This belief had often irritated a young Caleb, but not his mother, who evidently was endeared to Noah, even allowing him to have the liberty of naming his newborn illegitimate son.

Caleb Price was supported financially by his father for the most part but was rarely given an audience with him. It was a well understood necessary discretion, particularly to protect his father's reputation. That being the case, his father's support and clandestine patronage was much appreciated. Ms. Price was a goddess in his eyes, howbeit a goddess that worked from dusk until dawn in order to supplement the patronage received from Noah, but more so to supplement her dignity and self-respect.

The captain reminisced about the early days at Port Hartford on the docks and his employment being arranged at the very *word* of Noah Samuels. He often reflected on the joy he experienced from being able to support his mother. His thoughts detained briefly on the second voyage he embarked on, from Savannah to West Africa. It was also funded by his father and now just a blur to him. The ordeal, the stench and horror of it all forced him to pause in thought, seemingly lost in time. He stood up slowly.

"Damn it," he whispered above a hair's breadth. He had tried many times to put the ordeal behind him, but now he was having difficulty. Captain Price needed a clear mind on this day, with no unnecessary distractions. Once again, he breathed deeply and hardened himself. He was ready for the task at hand and he encouraged himself, as he had done throughout his life. He had no illusions about the situation. He knew that he was in a struggle for his life and that of his crew. Losing a member of his crew was simply unacceptable, that was always his conviction.

The winds had increased, and likewise the surf, as a light rain fell. Captain Price chose Manu and Tullo to accompany him, and as they each rowed together in unison they took in the view of the port. They had frequented it several times before, but never in this rough weather. There were no ships docked, which was understandable considering the conditions. Small vessels were scurrying to shore in hopes of securing their crafts on land. Tullo briefly locked eyes with Manu at one point, while seated in front of the captain. Price could discern the visual exchange between the men, which contained worry, and possibly fear.

As the craft approached the beach and was secured, Captain Price stepped out onto the beach, and into a foot of water as he made landfall. He turned and instructed the crew.

"Gentlemen, remain five paces behind me and no more. Your charge is to be alert, watchful, and ready. Let us make way," he ordered.

"Aye, aye, Captain sir!" they chimed nearly in unison. They both were hoping that Captain Price might be delayed an hour or so during the impending negotiations, which would be enough time for them to have brief sexual relations from a prostitute, choosing from the hundreds of who resided in and around the port.

Even during a typhoon the commerce of prostitution showed no trepidation of nature's fury, as coin and sexual satisfaction would be exchanged, as it had been since the dawn of mankind. Captain Price could read their visage and knew their thoughts. At times he also indulged himself with the temporary warmth of a woman, to ward off the disparity of loneliness.

They made their way off the beach and headed toward the main thoroughfare and traveled north near the Great Statue of Buddha. There was a brothel to the left, where the local *Co Hong* resided for business and pleasure. The *Co Hong* were specially designated Chinese agents through whom all foreign trade was conducted. After the end of the First Opium War six years prior, these intermediaries transacted all port affairs. Captain Price's primary objective was the attaining of three fit men who were seaworthy, to replace the three which were lost within the past two months. One man had fallen overboard during a storm and the others had either deserted or became casualties at the port in Siam.

With the typhoon making landfall, he knew that there would be difficulties in attaining proper seamen. Who would risk joining the expedition during these conditions? He could find several drunken sailors to sign on, but he could not determine their fitness under inebriation. He did not care to hire second rate crew hands in general, and especially not on his last expedition.

The idea of transferring the vessel over to the oncoming captain in that manner did not please him. He ascribed to the ancient precept: "*Do unto the stranger as thou would have done to thee,*" which he practiced with regularity, making a conscious effort. He was determined to attain satisfactory replacements.

As they continued along, they witnessed the local folk scurrying in all directions. Everyone sensed the tension and distress in the air. The crudely made shanty structures loomed over the thoroughfare as the sky appeared to darken within a few blinks of an eye. The once steady wind gusted at regular intervals while making crude sounds as it whistled through the small alleyways. While the men pressed forward, lightning touched the earth and thunder followed.

Shu-Shay finally was able to close the door, despite the powerful winds which resisted him. He was soaked, cold, and trembling. He slowly walked up the stairs with the wooden cup in his hand, shaking, and trying to save every drop of water for his mother. He entered the room, and without closing the door, he walked directly to her. He knelt down beside her and brought the cup to her lips.

"Momma, drink," he said almost happily, in being able to provide her some relief. He poured out a little into her open mouth. She did not swallow. He slid his hand under her head in order to prop it up and give her more. That's when he noticed she was not breathing. Her chest was not moving. He stared at her. An emotion started to rise deep within him. It grew stronger until he could no longer contain it. He cried out loud.

"Momma!" He dropped the cup, fell on her chest, and held her. Shu-Shay ran his fingers through her hair and kept calling for her as he wept.

Several minutes later, Wung, the landlord, walked into the room. In his native tongue he addressed Shu-Shay.

"Your mother and father are gone," he paused. "Life is hard. Your tears will not help you in life, so stop crying. She owes money, and now you owe money. Can you pay me?"

Shu-Shay sat and remained silent. Wung's words fell on him as inaudible sounds. He heard them but did not acknowledge them.

"If you cannot pay, you will work for me. You will do as I say, for as long as I say until your mother's debt is paid in full." Wung waited for a response. There was none.

"Do you understand me?" He noticed the jade amulet around Shu-Shay's neck. He walked directly over and stopped. He looked down at him, as a predator would, ready to overtake his prey. Shu-Shay glanced up at him before looking back down to the floor. Then, without warning, Wung snatched the amulet from his neck.

"She hid this from me! I wondered where she had hidden it!" Wung held it toward the candle and marveled at it, as he had never seen one quite like it before. He smiled for a moment and then he returned to his normal demeanor, a bitter bully by nature and a very brutal man. "This is a small start to repay your debt!" he shouted. "Tomorrow, I will have her body collected and take you to a certain man. You will obey him!"

From deep inside Shu-Shay, a wave of anger poured over him. He jumped up and grabbed Wung's hands, trying to pry the jade amulet away. Wung, being much larger than him, stood still and towered over the youth. As Shu-Shay struggled with all his might, pulling and prying at his hands, Wung started to smile.

All at once, his demeanor changed, and his smile turned into a snarl. Wung turned and struck him with the back of his hand, on his temple. He fell to the floor and, while he was dazed and semi-conscious, Wung began to search the room for anything of value.

————————

"This is the third damn brothel, Chan! We need one more man, now! Not later!" Captain Price bellowed. His face was red, puffed with anger. Manu and Tullo were agitated as well. Their libidos having been deflated by the increasing bad weather, they were eager to make way back to the ship. Two new crew members stood behind them in eager silence.

"Not Chan problem! Chinese no want work for captain in storm! Chinese no stupid! Chan find captain these sailors, is very hard for Chan!" he replied. He was the only *Co Hong* engaged in business this night.

The captain pulled off his hat and ran his fingers through his hair. "Can you get me at least one more man within the half hour?"

Chan paused and looked down, he made a low guttural sound as if within deep meditation. The captain's eyes were fixated on him. "Come, follow Chan!" He turned and immediately headed for the door. Captain Price and his men followed behind as they exited the brothel and walked out into the storm. They made their way through the maze of shanties to the northwest section of the port, as Chan led them into a building and up onto the second floor.

"Wung! Wung!" Chan called out to him from down the hallway. Wung rushed out into the hallway and looked both ways. He saw his employer, the building owner, coming up the stairs. It was Master Chan, with five men, one of them a white man.

"Yes, Master Chan," Wung replied with due diligence in the Cantonese dialect, his tone reflected his station.

"Is that Coolie here, by any chance? I have employers that need a deck hand immediately."

"Master Chan, he is no longer! Word was received months ago of his death. In fact, his widow has just expired this night. I will have her body removed in the morning."

Chan seemed shocked at this news. "I demand the room be rented as soon as possible! How did the woman expire?" he asked.

"Spirits and opium. After receiving news of her husband's death, she killed herself."

"So, am I to understand that she paid her rent in full, while being a slave to opium and spirits? *Well?*" Chan shouted.

"Master Chan, I collected all that was of value. I have her son now, and he will work for you until the debt is completely paid, I can assure you," Wung responded.

The new deck hands were able to understand the conversation, but the captain and crew were oblivious. It was all gibberish to them. The men deduced the subject of discussion by measuring each man's mannerisms and reactions. Suddenly, the captain heard a sound which alerted him. It seemed out of place for the situation. It sounded like a boy crying. Captain Price dismissed it.

Chan began to chastise Wung, "You fool! I require money, not the labor of a boy! Now months behind in payment, who will make restitution? You will! That's who!" Chan shouted as Wung held his head down.

The captain heard sobbing again, but this time he could tell it was coming from the room behind Wung. As if drawn to the sound, Captain Price walked directly toward the room, followed by Manu and Tullo, while the other men conversed. Price was filled with angst, and the sobbing of the child perpetuated the feeling. The sound of children crying was distressing to him. He surprised Wung as he walked past him, and Wung made the mistake of grabbing the captain's arm.

Both Manu and Tullo reacted immediately and in unison. Manu wrapped his thick arm around Wung's neck, and arching backward lifted him off the ground, while Tullo came out and up with his blade, placing the tip under the left side of Wung's sternum. Chan's mouth opened wide in shock. Captain Price turned his head left, and assuming that Wung had handled him, looked in Wung's eyes. He had both of his hands on Manu's forearm, with his feet off the floor, helpless. Manu and Tullo both were resolute and looking at Price for his next command.

"Release him," he ordered while entering the room. At once, they released Wung who stepped back behind Chan. Price could smell the stench of urine and excrement fall upon him. That smell always reminded him of death, although different than the smell of decay. He saw the woman first. Mouth open, eyes shut, with her arms spread wide at her sides. He knew she was deceased. Then Captain Price noticed a boy in the corner, apparently crying over the death of his mother. Price was stunned at the sight. He had seen men killed dead and dying before, but the sight of the dead young woman in bed with her young son in despair was all very sobering. He felt the presence of death in the place, knew it was time to leave, and wondered why he was risking the lives of his crew and vessel to remain here any longer.

"What the hell is going on here Chan?" Price roared. "Where is the man you promised?"

Chan seemed unnerved at the show of force by the bodyguards and responded in a moderate tone. "The man now dead. His wife dead, too. The boy work for Chan now. If captain want, you pay Chan one silver liang, and take boy for ship. He become Coolie, like father."

"What can I do with him you idiot? I need a proven seaman! Good day, Chan!" Captain Price yelled, as he turned to exit the room. As he did, he caught the boy's eyes, which had stopped crying and had a different expression upon his face altogether.

"Let us make haste, gentlemen!" he ordered his crew. He was aware that time was essential, but he sensed that he was leaving something undone. Regardless, they needed to press on. He marched down the hall with his men following. As they walked to the stairway, Captain Price heard Wung shouting in Cantonese. He could hear a slap, followed by the boy crying again. When he reached the stairs he stood still, and the crew stopped as well. Price paused and breathed deeply, preparing for what he was about to do.

He turned about, walking between his men and back to the room. He entered the doorway with the crew behind him and saw Chan as he stood with his back to him. Wung was standing over Shu-Shay and delivering punishment. Price was infuriated. His initial impulse was to kill Wung, but then reasoned that he would have to order Chan's death as well. He further deduced that despite this storm, they could be successful in making the row boat and the ship within an hour. There were no other witnesses, save the new crew, who would definitely not show any dissent. Ultimately, he knew these actions and impulses could not be executed, no matter how angry he had become. He remembered the scriptures, and was grounded in the great commandment *"Thou shalt not murder."*

He grabbed Chan by the shoulders and pushed him out of the way, then snatched Wung by his long hair braid and pulled his head backward, forcing him to kneel. Captain Price balled up his right hand as he looked at the helpless man and struck him once between his eyes with a powerful blow. At once, Wung's body fell limp, dropping backward to the floor. Manu and Tullo sprang into action, cornering the only adversary left standing, Chan.

"You! Seku! You speak good English, come here and translate for me!" Captain Price ordered.

"Aye, aye, Captain!" the new hire responded.

Captain Price walked over to Shu-Shay and got down on one knee. The boy was scared and at the point of panic. Price spoke to him, pausing as Seku translated.

"My name is Price. Captain Price. What is your name?" Price asked calmly, as Shu-Shay stared at him, and then at Seku, who began to translate.

"Shu-Shay," he responded in a quiet voice.

"Well, Shu-Shay, first I want to say I am sorry about your mother, bless her soul. I'm sorry your father has passed on as well. To be direct, you have two choices: you can stay here and work for this man lying on the floor and Mr. Chan, or you may come with us aboard a big ship and work for yourself with other men. The work is hard and sometimes dangerous, but I can promise you that aboard my vessel you will be treated fairly and never unjustly punished, as this man has done to you. What I tell you is the truth. Now, it's time for you to make a choice. I have to know your answer at once because we must leave now."

Shu-Shay looked up at him. Price's white beard and blue eyes were so strange to him. He had not seen one of these *white* men up this close. Captain Price had stopped Wung from beating him, which is what Shu-Shay wished he could have done for himself. He looked at Chan, who had an expression of terror on his face, while the two men stood against him with their blades drawn. He then looked at Seku and the other men. Seku nodded his head and encouraged him.

"You should come with us. Your mother is no longer in that body, but you will see her again one day. She shall live once more, so don't worry."

Shu-Shay stared at Seku and then glanced at his mother's corpse for a moment. He nodded and stood up.

"Manu, give Chan one silver liang," Price ordered, "Seku, assist the boy, we must get to the beach! We move now!"

They hurried out of the room. Manu tossed the silver to Chan, and Seku led Shay by the hand. As they exited, Shu-Shay pulled away from Seku and ran back into the room. He stood over Wung, who had blood running down his forehead. He frantically searched Wung's pockets.

Seku came in the room and shouted at him.

"Boy! What are you doing!?" Captain Price called out from the hallway. "Seku! What is going on?"

Shu-Shay stood up and turned around, placing the amulet around his neck.

"On the way, Captain! Right away, sir!" he answered.

Shay ran up to Seku and turned one last time to look at his mother before locking hands with him as they made their exit into the hallway and down the stairs.

————————

Two hours had passed, since the storm had reached landfall, and it began to slow. All the fury of Mother Nature was manifest, as the might of the wind made walking upright nearly impossible. Manu and Tullo now led the group forward, while debris of all sorts whipped past the men. They attempted to run toward the ship, but their progress reduced to a brisk walk due to the unforgiving gale force winds. As they came down the main thoroughfare, which descended to the beach, the entire harbor was in sight. There were no small vessels in the water, and no sign of people. The storm had blotted out the sun, and the sky looked as if it were dusk, as it became very dark. The lightning periodically illuminated the landscape and the ocean.

Then she showed herself, the *Rainbow*. She had anchored with her sails down, but still heeling and listing heavily from the wind and waves. As they hurried along, their heads were down but Captain Price caught site of the ship's present condition and the direction of the winds. A spark of hope brought him added fortitude, which grew inside him, as he saw an opportunity. It was a reprieve and a blessing, no doubt from the Almighty. The outer winds of the storm were blowing parallel to the coast for the time being.

He immediately deduced that if these winds would hold their course, they might have a good chance of setting sail and riding the winds out from the coast, eventually cutting through. It would be difficult and dangerous, but the high winds could catapult the vessel, which would allow them to cover more nautical miles than without. He would rather it be without.

Captain Price wholeheartedly accepted responsibility during these desperate, critical moments, which might have humbled a younger captain, but he breathed confidence. He believed it was his destiny to overcome these harrowing situations.

The group arrived at the beach and saw a lone crew member standing on the beach with a lantern in his hand, guarding the rowboat.

"Captain!" the mate shouted. He was standing a hundred paces from them, and he saw them approaching without a lantern.

Captain Price interpreted the man's cry as one of desperation and hope and knew that the rest of his crew shared the same sentiment. The men onboard the ship were no doubt even more desperate, since they were on board a potential tomb. The group continued to press their way forward and finally arrived at the craft.

"Captain! Thank God! Thank God!" the sentry shouted.

"Is our transfer complete?" Price shouted over the storm.

"Aye, aye, Captain! Yes, sir!" the mate responded with fervor.

Captain Price and Shu-Shay climbed into the boat, as the rest of the men pushed the vessel into the water and jumped inside. They grabbed oar, and rowed as if their lives depended on it, which it did.

The captain and young Shu-Shay were in the middle of the craft, with Shu-Shay seated on the floor of the boat between his legs, as he held on tightly. The waves crashed on them immediately and were unrelenting in their assault.

Shu-Shay was terrified. He had no choice but to trust his life to these men and sat in quiet desperation. The rest of the men, however, were focused. They had seen storms and rough seas numerous times, and they knew what they must do to survive. They were not heroes, but they were brave. They were hardened, seaworthy veterans, seasoned, as it were, with strong nerve. Shu-Shay heard them rowing to a rhythm and count, almost a chant. In fact, they were cursing the storm, showing disdain and contempt for it, as if it were the manifestation of the Devil himself come to take their lives. As they approached the ship the crew lowered a rope ladder along with the other two ropes. They rowed close to the ship but tried to keep space so they would not be beat upon it and scuttle. They lowered the ropes in order to raise the boat, but now they used them to lift Shu-Shay. Seku secured a rope around his waist, and the other he instructed him to hold tightly. The deck hands were looking overboard and were astonished to see the boy brought aboard.

"Heave!" shouted Higgins at the top of his lungs, while Captain Price climbed the ladder carefully, as the wind continually beat him against the ship. The crew hoisted the boy and untied the rope, immediately casting the ropes back down to the landing craft.

As the men helped Captain Price aboard, Mr. Higgins stood before him.

"Captain! Our business is complete, and we are ready to lift anchor!" Higgins shouted.

"Very good, Mr. Higgins! Have Seku place the boy in my cabin, and prepare the crew to raise anchor and set sail as soon as everyone gets aboard! We will head south! I will take the helm!"

"Aye, aye, Captain!" Higgins responded, and was relieved that the captain was taking command. Higgins maintained his post until Seku came aboard, and then informed him of his orders, which Seku then carried out with a sense of dire urgency.

The crew was in action, climbing the masts and preparing to raise the anchor at the critical time. Either the anchor raised too soon, or the sails prematurely set could cause catastrophe. The final order would have to be given by the captain. Captain Price grasped the wheel and took command of the helm. The winds and rain furiously pelted him. He took notice of all the events transpiring through his muddled and water-logged eyes. Everyone was in position waiting, with the exception of the men hoisting up the lifeboat. They had not gotten the craft halfway up the hull of the ship when the clipper heeled back and forth and continuously slammed the boat into the ship's side. This made the hoisting much harder and a monumental task. Captain Price had to make a decision swiftly. They could not delay any longer, and the small boat was not a priority at this point

"Scuttle the boat, now!" Captain Price shouted. "Lower all sails full and by! Then recover and brace yourselves, men!" As the square-rigged sails were lowered, the full force of the wind took hold of the ship, turning it fifty-five degrees, and away from the south shoreline, bringing her parallel with the coastline.

"Raise anchor!" Price shouted.

A few moments later, as the ship was loosed from its shackle, it propelled forward at an amazing speed. No longer heeling badly, it still listed heavily. The fast-medium clipper stayed true to its name and design, cutting through the rough waters. Captain Price fought the wheel with all his might, to subdue it and bring the vessel under his will, as if it were a wild stallion being broken for the first time. The men had come down off the masts, and had secured their stations, with most of them going below deck. The ship streaked through the stormy bay and headed down the coastline to calmer seas. The winds were picking up and the ocean swells had risen, slowing the speed of the ship, as well as forcing ferocious waves to bombard the topside. Mr. Higgins stood by the helm, surveying the conditions, at the ready.

"How are the masts holding?" Captain Price asked.

"All is well, Captain!" he shouted back.

"It looks that we shall make it past this beast!" Price shouted with emotion. He wanted to give Higgins some encouragement, perhaps even some inspiration, to strengthen the First Mate, who in turn would strengthen the crew. Captain Price believed in the unity of all, in the endeavor of one common purpose. It was the closest thing to true family he had ever known, and he craved their solidarity. Not just these men, but also every crew which he had sailed with from his youth. He might have despised or befriended some, notwithstanding they all had to work together in order to survive, and hopefully to do much more, even to thrive. He knew that good or bad tidings of any kind aboard an isolated vessel would spread like a plague. Price brought these lessons with him through life and regularly applied them, and he hoped that Mr. Higgins might do the same.

"We will maintain this heading as we come out of her grip! I will plot our course soon after!"

"Aye, aye, Captain!" responded Higgins, who looking away, parting his lips with a tempered smile.

Meanwhile Shu-Shay lay on the floor of the captain's quarters, holding onto a foot post of the bed, cold, hungry, and sea sick. The healing and listing of the ship made him nauseously ill. The foot post became his anchor, without which he would easily find himself rolling the measure of the room. He could not vomit because he had no contents to dispel, and had to be content with being nauseated, starving, and dehydrated. He thought about his mother. He could not truly fathom that she was gone.

For a moment, he thought that maybe she was still alive. That hope fleeted as quickly as it appeared, and dread began to set in. He opened his eyes to see the room spinning. Along with the noise and the arbitrary motion of the vessel, his senses were numb. He started to panic, and the fear inside him grew uncontrollably. It was as though the ship was turning upside down, with him inside this small room. He did not want to be alone and drown in this small room. His parents were dead, and he believed that this was his end, to die like his father at sea. Still, he would not let himself drown in this small room alone. Immediately he let go of the foot post and started crawling to the spinning door. The ship listed and healed, and so did Shu-Shay, who rolled into a desk and then into the wall.

Once he located the door again, he crawled with more determination. Approaching it, he grabbed hold of its latch and pulled himself up while his legs were buckling. As he opened the door, the ship again listed suddenly, sending Shu-Shay sliding out of the captain's quarters. He found himself holding on to the door latch, which had become his anchor of salvation. In the next moment, a wave crashed down upon the entire vessel and that salvation was now gone, and so was Shu-Shay. He had washed across the deck and now lay helpless and barely conscious against the rail.

He was below the helm, port side, unknown to all except Mr. Higgins, who was the first to recover from the wave.

"Captain! Port side! The boy is on deck!" Higgins yelled, as he made his way to Shu-Shay. He stopped short and held fast as the vessel listed again and descended. This was a precursor to another large incoming wave. Higgins quickly braced himself as the wave crashed on deck and dissipated. Captain Price and Higgins looked around for the boy, who they located closer to the stern.

"Take the helm! I will recover him!" Captain Price ordered. They swapped positions at the helm, as Price quickly made his way down the steps toward Shu-Shay. The ship then heeled and listed heavily again. Captain Price made a dash toward Shu-Shay without hesitation, and as he lunged forward he grasped the railing supports firmly. He pulled them both together tightly, and he secured them to the rail of the vessel. The next wave pounded them again and dissipated. Captain Price moved into a crouching position and held him by his ankle. He moved forward, pulling Shu-Shay over the watery deck, and directly to his quarters under the helm. He entered the room and picked up Shu-Shay, laying him across his bed. He went back to the open door, and, bracing himself in the doorway, he called out to Higgins.

"Higgins! Summon second mate Swanson to the helm! Have the new hand called Seku report to my quarters now!"

"Aye, aye, Captain!" Price heard him sound off fairly, with no noticeable panic in his voice. He closed the door and sat down next to the boy, assaying his condition. The lantern light was dimming and needed to be replenished with oil. He would have Seku perform that task and explain his reason for leaving the boy unattended when he orders were given to take the boy to the cabin.

Shu-Shay looked lifeless, but he was breathing. Price finally got a look at this lad close-up in detail. He had some minor cuts and bruises, especially on his knees. He pressed on the boy's ribcage, as well as his stomach, and then moved up to his head while trying to determine if any indention was present on his skull. He listened for any indications of pain from the limp boy. As he moved along his head, Shu-Shay released a low moan. Price pressed the area a little harder, and he moaned again, in a higher pitch.

"You almost got yourself killed boy. Why in the world would you walk out on deck in this fury?" He spoke rhetorically, in a gentle but firm voice. He did not ask the boy expecting an answer, knowing full well the boy spoke no English. He would have to wait for Seku to report and to translate any responses from the lad. Captain Price stood up, keeping his bearings and moving with the motion of ship, retrieved a secondary blanket from the small dresser mounted against the wall. He laid it over Shu-Shay and tucked it under his legs, the sides closing any opening for the cold air to enter. He looked at him in the flickering lamp light. He began to ponder his decision. Why had he brought this child aboard? He risked this boy's life in the interim, and for what? He was consoled with the knowledge that the boy was now in a better place.

After a few moments of reflection, Captain Price convinced himself that the right decision had been made. Although he was a man moved by his passions, the end did justify the means. To Price, the boy had a chance to live and grow into a man. He knew that life could be unforgiving, and usually was, but help at a crucial time could make a world of difference, if the recipient made proper use of it.

While they sat, Captain Price noticed that the frequency of large waves was decreasing, along with the instability of the ship. He was confident that all was well and believed that they had escaped from the worst of the storm.

There was a knock at the door.

"Come in!" Captain Price shouted.

It was Seku, who entered, securing the door behind him. Standing tall, cold and soaked, he reported.

"Yes, Captain, reporting as ordered, sir," he replied.

"Why in the hell were you not here with the boy? You were given simple orders to take the boy to my cabin, were you not?" Price inquired sternly. "The lad wandered out of this room and was nearly washed overboard! Mind your words in response. Now I require answers, Mr. Seku."

"Captain Sir, I brought the boy to the room as Higgins ordered. Tullo then told me to come with him and secure the foremast ropes. I placed the boy in here safe." After a moment, Captain Price looked away and to the boy. Seku had performed correctly in the captain's estimation, and Price knew he would have acted with the same prudence.

"Very well, Mr. Seku, your answer is acceptable. I will need you to perform special duties for me. The boy must learn to speak and understand English, to some degree. After he fully recovers, he will be your shadow while you perform your duties. Also, teach him about the vessel. You will be solely responsible for his wellbeing and care. During the interim, the boy will sleep in my cabin, so I need you to prepare a pallet with blanket and pillow. Do you understand?"

"Aye, aye, Captain." The Captain stood up slowly and continued his instructions.

"Also, please refill my lantern, and get the boy some soup from the galley and some water from the scuttle bucket. He is malnourished but needs water first. Hopefully, he will not take to fever. The morning will tell us more of his condition. You are dismissed, and thank you, Mr. Seku."

"Aye, aye, sir." Seku responded, briefly looking at Shu-Shay, as he left the cabin.

Captain Price walked to his desk and sat down at his chair. He reached into the lower right-hand drawer and brought forth a flask of his favorite spirit, brandy. He took out a small cup and poured himself a drink, and after that, another. He held the glass on his chest as he took his hat off and stared at Shu-Shay. He took a long, deep breath and exhaled as he looked at the boy in his bed. He shook his head, smiled softly, and chuckled to himself.

Two

TRUE RELIGION

It was morning, and as a ray of light shone through the sole round window in the Captain's quarters, Shu-Shay opened his eyes. The ship no longer tossed violently as before, and the wind had ceased howling; all was calm. The smell of fresh ocean air permeated the room, and the call of the seagulls outside echoed. He looked around and slowly sat up. His last recollection was of sleeping on the bed. Now he found himself on the floor, laying on a makeshift pallet of bedding.

Though it was comfortable, he did not know how he got there or who put him there. He remembered a man called "Seku," who had given him food and water. He recalled the man feeding him because he was too weak and battered to feed himself. He was hungry, and his entire body was very sore, feeling like the beatings he received from the local bullies. His thoughts turned to his mother as he stared at the light shining through the window. He was very sad, isolated, and alone. He began to frown, and he prepared for the inevitable emotion building up, and the sobbing that would soon follow.

As tears welled up in his eyes, he blinked as they poured down his cheeks. He cried quietly but made an effort to restrain his sadness. He did not know why he was trying to quell his grief.

After a short while, and just as suddenly as he fell into despair, his demeanor changed. Quickly he dried his face and wiped his runny nose with his hand. He was wary that someone might see him weeping. His stomach was cramping and he felt sick, so he thought to search for Seku or the captain. He stood up, barefoot and clothed only with his loincloth. As he took a step, there was a noise at his feet as he moved. He looked down and saw a small bell tied to his left ankle with a piece of ribbon. Wondering how it got there, he knelt down to untie the knot. After a few minutes of struggling unsuccessfully, his hunger and weakness grew in intensity, so he abandoned the endeavor and made his way to the cabin door.

He was full of trepidation from his last experience of opening it. He put his ear to it, this time listening for any commotion on the other side. He heard the faint sounds of men speaking and someone whistling a melody. He cautiously opened the door and suddenly felt it pull away from his grasp. He was startled and let go of the handle. He slipped as he turned to scamper back into the room and found himself on his stomach. He faced toward the doorway and tried to crawl into the sanctuary of the quarters. Seku stood on deck outside, laughing. Seku addressed Shu-Shay in Cantonese.

"Ah, boy! I see you are a fast learner, good! I heard the bell and knew you were awake and moving." Seku helped him to stand and knelt down to undo the knot.

"Since you are now my responsibility by the Captain's orders, I had to keep an ear on you while I was working and you were sleep." He looked up at Shu-Shay, who stared down at him and nodded. "Looks like you almost loosened it. I bet you never saw a knot like this, eh?"

Shu-Shay shook his head.

"Well, this is a Prussic knot. I will teach you to make this and others." He removed the ribbon and bell from Shu-Shay's ankle. "I will also teach you English as best I can. Captain Price has instructed me to do this too."

Shu-Shay looked up at Seku, eyebrows raised with a troubled expression.

"Speak, boy, you are not a mute," he demanded. "What is wrong?"

"Sir, I am hungry. Please, may I have more food and water?" Shu-Shay humbly asked.

"I knew you would be hungry by now," Seku responded as he attempted to place his hand on Shu-Shay's forehead, to inspect him for fever. Shu-Shay reacted at once, covering his head with his hands, thus protecting himself. Seku halted in amazement at the boy's reaction and spoke in a calm voice.

"Shu-Shay, I am not going to hurt you. Let me check you and do not be so fearful." Seku checked his forehead for signs and found none. "You have no fever, so no more broth for you. You are able to eat fish and even hard tack, that is if your teeth can cut through it!" Seku said, as he chuckled. "Come, follow me to the galley. Stay close at all times to me and don't wander off from my side."

As he started walking, Shu-Shay came out of the room onto the deck. The sun was in full glory, and so bright that he had to squint and shade his eyes. The skies were a soft blue and, looking around, he noticed there was no land in sight. It seemed he was in another world altogether. Seku stopped to give him a moment to survey his new surroundings. Shu-Shay saw men moving about everywhere and doing different things. Many were working with hammers, and others looked as if they were sewing on the sails. Several men were on their knees scrubbing with brushes. There was a constant breeze, and as he looked up, he marveled at the towering masts of the ship and at the men who sat atop them! Wonder and amazement filled him as Seku watched him with a grin.

"Come on now, cow eyes," Seku told him as he caught hold of Shu-Shay by the hand to lead him away. He briefly saw Captain Price, who was at the helm of the ship, with his eyes fixed on him. The large white man with the bushy, white beard and blue eyes wore a happy expression on his face. He stood stoically, holding the great wheel and moving fluidly with the motion of the vessel. Captain Price winked an eye at him. Shu-Shay wanted to wave at the Captain, but he did not know if he should, so he declined.

Seku led him to the galley, where he seated him. He left and returned with water, dried fish, and very hard, stale bread. Shu-Shay did not take long in devouring the food. Seku was amazed at the young lad's ravenous appetite. He finished the portions, but wanted more. As he looked at Seku and then the empty plate, his eyes advocated a silent plea. Seku understood.

"If you were well, you would not receive more rations during this sitting, but Captain Price ordered me to see that you become healthy and strong, so I will give you a little more. I notice you eat quickly, so quick that your stomach does not believe you have eaten anything. Wait a while before having another portion. Now listen to me and remember the things I tell you."

Shu-Shay nodded and sat silent and attentive.

"We are on our way to San Francisco. I have been many places, but I have never been to the great port there. It is a place where our people live. The captain has told us that the voyage will last three months, or ninety to one-hundred days. You are to serve as a cabin boy to the captain. This is good fortune for you, as you will receive privileges above the crew. I am to instruct you about your duties. If you have a question, you ask me. "First, watch out for yourself when I am not around you. Be alert, because anything can happen out here at sea. When I or anyone tells you to do something then do it at once, right away. If you do not understand, then ask and make sure you do it correctly the first instance. After you finish your task, check it again to make sure you have done it properly. Do you understand?"

Shu-Shay nodded his head.

"No, Shu-Shay. Answer by speaking, always. I want you say the words 'Aye, aye, sir', but if the captain gives you an order, you will say 'Aye, aye, Captain!' Now repeat this for me." Shu-Shay paused for a moment and then made a try.

"Aye, aye, aye, sir," he replied. Seku chuckled.

"No, Shu-Shay, just say 'Aye, aye, sir.'"

"Aye, aye, sir," he responded with a smile.

"Good, Shu-Shay! Very good!" Seku replied with encouragement. As they continued to sit, Seku watched him looking about the galley. There was something special about him. Seku had experienced and seen many things in his life, but took notice of this youth. The boy who had lost all and was nearly devoured by the vultures back in Canton, somehow survived the storm and now sat before him. It was a sign of how special he must be. Seku was inspired but did not know to what extent. Still, he felt a stirring inside himself and a kinship with Shu-Shay.

"All right, another serving of hard tack for you, then we shall work," Seku said.

"Aye, aye, sir!" Shu-Shay replied with a smile and a sense of tempered excitement. From that moment on, Seku was intent on transforming him into a first-rate cabin boy who could speak and understand the English language to the Captain's satisfaction.

Therefore, Shu-Shay was his shadow from dawn to dusk. Seku taught him what was required, then more, and was surprised at how quickly the boy learned. He unceasingly asked all sorts of questions. Nature, history, religion, and even astrology were common subjects of his inquiries. His eyebrows always peaked with curiosity as he waited attentively for an answer. During the journey the weather was most pleasant, notwithstanding the long days and nights, which seemed to perpetuate boredom.

The crew embraced the boy who became a reminder of their children left at home or in unknown places during travels and expeditions. Many hardened men viewed Shu-Shay as what they once were, little boys showing toothless grins through their bearded chins. The presence of youth was a welcome addition during the monotonous voyage to San Francisco.

Seku would bring a daily report back to Captain Price of Shu-Shay's progress, consisting of what he had learned, what he could do, as well as his general demeanor and well-being. Each night Seku would bring him to the captain's cabin before himself returning to the berthing quarters. This routine was repeated daily. Seku would leave Shu-Shay at the door and bid him good night. He would knock twice at the door, and Captain Price would respond.

"Who is it?" the Captain would inquire.

"It is Shu-Shay, Captain sir. I request permission to retire to quarter's, sir." He would respond in his high pitched, but loud and confident voice.

"Granted," Price would respond.

Shu-Shay would come inside and close the door, walk to his bedding on the floor, and lay down to sleep. By lantern light, Captain Price would review the quartermaster's plots and charts, and maybe have a smoke from his pipe coupled with a glass of brandy. He wanted to ease Shu-Shay into his duties without making him nervous, hence the Captain's usage of the redundant reporting procedures.

Captain Price had never required a cabin boy during his command. He believed he did not need help to either take his boots off or clean his cabin; he needed no personal butler or errand boy. These amenities, in his estimation, were for those of his peers who were inherently soft, vain, or lazy. He counted it all as nonsense and left that privilege to the high and lofty minded *peacocks* of the company. There were also other captains who had diabolical motives for sailing with personal cabin boys.

While women were specifically restricted from sailing on company manifest voyages, Price had known his peers to take aboard a young girl in the guise of a cabin boy, complete with head shorn to have relations with during the voyage. Others would use cabin boys for their pleasure, likewise, sodomizing them at will. He could remember his only expedition to Africa, and how the captain of that vessel indulged in the same moral abomination.

As Captain Price sat with pipe in hand daydreaming and watching Shu-Shay, he thought back to that time. He remembered the yells and whimpers coming from the captain's quarters, which told the story of what was happening inside. The crippled walk of the poor cabin boy who hobbled around deck in constant pain, confirmed it. Then one day the boy went missing. They all knew what had become of the lad, who had no doubt ended his own suffering by jumping over the side of the ship.

Captain Price partly blamed himself for the events. He believed that being a witness and knowing the abuse was occurring, but not stopping it, made him somewhat responsible for the outcome. He knew that if he spoke up, the captain of that vessel would have placed the young Caleb Price down below-deck, in stocks, then simply resume raping the lad, or maybe not, so he debated with himself. He poured himself another glass of brandy and continued to stare at Shu-Shay, thinking and reflecting.

"I will never know now." Captain Price mumbled, as he stood and turned to look at himself in the small mirror mounted on the wall. He stared into his own eyes, trying to recognize who he had become. The longer he stayed out to sea, the more he felt as though he was losing his bearing on who he was, not as the captain, but as Caleb Price. His wife, whom he was in love with, had long since departed this life. She had died from typhoid fever during the second year of their marriage. With much grief and despair, he survived, while pressing his way forward. He had not accomplished his goal of having children, but he built a solid reputation in the merchant shipping industry, and he was proud of that.

Even still, he knew the years spent away from civilization had started to change him for the worse. He had wanted to see and experience new places, as spoken about in the taverns and social circles, reflecting on how the world had transformed over the last twenty years. His life was at a crossroads, and, in maverick fashion, he was determined to lay down his commission. Many of the company underlings regarded the commission as a great achievement of station to aspire to, and others were willing to sell their soul and conscience to achieve it. He planned to embark upon a new beginning for himself, returning from whence he came.

Price turned from the mirror and extinguished the lamp, as the *Rainbow* streaked through the ocean, only weeks from San Francisco.

———————————

During the final weeks of their return voyage, Captain Price took note of Shu-Shay's progress. He tested him and challenged him constantly with conversation, either correcting or praising the boy as needed. At dusk, while he would be involved with business at his desk, Shu-Shay would be sitting up on his bedding, his mind racing with thoughts, curiosity, and wonder. Many lessons taught by Seku were taking effect on him. During the past three months he learned every part of the vessel, maritime commands, nautical terms, and a variety of other things. Most lessons were useful, but others were unfitting for a young lad to know. This was somewhat to be expected, as Seku and the crew were not delicate men, and most were not even moral.

Shu-Shay darted throughout the vessel, running errands and helping deck hands or Seku as best he could. One day he left the side of Seku and stood beside the captain at the helm. It was a natural inclination of Shu-Shay himself, of whom he took notice. Price was well pleased with him, although not vocally. A smile was his way of signifying approval. The ship was but a few days out from San Francisco when Captain Price called Seku to his quarters, to commend him for the tutelage he provided to Shu-Shay.

"You have done fine work with Shu-Shay, and I am pleased with his progress. After we dock and transfer this vessel to the next captain, I would have you continue to instruct the lad who favors you as an uncle of sorts. This affair I cannot order, but only ask of you."

"Thank you, sir. He has learned much but has more to learn still. I will always be near to him, Captain, I give you my word,"

Seku replied humbly. "He may think me his uncle, but he thinks you his father."

"What do you mean by that? Explain yourself please," Price inquired.

"The boy is always talking about you, and now he is your shadow. He looks at you and is happy. He asked me where your wife and children are, but I told him I know nothing of your family. He understands that you saved him, like his father would have had he been alive," Seku replied.

Captain Price sat back in the chair as he pondered the words spoken.

"Yes, I see. He is a fine boy of good heart, and his presence has lifted the morale of the crew," Price responded.

"Aye, Captain. Indeed. What you did that night in Canton I will never forget. In truth, I can only hope our new captain is half your worth." Price remained expressionless.

"Seku, that will be all, you are dismissed," he replied, hunching over his desk with a magnifying lens. Seku's words were upsetting for him, and he felt somewhat uneasy and troubled. He was not sure what was bothering him, but he knew it had to do with the future of Shu-Shay. He detested his ambivalent mood, and dismissed the words of Seku, counting them as mere pander.

Price reviled flattering words and vain persons alike. He believed that regardless of man's accomplishments, all were common folk, mere flesh and bones along with a heart that beats without promise, and that every man should temper his estimation of himself with that understanding. He resumed his survey of the quartermaster charts, as the sun began to set upon the horizon.

———————————

The next week arrived, and thoughts of making landfall ignited the men with feverish anticipation and hopes of carrying out plans abounded. It was the precursor to the end of boredom and monotony, and like tales of the dreaded black plague, it consumed the entire ship.

They would have at least a seven- to ten-day turnaround to refit the vessel to standard, and to the new captain's expectation. During this time the company shipbuilders would be hard at work, and the crew compensated before they departed on liberty. Everyone had plans, and Shu-Shay would stand around listening to the men and all the stories, trying to understand as best he could. He had never seen the crew as happy as now since they had left China in the storm. He remembered his mother and felt the demise of his happy mood, as sullenness replaced the former. Looking at Seku, who was also engaged in the banter, he patted his leg.

"Seku," he said, waiting for his attention. Seku acknowledged him smiling.

"Yes, Shu-Shay, what is it?"

"I tired, Seku, I go sleep. Goodnight, Seku."

"You look tired. Goodnight, Shu-Shay," he responded, and put his hand on Shu-Shay's head, giving him ever so subtle a nudge toward the captain's quarters. He made his way to quarters, knocked, and requested permission to enter, as was his directive.

"Come in, Shu-Shay," Captain Price responded. He entered and closed the door behind him.

"What have you been doing, Shu-Shay?" Price asked him, looking over his spectacles.

"I hear the mates talk when we come to San Francisco," Shu-Shay responded slowly, trying to perfect his speech in hope of pleasing the captain.

"What do you hear them say? Tell me the words of the men," he replied with a smile, his eyes fixed on the boy. He opened his middle drawer to retrieve his brandy and drinking glass.

Shu-Shay's demeanor changed as excitement took hold of him. He wanted to show Captain Price how well he could speak. He walked up to the desk. A lone lantern was sitting between the two, illuminating their faces. Price waited with enthusiasm to hear the tales of the crew as spoken of by this young lad. He had seen the boy grow and change drastically in only a few months.

"Peter say he going to buy a dress and ribbons for his lady-friend and sent them to New York with letters and ask she to be married with him!" Captain Price raised his eyebrows, holding his lit pipe in one hand and glass of brandy in the other. He chuckled at the boy.

"I see, he shall ask for his lady's hand in marriage. I see. I suppose that Mr. Peter Hardwick, should he receive the desired response from his lady, will not be long for this ship, or any other for that matter. If there is marriage, then children will surely follow. She shall need him, and if he is not near to home his newfound wife may not tolerate his extended absences," he responded. He emptied the glass of brandy, then filled it again.

"Either way, it will be the next captain's affair to replace the man. I would not blame any man who was truly in love for leaving an occupation in order to be with his woman. I'm rambling on, Shu-Shay. Continue to speak; tell me more."

Shu-Shay was trying to sort out all of his words and meanings, but the awkward silence prompted him to continue.

"Davis say he is going to have teeth pulled on, the most hurtful one by the dentist! Oh, and buy a new knife. Beaver and Snail say they are to get drunk for many days! Seku want to have new tattoo. Oh! Manu and Tullo say they will get four women and drink, and Tullo said he will stick his," Shu-Shay paused, looked down at his genitals, and back at Captain Price, whose eyebrows and glass raised in curiosity. "Stick it in three holes of the woman, and Manu said he would do that, too!" Captain Price choked on his brandy. As he coughed and tried to catch his breath, he motioned to Shu-Shay with one finger, back and forth.

Shu-Shay not knowing what strange sign language the captain was displaying, continued speaking.

"Captain, how do you put in three holes? I no understand. I ask them, but they laugh at me."

Captain Price regained his composure, and, after clearing his throat, firmly responded, "Shu-Shay, there will be no more talk about women, or the holes of women! No more! Do you understand me?" Shu-Shay replied with eyes wide.

"Aye, aye, Captain sir."

The captain restrained pouring his anger out on Shu-Shay, who he felt was the victim. Instead it should be for the men responsible. In their ignorance, they exposed the boy to tales of lust and their whorehouse escapades. Despite his first reaction, Price also blamed himself, for he should have known this would happen.

"I don't blame you, Shu-Shay. You are a child. It is as much my fault as it is my crew's that you were privy to the personal tales of men. Remember to have respect when speaking of women or to women. Never talk of their bodies or their nakedness. When you grow up you will have a lady-friend no doubt." Shu-Shay, understanding most of his last words, stood attentive. He took hold of the jade amulet around his neck and looked at it. Captain Price wondered why the boy had such affection for the charm and had never taken notice of exactly what it was.

"I see you are always wearing that charm. Come closer so I may see it." Shu-Shay took a step and leaned over the desk, displaying the jade amulet to him. He examined the piece, noticing it was petite and exquisite, but yet simple. The edges were fine and the small engravings unique. Captain Price had never seen anything like it, all his years at sea. It was majestic. He was astonished that one of the crew had not stolen it in stealth, an event easily blamed away on an irresponsible child who had been out to sea for three months.

"Where did you get this from?" the Price inquired. Shu-Shay started breathing very hard and his face started to lose composure. He was trying to fight back his tears with great effort. Captain Price could see he was becoming visibly shaken by his question, and as he was about to withdraw it, Shu-Shay answered.

"My momma gave it to me. My father gave it to her." Captain Price put down his pipe and brandy, slowly got up, and walked over to him. He knelt down on one knee and put his hand on Shu-Shay's shoulder.

"When you get older and become a man, you can give it to your woman. She can then pass it to your son, just as it was passed on to you." Shu-Shay stood silent but listening, understanding.

"Does it have a name? What do you call it in China?" Shu-Shay looked up slowly and answered in a soft voice.

"Hu-di-eh."

"Come again, son? How do you say it?" Price inquired, his eyes squinting.

"Hoo-di-eh." replied Shu-Shay slowly.

Captain Price smiled. "Take care and give it to your true love only."

"Aye, aye, Captain," Shu-Shay answered as he fought back a coy smile. The captain returned to his desk, and Shu-Shay lay down on his bed.

"Goodnight, Shu-Shay," Captain Price spoke as he began to turn off the lantern.

"Goodnight, Captain," Shu-Shay responded as he turned over on his stomach, beholding the captain, until darkness fell upon the room.

Price removed his boots and suspenders and lay down, but he started to worry. He realized the frailty of the boy, and he felt the weight of his loneliness. To lose both parents was a tragedy that even Caleb Price could not imagine, nor would he wish such a thing on an enemy. He worried about the boy's future, when he would no longer be under protection.

Being a cabin boy was not in Shu-Shay's best interest, and Price hoped that the boy would have a chance to succeed in life. The boy deserved such a reprieve. After thinking about it, he concluded his plan of action. If the oncoming captain had his own personal cabin boy, then he would stay in the care of the

Missionaries in San Francisco. If a cabin boy were required, Shu-Shay would be fit for that service. As he grew older, he would have the opportunity to gain position aboard the vessel, and with Seku as his mentor, he would do well.

They would be making landfall within a week, and Price would inform him of his possible departure to the Mission, if the situation dictated such. Captain Price believed his decision was a moral one. He had read in the Psalms earlier that night where it said, "But you do see, for you note mischief and vexation that you may take it into your hands; to you the helpless commits himself; you have been the helper of the fatherless."

On the remembrance of those thoughts, he slept.

"Land ahoy! Land ahoy!"

The cry came from the crow's nest. All the deckhands made their way to the bow of the ship in anticipation of a glimpse. Shu-Shay weaved between the other deck hands as he scurried forth to the bow.

"Seku! Land! Land!" Shu-Shay shouted in excitement, pointing to an ever-so faint glimpse of the coast on the horizon.

"Soon we will all smell the land," Seku replied with a smile. The entire crew let out a hearty and cheerful cry as they embraced one another with gratitude and not attempting to restrain themselves. Captain Price and Higgins looked out at the men from the helm, then at each other and smiled themselves, shaking hands.

"You are to be commended, Mr. Higgins, for your duty well done. Upon my resignation I will deliver to the company my letter of recommendation that you be considered for the next available command." Higgins' eyes widened in surprise as Captain Price continued:

"I have taught you everything I know, Higgins, and you are ready."

Higgins face became flush from hearing these unexpected, but much appreciated accolades, as he nodded. "Captain Price... Sir, it has been a pleasure and a blessing to serve with you these many years. You have taught me most of what I know, and I will forever be indebted to you." Captain Price smiled and nodded.

"Mr. Higgins, make ready the charts from the quartermaster. I estimate we'll be moored by noon. Let the men set foot on land for a short spell before unloading the cargo. I will go directly to the Company and meet with Mr. Brady to execute my affairs. Bring the completed manifests to the packet office as soon as they are ready."

"Aye, aye, sir," Mr. Higgins responded over the cheers and song of the elated crew.

The excitement on the ship reverberated throughout the vessel as everyone craved the thought of making landfall. The morning passed quickly, and the vessel was moored by noon. Captain

Price stepped out onto the dock, put his hands on his hips, and inhaled the aroma of land. He turned about and looked at the *Rainbow*. His last voyage was a success. He smiled as he left to complete his business. The main office was not located on the wharf, but rather further in town. Captain Price strolled down the thoroughfare, observing all his surroundings.

It was a joy to look at new faces after having sailed with the same crew for months. The smells of town life filled the air as Captain Price bought a small bread loaf and an apple from a local vendor along the way. As he ate, he marveled at the women passing by him beside the thoroughfare. He had been without the company of a female for the past several months, and each woman stirred his attention. He found the lot of them increasingly attractive, whether they were thin, plump, or perfect. While he walked, ponderings arose of him taking a detour from his affairs to visit a brothel. His nature awoke, and a maverick spirit began to take hold of him. He smiled and discarded the notion. Being true to his reputation and character, he would conduct business first and entertain his personal desires later.

Captain Price arrived at the Main office of the Merchant Company. His resignation process was quick and forthright. He also delivered his recommendation letter for Mr. Higgins and briefly discussed his mercantile trade prospects back in Connecticut with the merchant controller.

He received information that Mr. Livingston would be the ship's next captain. Livingston was new to the company, and from England. It was unknown if he had a personal cabin boy, but a runner was dispatched to inform him the *Rainbow* was moored and the crew at his disposal. It was now Captain Livingston's vessel. Captain Price shook hands with the controller and returned to the ship. The walk back seemed shorter to Price, who seemed to quicken his step with a sense of urgency. His few belongings were packed and on their way to the Coach Station.

He would go back to and greet Captain Livingston, perhaps answering any of his questions. The disposition of Shu-Shay would have to be discussed, and if his cabin boy service would be needed. He planned to catch the eight-o'clock stagecoach to begin the circuit which would take him to Connecticut. If he could conclude those affairs and leave promptly, he would have time to visit a well-reputed brothel he had passed earlier. With this thought, he increased his pace.

Back on the *Rainbow*, the crew was nearly finished offloading the cargo from the hold. Shu-Shay was right behind Seku, doing his part and carrying anything he could handle. The men were making haste with the offloading, motivated by thoughts of women and strong drink. Captain Price made his way to bridge and had a few words with Mr. Higgins, who then walked down and stood on the deck below. Higgins shouted out and addressed the crew.

"All hands! Gather 'round! Captain Price would like to say a few words before his departure! Gather 'round!"

The men mustered and assembled themselves while looking up at Captain Price who stood at the helm. He addressed them with his commanding tone:

"Men. I apologize for taking you away from your duties, and it is almost unforgivable that I, or any man, should come between this crew and the pleasures that await you all in town. Not to detain you all any longer, but I must give thanks. Each one of you has served this vessel in an excellent manner. Over the many years we have all encountered trials and tribulations upon these waters; events that simply would have broken most land dwellers! Yet in every situation, you pulled together and showed why you are more than men—indeed, you are sailors!" They all raised a shout in response. "I am proud to have served with you, and I thank you for bringing me back to these United States from my final voyage. To the crew: I pray the Almighty bless you all!" The men burst out with applause and cheers as Captain Price waved them back to their duties. He watched them disperse and a feeling overcame him. He knew that this chapter in his life had finally ended. He felt forgotten already and sensed the sharp sting of truth: that his time had passed.

As Price spoke with Mr. Higgins, a wagon was approaching. Out of the drab grey and brown back round, a lone red-silhouetted passenger stood out. Another wagon followed close behind, with the front seat occupied by luggage. Higgins stopped talking, as he noticed the object of the Captain's attention. The wagon arrived at the crossing. Out stepped a thin man dressed in very elegant attire, complete with full ruffles and English pomp. It was no doubt Captain Livingston, Price surmised. As Livingston approached the gangway to cross over to the vessel, Price and Higgins met him.

"Good day, Sir. Captain Livingston, I presume?" Price inquired.

"You are correct. Good day to you, sir. Captain Price, I assume?" he replied.

"Yes, very nice to meet you, Captain," Price replied. The two shook hands. "The vessel is ready for your inspection; all the crew are accounted for. The cargo transfer is nearly finished, and I estimate completion in two hours. Do you have any questions for me in the interim?" Captain Livingston seemed preoccupied with taking in the surroundings, and after pausing for an extended duration, finally replied.

"No questions, thank you. I shall rest tonight and make a full inspection on the morrow. Best fortune to you in your future endeavors, Captain Price. You need not delay any longer. It was a pleasure to meet you. Good day, sir." Livingston showed a faint grin as he nodded and proceeded past them, with baggage carriers following.

Captain Price was somewhat shocked by Livingston's abruptness. Then he remembered Shu-Shay. "Captain Livingston, there is one matter I would like to discuss." Livingston stopped and turned with an irritated expression on his face.

"At the port of Canton, I took aboard a Chinese youth, ten years of age. He his proficient in the English language for his age, been taught the duties of cabin boy, and can perform them diligently. I was unsure if you required those services. If you do not, then I will take him to the Baptist missionaries." Livingston paused and seemed surprised.

"My cabin boy disappeared at port a month ago without any indication of his whereabouts. I may be able to use the services of the lad. Bring him forth, so I may inspect him." Captain Price turned and called for Shu-Shay.

"Shu-Shay!" Price called out. A few moments later, he came running up to Price.

"Yes, Captain sir!" Livingston's eyes widened as he began to walk around Shu-Shay, inspecting the boy. Shu-Shay stood still, but watched the strange man dressed in bright red clothing as he circled. Livingston smiled at Price.

"I do believe I can use the boy's service. Indeed, I shall. You made a very good selection Captain Price, I compliment your taste." Captain Price was somewhat confused and unsettled by Livingston's compliment. Livingston looked down at Shu-Shay.

"I am your new master and commander, Captain Livingston. I want you to go to my cabin and wait for me. I would like to assess you properly." Shu-Shay stood motionless, unsure of Livingston's orders due to his English accent. He did understand to report to the cabin and wait, but the rest of his sentence was unknown to him. Livingston hardened his expression and raised his voice to Shu-Shay.

"Run along, now!" Livingston barked. Shu-Shay scurried past the men to the captain's quarters. Price was shocked, and dismayed by the episode that had just transpired before him. He looked at Livingston who never returned Price's glance as he made his way aboard the ship with Mr. Higgins now in tow.

Captain Price's nostrils began to flare as he became angry. He marveled that he did not even have an opportunity to say a proper goodbye to Shu-Shay. Price stood alone, not feeling visible to anyone else. He sighed and turned about, replacing his thoughts and emotions with his plans. He headed toward the brothel, which he had seen earlier in hopes of spending time in the company of a woman. He made haste to his destination for within a few hours he would begin the first stage of his journey to Connecticut.

As night fell, the docks began to empty, and the various ships in mooring floated silently. Howbeit, ruckus and riotous celebration could be heard from every tavern in the vicinity. The many expressions of music weaved themselves into a potpourri of sound, lacking order, but full of human emotion.

Captain Price, having satisfied his manly desires, lent his cheek to the woman he had just engaged with in relations. As she kissed his cheek, he smiled at her and looked deep into her eyes. He marveled at her natural beauty. He had chosen her because she had favored his deceased wife, though in her mannerisms only. He gently ran his fingers through her hair as she closed her eyes momentarily, basking in his affection.

While much of society showed disdain for prostitutes, he did not share this popular opinion. In fact, he believed the contrary, looking at the prostitute with empathy and affection. He saw those who practiced prostitution as desperate individuals, overwhelmed by events of life and circumstance, and that any woman or man without hope would also be capable of the most shameful acts. The self-righteous opinions of hypocrites only added to the prostitutes suffering instead of offering help to those in distress. Captain Price embraced her brown eyes for the last time, knowing he would never see this woman again.

"My best wishes to you, young lady. Goodbye," Captain Price said as he walked away down the hall and out the brothel, happily making his way down to the waiting stagecoach. He seemed indifferent about his future but felt youthfully excited and confident.

While strolling along he passed a tavern, which was exceptionally boisterous, he caught a glimpse inside and observed a frenzy of frolic, the likes of which he had not seen in decades. In the midst of all the folk, he noticed Seku with his arms crossed, leaning back against the counter. He was the only patron, motionless and staring toward the ground while the others moved to and fro in a clamor. Captain Price stopped walking, and curiously watched Seku. Not wanting to go inside, he called out to him. The noise was deafening, so he called out again, but much louder.

"Seku!" Seku looked toward Captain Price as he stumbled forward toward the door, heavily intoxicated.

"Captain! Captain! Come inside, drink with us!" Seku slurred, his foul breath preceding his every word.

"No, thank you, Seku. I am headed to the stage, and at eight o'clock I depart. I saw you and wanted to bid you farewell," Captain Price paused. "Please watch over Shu-Shay and see that no harm comes to him." He patted him on the shoulder. "Farewell, Seku." Seku looked dumbfounded as Price turned to walk away. He grabbed his arm, gripping it tightly. Price looked at him as his temper began to awaken. Seku pulled him even closer, and with his teeth gritted together, he croaked a question.

"You would leave the boy to that man?" They stared at each other in silence. Captain Price suddenly pulled his arm free of his grip. He responded:

"Captain Livingston seems to be a hard and pompous man, I would agree, but you know that every captain has his own way about him. You ought to mind your manners, Seku, and never handle me again. I count such as disrespect. It is not deserved, nor appreciated."

Seku ran his hand through his hair while trying to steady himself.

"I'm sorry, Captain. Forgive me, eh? Answer me this: Why does the Red Rooster Captain still keep Shu-Shay on the ship?" Seku slurred, as he tried to fasten his eyes on Price. He continued, "All the crew leave, except Tullo stand watch. Shu-Shay does not leave! I saw! I saw the Rooster look at Shu-Shay like he was a girl!"

Captain Price was infuriated with himself. He did not want to believe Seku's report; he would have to investigate these accusations himself. He surmised that the benefit of any given doubt must be laid to rest. He responded to Seku.

"I will say farewell to Shu-Shay before I leave this place. I will see for myself how he is being treated. Worry not, I will see for myself!" Seku bowed with respect.

"Thank you, Captain," he replied, and stumbled back into the crowd of drunken patrons. Captain Price went straight away to the *Rainbow*, with quickstep employed. He passed the coach station, where he saw the driver was napping and the shotgun rider cleaning his weapon. Nearly arriving to the *Rainbow*, he tried to keep his calm, shielding himself from the constant barrage of thoughts darting through his mind. Price's conscience told him that Livingston was just not to be trusted, and that Shu-Shay was at his mercy. He blamed himself while arriving to the gangway, where Tullo stood watch.

"Evening Captain!" He said, greeting him with enthusiasm. Captain Price responded.

"I want to bid Shu-Shay farewell. Is he still on board?"

"Yes Captain, with Captain Livingston in his quarters."

"Thank you Tullo, I shall only be a moment." Price walked past him and made his way to his former room. When he got to the door, and listened, he heard no sound. He knocked three times. After a long silence, he knocked again. Captain Livingston answered in a low voice.

"Who is it?"

"It is Captain Price. Excuse me for this unannounced visit. I would like to have a few words with Shu-Shay. Thank you, Captain." After a long silence Livingston replied.

"Shu-Shay is sleeping Mr. Price. I would appreciate if you would return tomorrow. Goodnight." Caleb Price was furious. He had to see Shu-Shay; he had to look at him in his eyes. Price began to knock on the door without ceasing. He looked across the ship at Tullo, who seemed agitated and curious at the unfolding events. The inside latch could be heard, as the door to the cabin was unlocked by Livingston, who opened it a few inches. Barely visible, he stood clad in a night garment as he yelled out at Price.

"Good God, man! I told you to leave! You are no longer the captain of this vessel! Remove yourself, or I will have you removed at once!"

Price seemed impervious to Livingston's comments, as he looked passed Livingston for a sign of Shu-Shay. Then he saw a glimpse of him and was appalled. Price was enraged and pushed the cabin door open with his full force. This resulted in Livingston being struck by the door and propelled backward. As it was completely open, the truth was revealed. Shu-Shay lay there on the captain's bed, face down and completely naked. Price stood still and without expression. Shu-Shay turned his head from the wall toward the door and looked at him. His eyes were filled with tears, while shame and desperation emanated from his stare. Captain Livingston regained his bearings and looked up at Price with utter hatred. He yelled for the watch.

"Boatswain mate Tullo!" He cried out, as Price walked into the room.

"Shu-Shay, get up and put on clothes. You are coming with me." Shu-Shay sprang up to put on his trousers and his top. Livingston yelled out for Tullo again while Captain Price took Shu-Shay by the hand, leading him out of the cabin to the gangway. As they approached, Tullo blocked the way. Price let go of Shu-Shay and took hold of the dagger under his jacket in the back of his trousers. He walked up to Tullo.

"Move aside, Mr. Tullo, or I will bleed you where you stand," Price said firmly, as he and Tullo stood facing each other. Tullo smiled, extended his arm and gave way. Livingston came out onto the deck following behind Price and Shu-Shay and shouted to Tullo.

"Damn it, Tullo! Stop the boy!" Tullo looked at Livingston, and then Price.

"Godspeed, Captain Price," Tullo said as they passed.

"Godspeed to you, Tullo, and God help you all aboard this vessel."

He led Shu-Shay off the ship and away by the hand. As they walked toward the stagecoach, both hearts were beating furiously. Price wondered what was to become of the boy. Had he been brought a thousand miles from the slums of China, only to serve the pleasure of a rapist? It was unacceptable to stand by idle. When they arrived at the coach, Price kneeled and looked at Shu-Shay, who was no longer crying.

"Are you hurt?" Price asked.

"No."

"I am sorry. I did not know that man or that he would mistreat you," Price explained, as Shu-Shay lowered his head.

"I would take you to the Baptist missionaries, who are like the missionaries who taught Seku, however, I fear that monster would find you there and take you back." Shu-Shay started to frown, which was a prelude to his tears. "Or if you want to come with me to my home in Connecticut, you are welcome." Shu-Shay stood quiet. "I am starting a business there, a hardware store. You could help me and work for me, if you want. If not, then along the journey, when we get far from this place, you can choose to go your own way. I need to know your answer, because I must leave now." Price awaited his answer.

Shu-Shay looked up at the him. "Aye, aye, Captain," he responded.

"Are you sure, Shu-Shay?"

"Yes, sir," he responded, nodding his head in affirmation. Captain Price opened the door to the coach and helped him climb up. The driver who had been watching and listening, addressed Price.

"Sir, you need to pay for the new passenger."

"When we get to the next town I will pay the boy's fare. Now, let us make time, gentlemen." Captain Price climbed inside and shut the door.

Uncertain of the future and shaken by the sudden change of events, Price was certain of one thing: that his actions were right. Price looked at Shu-Shay and then into the darkness, thinking about a great many things. The stagecoach rocked back and forth, as it negotiated the uneven road. Sleep was heavy upon him, and he started to drift toward slumber when he heard Shu-Shay's faint small voice.

"Thank you, sir," Shu-Shay mumbled, as he lay on the seat with his eyes closed on the precipice of sleep, unaware he had spoken a word. Price watched him until he drifted off as well, while the coach rolled along through the darkness.

Three

INTO THE ABYSS

That same year, within the land of Nigeria, the small village of Osugun was full of excitement. The annual festival of the Odun Egungun was on the morrow and the people were enthusiastic. The folk were making final preparations before they made the journey to the Oyo capital. The African Oyo Confederacy was comprised predominantly of the Yoruba tribes, and had collapsed decades earlier. For the past two hundred years, they were the richest and most powerful kingdom in Nigeria.

Their main commodity was slaves, of which millions of men, women, and children were sold and traded to the Europeans at ports to the west for cloth, metal goods, guns, and such. These items in turn were commonly exchanged with Arab traders in the north for horses. The Oyo also taxed all other commerce crossing through the kingdom from Hausa Land. However, the Aro Confederacy was now the dominant governing power in the region, centralized at its capital Arochukwu. They consisted primarily of Igbo and Igbibio people, and they exploited and expanded the successes of the former Oyo Kingdom through increased trade and regional alliances. This was the annual Yoruba festival to honor the dead, in which ceremonial décor was worn in the form of costumes. The majority of people from Yoruba tribes in every territory would assemble to participate in this sacred ceremony.

Ten-year-old Chimanda and her younger brother Soja were both occupied with twigs in hand. They were lightly tapping a spider's web trying to summon the creature to show itself. There was one insect caught in the web, wound with silk in preservation for the spider's later meal. They took turns and waited, but Soja almost broke the web twice while imitating his older sister's action.

"Not so hard, Soja! Tap it lightly like this." She tapped the edge gently. At once he attempted but demolished it in his excitement.

"Soja, no!" He looked at her and laughed, as it was now ruined. Chimanda loved her baby brother dearly, even as if he was her child, but at this moment she wanted to slap his hand. They both heard their mother's voice and looked up.

"Chimanda! Soja! Come!" Their names echoed through the forest.

"Come on, Soja, it is time to go." Chimanda grabbed his hand and pulled him along back to the village.

From afar, Ugonna saw them moving toward the village and went back inside her house. Her husband, Akin, having gathered up food planned for the trip to the festival, brushed past her.

"Excuse me, wife," he turned to look at her while walking out the entrance. His tone resonated inside her as she watched him pass by. She felt appreciation and contentment by his manners and subtle words of consideration. He had been a good husband to her, never raising his voice in anger, nor making demands of her, but always asking. He was special to her, and she truly understood and cherished him. She walked outside where he was storing food and water inside a large satchel.

The journey to the capital would take six to eight hours on foot, and it was times like these in which Ugonna wished her husband would have kept his horse, making the trip easier and faster. She recalled the years past and the disbanding Oyo Confederation. Before Akin took her as his wife, he was given a horse as a parting tribute for his loyalty and faithful service by the Oyo Mesi, the ruling council of the Confederacy; it was a great honor. She also recalled her family's objection to their marriage, due to Akin being from the Yoruba people and she from the Igbo. There was much contention about their plans for marriage, but ultimately it was her right. So, she married the man she loved, contrary to her family's wishes.

"I am going to my brother's village to get the yams he promised us, and, when I return, we will leave," Akin said, as Chimanda and Soja came running toward the house from the clearing.

"Children, I will come back soon," he shouted to them.

"Yes, Papa!" Chimanda responded.

Akin stared at Ugonna, admiring Ugonna's irresistible beauty and grace. At times, he would pause to look upon her in subtle disbelief, wondering why a woman such as her would choose to be with a man like himself. He did not feel worthy of her love and would never divulge this to her. He glanced at Chimanda and Soja. She was his first-born child and more precious to him than the rarest of gems. She had something very special about her, in her spirit, which shone forth through her eyes. This was not just noticeable to himself, but to everyone in the community, and he truly felt blessed. Akin smiled and abruptly left the village toward his brother's dwelling, which was an hour away. Chimanda and Soja came running up to Ugonna.

"You can play, but do not leave out the village. When your father returns, we will leave. We want to set close to the ceremony."

"Yes, Momma." They went into the house and sat on the floor for a while. When she laid down, Soja did likewise, mimicking his older sister.

"Do you need something to eat? Are you hungry? Your father will not want to stop on our journey." Chimanda looked at Soja.

"I want yam," Soja said.

"We have no yams until your father comes back," Ugonna told him. Chimanda wasn't hungry, but she was sleepy, and pulled Soja closer to cuddle with him.

"I'm not hungry, Momma. I want to nap," she replied, and closed her eyes.

———————————

A few hours had passed and most of the villagers had already left. Ugonna started to become frustrated and angry at her husband's tardiness, as she and the children sat out in front of their house. The longer she waited, her frustration exponentially grew, and she contemplated walking to her brother-in-law's dwelling, possibly meeting Akin along the path. She stood up.

"You children stay near the house. Do not leave the village to play. I am going to your uncle's home and see what is delaying your father!"

"Yes, Momma," Chimanda responded, as she tended to Soja. Just then, sounds could be heard outside. There was a deep, rumbling coming from the north, the direction she would be heading. Ugonna stood still while keenly listening to discern the source of the sound. The rumble rose in intensity as a large group of warriors appeared through the clearing, their numbers increasing with every passing moment. Ten men mounted on horseback, followed by twenty-five light infantry foot soldiers marched toward the village. Signified by their colors, Ugonna recognized them as Aro Confederates.

Startled, her heart rapidly beat in her chest as she began to worry. Firstly, Akin was late, and now these men had arrived for some unknown purpose. The cavalry rode directly through, as the soldiers sprinted behind them along the path in a two-man column formation. The village was nearly empty by this time, save a few elderly and disabled folks along with their caretakers. Only a handful of people remained outside to witness this alarming sight. Although this was a Yoruba community which bordered Aro Confederate lands, Ugonna had never witnessed their military presence inside her husband's village. She looked back at her children.

"Go in the house, now!"

Chimanda grabbed Soja by the hand and pulled him through the cloth at the doorway entrance. She wrapped her arms around him tightly while anxiously looking through the opening. The men poured into the village and marched toward Ugonna. They crowded her yet remained two arm's-length distance from her. Their captain was on horseback, making his way through the soldiers while his eyes were steadfast on her. They parted their ranks, as he stopped his horse short of her.

"Woman, are you the wife of Akin, captain of the Oyo Mesi?" Ugonna bowed her head.

"Sir, I am the wife of Akin, a former captain of the Oyo Mesi. How may I be of service to you?" She made a great effort to hide her fear and the overwhelming feeling of dread.

"Your family has been offered as restitution by the Oyo Mesi, to the Aro Kingdom for offenses committed. We know you have a son and daughter. Where are they?"

"What do you plan to do with us?" Her voice trembled and crackled.

The captain paused. "You are sentenced to slavery, along with your daughter." Ugonna went numb as she stared through him in disbelief, speechless. Where was Akin? What crimes had he committed? Why? Why, pray Chukwu, was this happening? Chimanda and Soja were viewing the scene, and although their mother's form was obscured by the soldiers, they could clearly hear the conversation. The captain's eyes widened with anger as he dismounted.

"Woman! Tell me where they are!"

She became angry and defiant. "I want to speak to my husband!"

Her words were met with momentary silence.

"You may see him in the afterlife. He walks with his elders now." The words penetrated her, although she somehow expected them. The strength left her legs as she fell to her knees. She began to sob uncontrollably and cried out. "Akin! My husband!"

The captain seemed unimpressed with her weeping but thought it futile to press her further. He turned to his company.

"Search the village for a small boy and girl!" The men shouted in assent and dispersed in all directions. Concern for her children's safety brought Ugonna back to her senses. She stayed on her knees and sat upright, pleading to the captain.

"Please, spare my son and daughter. I beg you! Take me and do whatever you like but have mercy on them!" He looked at her without emotion or expression.

"You and your daughter will be sold. Your son must forfeit his life, lest he return as a man to seek revenge in the name of his father. It has so been ordered." His words destroyed her, yet also empowered her to fight for them the only way she could.

Ugonna inhaled as deeply as possible. "Chimanda! Soja! Run! Run! Ru—"

She was struck on the head by the butt of a rifle and silenced. She fell down, lifeless, as the soldier prepared to hit her again. The captain held up his hand.

"Enough! Do not kill her fool; she is worth nothing dead!" He focused on the house behind her.

Her words had not been in vain. Although terrified, Chimanda looked into her brother's face and whispered, "We have to run. Just keep running and don't stop!"

She pulled him out the back of the house and down the south path out of the village. As they went into the forest, she pushed Soja in front of her, prodding him to keep running rather than trying to drag him. The soldiers were in pursuit at once and Chimanda could hear them getting closer.

"Soja! Soja! Run off the path! Keep running!" He ran into the jungle, just like when they played the hiding game together. Chimanda stayed on the path as her little brother forked to the left and out of her sight.

"Run, Soja!" she whimpered. Her long skinny legs began to tire as desperation enveloped her. She felt a hand grab onto her hair, and then she was on the ground. She lay still, covering her face in terror.

"Fan out and find the boy!" a voice shouted.

"Get up, girl!" another directed.

Chimanda was disoriented and confused as she was snatched up to her feet. Other men came over to quickly tie her wrists and place an iron band around her neck, which began to dig into her skin. They took her back to the village, where Ugonna now stood, also shackled.

Other captives were ushered into the clearing. The faces of these people looked different to Chimanda as they were from other villages. She approached her mother and cried out. Ugonna saw Chimanda and tried to run to her but was stopped by the neck iron chained to the other captives. Chimanda broke free and ran toward her.

They pressed against each other with bound wrists, trying to embrace. Alas, it was a sorrowful sight. All the women were weeping, while the men had mixed reactions. Some showed signs of resistance, indicated by bruises and bleeding. Many looked enraged and wide eyed, while others appeared broken and dismayed. The Aro raiding party began to organize the captives into two rows. They pushed or struck the unruly and slothful to impose their will. Ugonna looked at her crying daughter.

"Chimanda, where is Soja?"

"I don't know, Momma. I told him to keep running, off the path. He ran and disappeared."

"Chukwu will protect him," Ugonna muttered, as she began to entreat her god. "Pray to Chukwu."

"Yes, Momma!" Chimanda cried out as they both prayed. After several minutes there was a small commotion in the clearing. A group of soldiers ran to the captain.

"We could not find the boy," a soldier reported. The captain's frustration was apparent, as he grimaced in anger.

"Your report is unacceptable! You five will continue to search until dark! We head through the pass toward the river and Biafra. We cannot stop until we arrive, so at sunset, double your pace and meet us there tomorrow. If you men are encountered by any Oyo who resist you or this lawful mandate, you will defend yourself and the Aro Kingdom's honor! Even unto death! Do you understand?" They bowed in acceptance, turned, and sprinted off into the woods. Ugonna subtly glanced at the exchange, and listened to their report. She thanked Chukwu, and believed her son had a chance to escape. The captain mounted his horse and surveyed the captives.

"Move!"

The caravan of slaves began to walk, while being chided to increase their pace. They went down the south path leading toward the Bight of Biafra, a major slave-trading port. The captain was pressed for time but would attempt to complete his mission by any means necessary. European and American slave ships were on very constrictive schedules due to England's maritime patrols along the coast. The British attempts at stopping the immoral trade were increasingly successful, especially in the north at the Bight of Benin, another high-volume slave port.

They marched the captives all night, with little time for recuperation. The irons caused nearly everyone to bleed and bruise. Several hours into the torturous journey, the pain of separation and confinement gave way to surviving the hardships of the march. Continuing their progress without stopping was of monumental importance. Those who fell down due to weakness were beaten relentlessly until they rose to their feet. The captors were willing to sacrifice the lives of the weakest. The bound folk were ignorant of their destination, and also that their will to survive would be tested beyond their measure and their control. The night seemed endless to Chimanda, as she wondered if her father had truly been killed. Would he come to rescue them? Had Soja been captured? These thoughts were replaced with the concern of biting insects. Unable to scratch or brush them off, she continued on with the others in great discomfort.

The only consolation for the condemned was the brightness of the full moon which illuminated the way. It was the only constant during this hour which remained the same, untouchable and dependable. They all felt complete desperation, even of life itself.

They reached the river and boarded waiting canoes. The captain and the majority of his party watched as they paddled down the Niger, toward the delta and the Cross River. This brief period of rest was welcome, but their bodies were wracked with hunger pains. They were given only water, as the soldiers ate their own provisions, not offering a morsel to the prisoners.

Shortly after sunrise everyone noticed the smell of the air and how it had changed. Recognizing that the ocean was close, some sat upright to gather their bearings. They needed to remember how to return to the villages from whence they had come. There were ten people connected together in each of the two boats, with five soldiers in escort. They were bundled into a cluster, with each person trying to stay close to someone familiar, but the order in which they were chained made it difficult. Chimanda was originally attached to the main chain opposite Ugonna but had long since crawled close enough to embrace her leg. A few hours later they arrived at the mouth of the delta, where several small boats and people were gathered. They disembarked and were led down the riverbank and were astonished. The banks were lined with hundreds of Africans and many white skinned men. Chimanda and the other captives were amazed at these white men, having heard of them but never seeing them.

Their world was in chaos, and the hope of rescue by their respective villages was paramount as they were placed into holding pens on the beach. Food and water were given for nourishment, lest they perish before the great voyage that lay before them. As the sun rose and the noon hour approached, the activity at the port dramatically increased. The slavers with their human cargo made their way onto the beach from different locations and routes. Chimanda fell asleep from exhaustion, as did a few others. Ugonna remained awake, staring aimlessly at the beach. She was numb and, while holding her child, thoughts overwhelmed her mind, yet none offered any solace.

The main building was full, as well as the holding pens on the beach. Unable to add any more human livestock, the overflow of slaves was seated on the sand, shackled together. Ugonna recognized most of them as Igbo and Yoruba, along with several other tribes. She noticed the many Muslims among them, and people from the north by their languages, mainly Kongo, Kikongo, and Ki Mbundu. There was no resistance from the people as they were all equally weary. She thought of how they each were taken. Who did they leave behind? Would their tribesmen come for them? Chimanda had woken, and Ugonna looked down as she opened her eyes. Looking up at her mother she began to cry.

"It will be all right, Chimanda. Chukwu will provide a way for us. He will protect us."

"Why is Chukwu waiting?" she exclaimed in between her sobbing. "Where is my Papa?" Ugonna rocked Chimanda in her arms but had no other words to ease the pain. She noticed other men who were bartering with the whites. By their mannerisms, clothing and language, they appeared to be the Arab merchants Akin had once described to her. She briefly remembered things that he had shared with her about what lay beyond their lands. He spoke about different customs of certain people, mentioning their gods and beliefs. The numbness was replaced with anger as thoughts of her deceased husband filled her mind.

"Is this how it will be? Taken from our lands in silence?" She whispered to herself. Her jaw began to tremble.

Chimanda's weeping subsided as she watched her mother change. Ugonna noticed the captain of the raiding party speaking with two Arab merchants. They appeared from a group of tents under the shade of nearby trees. A merchant adorned with a turban, led the men over to holding pens. He expeditiously inspected the human cargo as everyone sat quietly, not wanting to attract attention. After a short while he walked back to the group and spoke with the captain again. They both nodded in agreement and dispatched their seconds, who in turn hurried themselves in opposite directions. They returned shortly with crates and other goods which they exchanged with each other.

Ugonna realized then that they had been sold. Overwhelmed, she stood up on her feet and grasped the posts, yelling the Igbo cry for danger. The other captives looked around at her. Repeatedly, she yelled out of desperation. Slowly, the other women rose to their feet in unison, each one calling out at the top of their lungs. Most thought that perhaps their villages were looking for them and the cries might help them to be located. On the other end of the beach, a cluster of captives joined the call, and then another. The captain walked over and ordered the gate to be opened and proceeded to grab Ugonna by her neck in preparation to strike her.

"Wait!" the merchant yelled in the Arabic tongue, which the captain understood.

"Look at her. Does she look afraid of you? Will your fist silence her without damaging her beautiful black skin?" The merchant posed. "She is my property now and I do not wish her skin or her beauty marred! Do not damage her outwardly to punish…but you may damage her inwardly and make an example for all to see. Two men. Now." He clapped twice. The captain commanded two of his men to perform the task.

As the section of the beach continued to erupt with the cries of the captives, Ugonna was removed from the others, walked a few paces to a small clearing, and raped publicly. Their verbal rebellion continued during the violent encounter with the first man, but slowly fell silent as the second soldier completed his assault with gladness.

Ugonna felt and thought nothing. Her blank stare was that of a dead person, without spirit and absent of life. The men dragged her back into the pen and shackled her to the others. She lay still with her mouth open, staring into the sky. She could not hear any sound and showed no response as the horrified Chimanda fell on her mother's chest. Everyone remained silent in fear of reprisal as the final trade agreement was completed.

The task of loading the human cargo began. These slaves would initially be loaded "tight pack" aboard the vessel, but through the attrition of death would eventually become "loose pack." Hopelessness abounded as most finally accepted the truth: no one was coming to save them.

They were transported to the ship called the *Baron Barksdale* by groups of three smaller boats, along with other goods. This took most of the afternoon, as males were separated from females and packed tight, close together, between decks. Most slave ships were large cargo vessels, specially modified with layers between, or "tween" decks, for the purpose of maximizing capacity. When all the captives were finally stowed and secured aboard,

Chimanda found herself five persons across from her mother, who remained silent and expressionless.

All the females lay on their back with their shoulders touching, while the males lay like spoons on their sides. Chimanda had called out to her mother several times, but she received no response. The heat was almost unbearable as the air was hot like steam and offered no relief or satisfaction. The space began to fill with the stench of excrement, urine, and vomit as the vessel set sail into the abyss, to a place unknown. The captives were absent of hope and full of despair. Most of the adult females, and a majority of the males, wished for a swift death, rather than endure another hour of the torment which was their present reality. One could not imagine that only a day before all of the souls were content and happy folk, common folk, no less, living in their villages. Now beaten, thirsty, exhausted, and half sane, they found themselves as different beings, trying desperately to make sense of their situation. The intense heat subsided as the ship made headway from the Bight of Biafra, or Old Calabar as most Europeans called it, into the heart of the Atlantic Ocean. Their destination was Charleston, South Carolina. The modified vessel was built with small openings to help move air through the cargo hold; that is if any wind were present.

Chimanda concentrated on her breathing and took in as much air as possible. She felt as though she could not get enough, no matter how deeply she breathed. She shut out the world as she closed her eyes and drifted off into darkness.

———————————

She woke the next morning in the dark with a terrible headache and the intense need to urinate. Looking around through the dark, she noticed the sun showing through imperfections in the vessel, like blades of grass made of light. Her need became so intense she could no longer restrain it and released herself, urinating where she lay, weeping from shame and sorrow. She was sorry for the person under her and for herself, but immediately thought of her mother.

"Momma!" she cried out, looking and listening for any sign of her. There was none. She called out her name several more times. She suddenly heard rumblings, and after a short while heard what sounded like a drum. This lasted for nearly an hour before subsiding.

The crew opened the compartments containing the females and children. Elongated chains connecting the feet of the captives were pulled through each row, allowing each person to move independently. The light was blinding, as all of the slaves were reintroduced to the Sun. They stumbled as they made their way, single file, onto the deck, to the clamor of the crew. Some could not walk and dropped to their knees, while others stood motionless. Those left behind were roughly handled and chided, while determining their condition, as the rest were led topside and seated.

As they came through the hatch, all were doused with buckets of seawater by the crew in an attempt to wash away the stench and stout odor emanating from them. They were given food and a pannikin, which contained their daily ration of a half pint of water. All this was devoured without sense of taste or savor. As she was being led atop, Chimanda looked around frantically for Ugonna and was deeply troubled when she didn't see her. Some of the crew came from below decks with the remaining slaves, her mother being among them. Chimanda wanted to call out to her, but remained silent, hoping Ugonna would look her way. They sat the women near the hatch from whence they emerged and gave them their rations. Chimanda watched as Ugonna sat expressionless, not responding to the food or water given to her. The sailor giving out the rations noticed her despondence and that she did not drink. He poured it in her mouth and watched it drain onto her lap.

The captain of the vessel reviewed the condition of the living cargo. He gave instructions to the first mate while selecting certain women. He informed the entire crew of the order. At the behest of the crew, all the women and children rose to their feet and began to hop and move, while the cabin boy beat his drum. They moved indiscriminately as Chimanda noticed her mother and two other women. They were led into another hatch by members of the crew without struggle. Chimanda was saddened by seeing her led away and dreaded what harm might come to her. She was correct to fear her mother's fate, as the Captain was a very shrewd man, but very practical in his own estimation. He valued the morale of his men and understood the importance of entertainment to bolster such.

It was a fact that a certain percentage of the slave cargo would expire during the voyage. He had witnessed up to thirty percent of cargos lost during previous voyages, and knew the weakest were usually the first to die. Unfortunately, Ugonna was marked as one of those slaves. The captain reasoned that rather than they perish without providing any profit, a portion of the weak females be relegated for the crew's entertainment and pleasure. This would avoid risking the impregnation of the more robust females, and not jeoparde the quality of the remaining cargo. The weak were destined to be exploited. When the exercise was over, all the remaining slaves were led back below deck. The hatch was closed, and darkness ruled once again.

Chimanda began to cry, but no tears would fall. Cries of the anguished and suffering filled the hold of the ship. She was mentally and physically exhausted and fell asleep. There were no fears of nightmares since none could compare to the waking horror of the present. Sleep was now every captive's hope, followed by the desire of a quick death. The well-aged realized that although the great waters separated them from their kinsfolk, the sweet release from this life would unite them with their ancestors, even from time primordial.

Four

STRANGER IN A STRANGE LAND

During the stormy months that followed, all the souls aboard the vessel were subjected to the temperament and whims of the ocean. Whether free or bond, all felt the same common emotion. Fear was the catalyst that unified them all. Nature illustrated that truth by inducing helplessness and desperation into all hearts, dousing the hope of those who had any vestiges of optimism. The brief unity between crew and captive was soon forgotten as the destructive tempests dwindled.

Time stood still for the slaves, but darkness, pain, sickness, and death continued for them. They did not know where they were going, when they would arrive, or how long they would be held captive. These basic unanswered questions further stripped the last remnants of hope from those who retained their mental or spiritual fortitude. It was these few captives who would at times muster a song or chant from their native land, encouraging all within earshot and themselves likewise. The songs would spread between decks and throughout the ship while the captain and crew observed. They allowed the cargo to keep their spirit about them, because in the spirit was life, and cargo delivered alive would lead to increased profits. The slaves either resolved to survive or had succumbed to death, with a few being betwixt.

Broken hearts and spirits killed as many men, women, and children as did dysentery. Although not cognizant of her decision, Chimanda had decided to live. She had not seen Ugonna since the first week and had stopped calling out to her. Chimanda's state of mind was only lifted in her dreams. She dreamt that her mother came and spoke to her.

"I love you, Chimanda! All will be well." The visions were crisp and clear to her. She held on to the hope that she and Ugonna would soon be together again. What Chimanda didn't realize was that a few days before her dreams started, Ugonna had succumbed to dysentery. During her last hours of life and despite her delirium she thought of Chimanda and Soja, as a vision of her late husband Akin appeared to her, comforting her with loving words and reassurances.

Ugonna was weak and despondent, yet still alive when she took Akin's hand and was thrown overboard along with two others. The sea absorbed their bodies without apology as it has always been willing to do. Undeterred, the pirate slave ship secretly made its way past Sullivan's Island and then onto its final destination, the Port of Charleston, South Carolina.

The morning Alabama mist had settled as the sun shone through the trees and into the window of Emily Walters' room. Her eyes opened to the sunlight as the petals of a flower would, ever so slowly. Suddenly, she sat up. Today her Papa was leaving for Charleston, in the state of South Carolina. She hopped out of bed onto the wooden floor, nearly slipping on her full-length nightgown. She ran down the stairs and out the front door, looking around frantically for her father, the Colonel. The wagon was near the stable and looked to be loaded with supplies beside another horse that was saddled. She could contain herself no more.

"Papa! Papa!"

"Emily! Come to the kitchen!" her mother Elizabeth shouted. She ran inside to the kitchen and saw the greatest man on earth: her father. He looked at her with a wide grin, his mouth full of biscuit and bacon. She ran around the table to his chair and threw her arms around him, just as he was taking a drink. As she squeezed him, he steadied himself and finished his cup of water.

"Ah, there she is! My baby girl!" He embraced his only child and kissed the top of her head. "I'm glad you woke up in time to see me off, Emily." She looked up at him with her sky-blue eyes.

"When will you come back, Papa?"

"Well, providing there are no storms or other inconveniences, perhaps next month. I want you to mind your mother. I don't want to return and hear a bad report. Is that understood, young lady?" The twelve-year-old nodded her head.

"Yes, Papa. I promise I will be a good girl." He smiled and kissed her on the forehead. His wife, Elizabeth, looked at them as her heart beat strong with approval. She was overjoyed by her husband's fondness and affection for their daughter but could not help thinking that he deserved more children, sons in particular. Had it not been for her barrenness, this could have been so. Emily's birth was difficult and nearly killed them both. She paused only for a moment to let the regret pass through her, never forgetting, but not dwelling upon it.

During her younger years, harboring such regrets had led to her deep depression and a consideration of suicide. She had often pondered how the act would free her husband to marry a more fertile woman if he wished. William Walters had risen to the occasion during those dark times, putting himself and his needs second, seeking only to comfort and care for his wife. He lay holding her many a night until dawn, and she had no doubts of his undying love.

He gathered his hat and made his way to the front of the house where he retrieved his sidearm from the table next to the door. Walking out on the porch he stopped and took a deep breath as he surveyed all his property and the beauty therein. The slaves had been in the fields since sunrise. Seven bucks and four wenches comprised his stock, and this journey to Charleston would hopefully yield him two more bucks. He was interested in slaves from the river Gambia region of Africa, or even the Gold Coast, if fortunes prevailed. Those were prized specimens indeed, and he had saved three hundred sterling in currency toward that effort. The addition of high-quality field hands would enable him to clear timber and farm ten more acres.

The overseer walked up to the porch. "Morning, Colonel Walters! It looks to be fine traveling weather for you sir."

"Good morning, Mr. Shannon. I have given you my instructions and expect you to have them completed before my return. Do you have any questions before I take my leave?"

Mr. Shannon paused momentarily. "No, sir, Colonel. Just know that I will look after your affairs as if they were mine," he exclaimed with a toothless smile. Walters was unaffected by the remark.

"Very well. I bid you all farewell." He embraced his wife, Elizabeth, and kissed his daughter on the cheek.

"Ned!" the Colonel shouted. A slave around sixty years of age came scurrying out of the stable.

"Yes, Massa Walters!"

"We are leaving."

"Yes, Massa Walters!" This was truly an exciting day for Ned. He knew this trip would take a good part of the month to complete. That meant weeks of freedom from field work in the Alabama sun. On the other hand, it would also be time away from his woman, Maggie, who worked in the big house. The thought had crossed his mind that the other bucks might try to press Maggie into relations during his absence. He eventually surmised that she wouldn't take on any other buck. She was Ned's woman, and like she had told him many times, she was only sweet on him. They climbed onto the wagon with a horse in tow.

"Get, get!" Colonel Walters sounded, as they started to move along their way. Elizabeth and Emily both watched their patriarch slowly disappear beyond the tree line and into the morning Alabama sunshine.

Colonel Walters planned to take the same route as always. They would make their way to Huntsville and follow the main road to Vienna and then turn south to Claysville. They would ferry across the Tennessee River to Gunners Landing, after which they would head south and rest up at Rosenant. The road east would keep the Coosa River on the right as they headed toward Rome. The rest of the trip was not negotiable, as the most direct route would be through Atlanta, Augusta, and then Columbia, South Carolina. There he planned to take a day to survey the state capital before heading directly to Charleston. The journey was indeed lengthy, but if not for Ned's constant banter, it would have seemed much longer.

As the days passed, Colonel Walters reflected on many things. He had come a long way during his fifty-four years of life. Born in North Carolina as the son of a county sheriff, he attended West Point in his youth. Graduating in the middle of his class, he was sent to take part in the Seminole Wars. Nothing could have prepared him for what he saw. Those years were followed by relatively peaceful days of promotion and the yearning of a life separate from the Army. He was assigned to gather up the remaining Creek Indians in the year eighteen thirty-seven to close the book on the Creek War.

Upon his father's death, Colonel Walters acquired his property and possessions. This provided the profits to start his small plantation. Ned was also an acquisition, and valuable in many ways. He was now older and grey but was still as spry as in the days of the colonel's youth. Ned had been taught much from Master Walter's father, which was passed along at every available opportunity. He reflected how Ned's presence eased the sorrow of his father's passing. Ned always spoke of the senior Massa Walters and told a great many stories of glory days far gone. When they made camp that night and as they sat around the fire, the Colonel probed Ned for reassurance on a matter.

"Ned, be sure you remember those African Ghana words, and don't forget to nod at me for those who understand them, before the auction begins. Our purpose is to get the two best bucks from the Ghana region. There are several ships supposedly filled with them as declared in the posting."

"Don't you fret, Massa Walters! Ned gone sort dem coloreds for you, likes the Lord gone separate the sheep from the goat! Yes, sir, Massa, don't you fret none at all!" His shiny eyes and broad smile gleamed. He always looked as though he was tearing, regardless of his mood, they were just watery.

"Oh, so you saying that you are the good Lord's equal Ned? You are separating on the same ground as the good Lord?"

"No, sir, Massa Walters! Ole Ned would never do such a thing! Oh, no, Massa, you know ole Ned don't have a bit a pride in his bones! Not even in my lil' finger!" Ned held up a crooked finger and smiled.

"That's good, because you remember from my scripture reading that pride comes before the fall. You are so old now, if you fell, you just might not get back up!" They both laughed. Ned laughed hard and long at the Colonels words, which was his ruse, and one among many which were rooted in self-preservation. They slept until daybreak and then continued on their arduous journey.

———————————

Ten days had passed since they began, and Colonel Walters had not slowed their pace, covering nearly twenty miles per day. Ned had begun to move slower, and grunt when waking up on the ground in the mornings. His old bones were feeling the effects from years of hardened servitude in the fields, the stables, and life.

Colonel Walters also felt the discomfort, being separated from his soft down bedding back at the plantation. He thought of his loving wife and precious daughter. He was concerned about his slaves and their well-being, but did not worry about them running away, believing in his heart that he treated them fairly. He did not work them to exhaustion and allowed them rest on the Sabbath, reasoning himself to be a just, God-fearing master. He knew other slave owners that regularly abused their own livestock. His main concern was his overseer, Mr. Shannon. Although, he had not discovered any act of impropriety by him, he had observed lust in the man's eye when overseeing one of the female field hands, Tabby. He feared Mr. Shannon would secretly engage in relations with Tabby while they were away. Other men in the community frequented their own slave quarters and many times impregnated the wenches, but he found this practice unethical, and immoral. It was an abomination in the sight of God to have offspring with a colored, and upon returning from the trip a close eye would be kept on Mr. Shannon.

He reminisced of his former company and their assignments in Mexico during the second year of the war, imagining himself back in the Army. After a few moments he mentally retreated from his disgust for the bloodshed and turned his thoughts back to his home in Alabama. It seemed that all recollections led him home. His family was the most important thing in his life, and everything was done for their sake.

Likewise, Ned thought about the plantation and his woman, Maggie. At this time, he was sickened by thoughts of one of the other bucks warming to her. He knew a slave named Jasper who always smiled when Maggie was around and it set Ned on fire. If something did happen while he was gone, he believed it would tell on Maggie's face. He wondered about these new field hands and whether Maggie would take a liking to one of them. In any event, hopefully Master Walters would not allow them to even speak to her.

"Hope not," Ned muttered under his breath.

"What you say there, Ned?"

"Oh, nuttin', Massa, just hopes we don't run into a storm on the way. It's been real peaceable like, all this way. Nope, don't need nuttin' foulin' up our journey!"

"Amen to that, Ned. Amen to that."

After another day and a half they finally made their approach to Charleston. It was noon, and they were famished. After hastily swallowing a good part of their food, they pressed on toward the markets. As they drew closer, the crowds grew increasingly dense and noisy. Colonel Walters stopped at a stable near to the market to give the horses a much-needed rest and shoeing for the return journey home.

"Keep pace with me, Ned!" Walters exclaimed, as he hastily walked to the north side of the Custom House, while Ned hobbled behind him, grimacing in discomfort as if tacks were in his shoes.

"Yes, sir, Massa. Ned right with you!"

Colonel Walters surveyed the courtyard off the street. All the entrances were guarded by auctioneer-hired men who appeared to share the same thuggish qualities and visage. The venue had changed since his last visit, six years prior. He could not see a way for him or Ned to get inside the building, let alone get close enough to the slaves before the auction began.

"Damn," whispered Walters under his breath.

"What to do, Massa?"

"What I came here for!" Walters was determined to achieve the goal of his journey. Slaves from Ghana were of the best quality. They were renowned among seasoned plantation owners for their endurance and strength. The work performed by only one man was equal to that of one and a half men, so in buying two he would be only feeding two slaves but receiving the labor dividends of three field hands.

During the next hours, dozens of slaves from Ghana were brought to auction as advertised, but the colonel was outbid by everyone. His frustration did not show, and he remained calm with his former military discipline intact. As the crowds dwindled, the prominent men made away with the finest of all lots, and Colonel Walters decided to make his charge. The last crop of slaves from Ghana were brought up and quickly secured by his bids. They were two fine specimens. One was slightly thinner than the other, but both had very good bone structure and hard musculature. He patted Ned on the back in excitement, happy with the ending auctions purchases.

"Them some fine looking field hands, Massa Walters! Prime field hands, prime!" The colonel nodded in satisfaction as the documents were drawn up and payment rendered, while Ned waited outside the building with the new livestock.

"Fine choice, Mr. Walters," the auctioneer complimented, as he shook the colonel's hand.

"Thank you, sir. It is said that these slaves from the Ghana region are among the choicest of field hands," Walters responded.

"Since they command the highest price, they should be among the highest quality," replied the auctioneer, his hands waving with emphatic mannerisms.

A man walked up to the colonel. "Sir, your negro is outside asking for you, and seems to be in a tizzy."

"Thank you." He walked out the door to meet Ned.

"What do you want, Ned?"

"Massa! I spoke the words just like you say to both dem bucks! The big one called Tom speak Ghana words. The other one you call James know only da words of dem Ibo African. He don't know not one of dem Ghana words! Massa, they trying ole trickery!" Ned's eyes were bloodshot with anger as if he had personally been injured in the exchange.

Walter squinted his eyes. "Are you sure?"

"Yes, sir, Massa Walters!" he pleaded.

Colonel Walters turned from Ned and walked back inside to the auctioneer, still poised and composed.

Chimanda sat on the floor of the holding room, which was once tightly packed with slaves. Twice she had been put on display, with no interest except by one bidder's child. As a youngling begs for candy, likewise the little girl entreated her father for a play mate but was summarily dismissed.

Chimanda had been thin before the abduction, but now appeared emaciated. Even so, she still retained an innate beauty, which emanated from her face and was solidified by her eyes. They were wondrous, piercing marvels, yet subtle and gentle. They were quite extraordinary. She was not chained or shackled due to her frailty and docility, and seemed almost forgotten, or so it seemed. One of the slave handlers approached the auctioneer as he stood talking with Colonel Walters and inquired of her disposition for the day.

"Sir, about the little one, she's finished for the day. What say you, me, and Otis mind her in our quarters tonight?" The auctioneer sighed at the unmannerly interruption.

"Very well. Just do not break the tiny black bird. Ensure she is to be able to walk tomorrow. Use only her mouth. Am I understood?" he answered and turned back to continue negotiating with the colonel. There was a misunderstanding as to the exact origin of his newly purchased field hand named James. The colonel had provided proof about the dialect spoken by the slave and had the position of leverage. The auctioneer was being pressed to compensate him through goods or merchandise as all sales were final. Colonel Walters continued his attack.

"Your offers of rice and grain are not nearly adequate, sir. Know that I will not leave this place until this injury has been rectified!" Walters maintained his stoic composure while the auctioneer removed his hat and ran his fingers through his hair.

"Very well, sir, I yield. What is it that would satisfy you? I would very much like this affair to be settled promptly as I have other matters to attend." Walters stood expressionless. He surmised that he had been cheated out a percentage of his property's worth but could not propose an adequate remedy. While pondering a solution, he noticed the slave handler pulling a scrawny girl across the room. He watched her being dragged, seemingly from weakness rather than stubbornness. She looked at the colonel and their eyes met. Walters came to himself and pointed at Chimanda

"That little one over there. I will take her in lieu of food or materials. We need not negotiate any further." The auctioneer turned with a look of surprise.

"Consider it done! Feed her and she'll plump right up! A fine bed warmer she will make until she is ready to work. An excellent choice, sir!"

"Draw up the papers right away. And your summations of my motives are incorrect. I have a young daughter who has no sibling, and they look to be near the same age. She will be a playmate until ready for field work or whatever I deem proper."

"I see. Well, right then, still a fine choice." The auctioneer walked to the document table, smiling.

"Bring her here to me now. She won't be putting anything in her mouth from your handlers." Walters added. The call went out and Chimanda was brought to stand at the document table. She kept her head down, trembling from fear and her weakened state. Colonel Walters stared at her while the papers were being completed.

"What would you like to call her?" the auctioneer asked, pausing with quill in hand. The colonel walked closer to Chimanda and lifted her chin gently until she looked into his eyes.

"I will call her Victoria."

The auctioneer paused momentarily. "A royal name? I must say, that is uncommon." The colonel was unaffected by his remarks. The papers were completed and the colonel started to walk out of the room. As he opened the door he turned to look behind him and saw Victoria behind him. He nodded and walked to the courtyard where he gathered Ned and the two other new acquisitions. They were loaded onto the wagon, as Colonel Walters mounted his steed and began their departure out of Charleston.

The passage back for Colonel Walters and Ned was marked with anticipation as they thought of their respective loved ones daily. Victoria sat in the back of the wagon, between James and Tom. For them the world had turned upside down, although their surroundings and treatment were much better than when aboard the slave ship. From the moment they disembarked they were astonished at the buildings, landscapes, and the smells in the air. They observed the white people with trepidation as they encountered a myriad of small towns en route to the unknown. Victoria was completely numb and felt like she didn't exist at all. Meanwhile, Colonel Walters and Ned kept each other amused as they conversed, passing the miles and the time.

The journey became a blur for the slaves as their will had long been broken. With no more tears to shed, they were emotionless.

It was an hour before the Alabama sun set, and the plantation was in sight.

"Oh, Massa! I see the promised land!" Ned proclaimed. "Thank you, Lawd!"

Colonel Walters glanced at him and smiled. "Yes, thank God."

Elizabeth and Emily were walking from the back of the house having just finished filling a small bucket with freshly picked pecans. As they strolled toward the front porch, both noticed the approaching wagon and horse.

"Papa!" Emily shouted as she pulled away from her mother's hand and ran toward her father. Elizabeth smiled and waved her hand in excitement as she followed behind Emily.

"William!"

As Emily approached the wagon, Colonel Walters set the brake and disembarked. He bent down and tightly embraced her.

"Papa, I missed you so much! I've been a good girl and listening to Mama! We just finished picking pecans and Maggie is about to make a pie with them!"

"I missed you as well, baby girl, and I knew you would behave yourself. I had no doubts and brought you something. Look in the back of the wagon." Emily smiled as she ran off to see while Elizabeth walked up to him. He stared into her eyes.

"Elizabeth, my dearest love. I have longed for you." She began to tear and broke her gaze while throwing her arms around him.

"Oh William, I am so glad you are home! I miss your presence the moment you leave!"

She squeezed him tightly as she inhaled deeply, relishing the scent of her husband.

"Dear, I believe this was the last time. If the good Lord wills it, the stock we have presently will multiply and hopefully bear fruit. Come, look what we own." They walked to the rear of the wagon where Emily and Ned stood. The men sat shackled, sitting upright, while Victoria lay on her side between them, unshackled.

"Papa, she is so tiny. How can she do any work?"

"Well, she isn't going to do any field work for a while. First, she needs to be tended and revived, so that is why we will not brand her today. For now, she will sleep in the cellar with Maggie. Go tell Maggie to come down here to fetch her. Her name is Victoria."

"Yes, Papa!" Emily ran off to the house to find Maggie. He turned to Ned.

"Take these two and locate Mr. Shannon. I want them branded and working tomorrow, clearing the new fields. Then you will tend to the horses and clean this filthy wagon! Do what you must and rid it of that powerful stench! In that order, understand? Then you can speak to your Maggie."

"Yes, sir, Massa Walters!" Ned replied as he hurried the two men down from the wagon.

Elizabeth was fixated on Victoria, who was still lying on her side.

"You gave her a queen's name, I see. What did you pay for her?" Elizabeth asked

"It's the first one that came to mind, and even though she is frail and pathetic, she has a look about her eyes. Besides, I paid nothing for her, but gained her through my skillful negotiation." Elizabeth put her hand on his chest and smiled.

"My wise husband." They both looked to see Emily and Maggie approaching.

"Welcome back, Massa Walters! We done miss you heaps!" she exclaimed.

"It's good to be home, Maggie. Ned will be around later tonight to visit you. I know you're wondering where he is."

"Oh, Massa, I thank you! Now what we got here, Massa? Looks like a little bird done fell out a tree!" Maggie walked up to the wagon and reached out to touch Victoria's leg. "Come here lil' thing. Come to Maw Maw and lets me take care of you." Maggie spoke in her soothing voice.

Victoria sat up with her eyes closed and faced her. When she opened them, Maggie was taken aback in surprise.

"Look at her eyes, Papa. I never saw eyes like that," Emily uttered. Elizabeth remained silent as Victoria got down off the wagon and was led away by Maggie. The grass felt good underneath Victoria's bare feet and holding Maggie's warm hand was soothing to her. Maggie led her to the room in the cellar where she slept and then got water from the well to prepare the wash tub. After it was filled, Victoria was stripped and helped to step in it. While she stood upright, Maggie began washing her and humming a spiritual song. The gentle touch of Maggie, along with the emotions carried by her song, overwhelmed Victoria. She felt an uncontrollable force growing deep inside and cried out.

"Iya!" Tears streamed down her face. Maggie stopped washing her and embraced her tightly while she wept.

"It gone be all right child, don't you fret now. You got to let it go." Maggie knew the word *Iya* meant "mother" in the Yoruba dialect. She had not heard it spoken since the time of her childhood before her own abduction. She bent over and looked in Victoria's teary eyes while lightly tapping her chest.

"Victoria," she said and then tapped her own chest. "Maggie." She did this twice as Victoria stood, sniffling but attentive. She took Victoria's hand and pulled it to her own chest, while whispering. "Maw Maw. Iya, Iya." Victoria understood, but started to cry again. Maggie hugged her once more. "Let it go child. Everything gone be all right." She resumed humming while washing her, and soon Victoria stopped sobbing. They finished the bath and Maggie wrapped an old piece of cloth around her and had her lay down on the bedding.

"You stays right here and rest. Maw Maw gonna bring you some vittles." Victoria didn't understand any of the words except for Maw Maw, but she did know that Maggie was kind. The feeling of being clean while lying on the straw filled mattress, put Victoria to sleep within minutes. The Alabama sun would soon set, and, after a few short days of respite, Victoria's indoctrination into her new way of life would continue.

Five

STATE OF THE UNION

10 YEARS LATER

It was the year 1863 and the Union was at war, the line drawn. In the North, it was known as the War to Save the Union, and in the South, it was the War of Northern Aggression. The great hope and ideals which were consecrated in blood and sacrifice during the American Revolution had been splintered and disfigured. The earlier decades were filled with upheaval and contention, both financially and morally. Taxes, tariffs, and trade disputes were among the main subjects of dissent between Northern and Southern states, specifically Industry versus Agriculture.

These contentions were only symptoms of the true sickness of America, caused by the subtle demise of the Statesman, which ushered in the birth of the Politician. Like a cancer, these greedy men infected the land and its inhabitants. The result was continuous death and decimation of the common folk by the common folk.

The past two years of bloodshed and violence left tens of thousands of dead, families and communities devastated. The Battles of Manassas, Antietam, Shiloh, Fredericksburg, and

Gettysburg were counted as victories by opposing sides, but the reverberations of destruction cried otherwise. The draft was instituted in the North and conscription in the South. The reaping of human crops was in full production and none was spared. White, Black, Native American, Mexican, and Oriental, whether free or bond were readily accepted by both sides for combat. Willingly or unwillingly they fought and died.

Caleb Price sat at the counter of his small hardware store reading the weekly news. Wearing his spectacles, he was intently focused on an article on the riots erupting in New York City earlier that year. It was in opposition to President Lincoln issuing the compulsory draft. He finished and took off his glasses in disgust, scratching his white bushy beard.

"It simply does not ever end," he muttered to himself. He went to stand and winced due to a sharp pain in his knee. He bent down and rubbed it. He had many such pains and aches indiscriminately arising at a moment's notice. At 66 years of age, the retired captain's health was good in general, and his store prosperous. He had built it upon a bluff off the main road. He could see the Connecticut River a few hundred yards away. He yearned to be near the water. The sea still lived inside him. Watching the flowing river carrying the ships to and fro pacified his longing for the seaman's life. He never ventured to the mouth of the river where it met the ocean. He felt it would torment him, so he kept it out of his sight. Just then he remembered something important.

"Shay!" he shouted. After a few seconds Shay walked in from the back of the store and stood before Price.

"Yes, sir?"

"Shay, I just remembered that the hammers and saws need to be delivered to the mill before evening. I meant for you to take them on your way to the market this morning. It would have saved at least an hour."

"I already did it, just as you said," Shay said smiling.

"That's my boy, very good," Price answered. "Now we need to decide on what we are going to have for supper."

"Well, sir, there is enough to put together some stew. We have some beef, some potatoes, celery, and also a few ears of corn. Do you want me to get it started?"

"No, you just finish repairing those two barrels and I will get it," Price answered.

"Yes, sir, it will take me about two hours, I think." Shay tapped the counter and walked off.

Price watched him as he went through the curtain and into the backroom. His mind was taken back to the early years when he first laid eyes on the skinny boy who was in dire straits. The years had been good to Shay, and to himself as well. He no longer wanted to be called Shu-Shay, and his wishes were respected. He had lived to reach twenty-one years of age, and, being stout and smart, he had turned out to be a fine young man. Taught to respect him and others, Shay was one of few words. He had learned many lessons, among those having the ability to listen much and speak less. Price had taught him to use his words wisely and sparingly.

Growing up, Shay faced the usual discrimination that a child who looked differently within a new community would, but he experienced no violence from other children. In time, many of the children befriended him. Price had believed Shay deserved to have a decent childhood. Some folk the community looked upon Shay as a sort of human trinket brought back from faraway lands by the once Captain Caleb Price. Price dispelled these notions on several occasions, making it clear that Shay was under his patronage. He stopped only short of legally adopting Shay and calling him his son. Never the less, Price ensured that his estate and belongings would be inherited by Shay. Price's dear mother had long since passed, and he considered Shay as his only son.

In Shay's eyes, Price was a father in every sense of the word, though he never addressed him as such. He felt that if the captain wanted to be addressed as such, he would give instruction to do so. The lack of conversation concerning the matter never arose and seemed moot.

Shay peeked through the curtains. "Sir, after I finish the barrels may I go fishing with Gus?"

"Yes, just be back before sunset so we can eat supper."

"Aye, aye, sir!" Shay said in an elevated voice jokingly.

"You get going or get fed to the sharks!" Price retorted humorously.

Shay completed repairing the two barrels earlier than expected. He got his pole and some crickets he had been catching since the day before in preparation and headed to a favorite bank along the river.

Sitting along the bank he could see a great deal of activity. There were boats and ships moving to and fro. Union soldiers were loading a frigate on the east bank. Folks were all around, fishing from boat and land. He cast in and waited. His mind raced with thoughts about the world around him, namely the war. All his friends had long since left and enlisted, most of them two years previously during the voluntary enlistment call. Only Gus was left. He was a free black man, born to free black parents. Both Captain Price and Gus's parents paid the necessary $300 for Shay and Gus to avoid the draft. Both were against the war effort and believed that diplomacy should be used to bring about peace. They had hoped that the enormous toll taken on both sides was more than enough incentive to end the bloodshed. Sadly, this was not the case. Shay looked down the road and saw Gus approaching. He was quite a bit taller than Shay, with a burly build. The two friends were quite the motley pair.

"Hurry up, Gus! Two have got away already and you need to catch up!" Shay shouted.

"You just don't worry about that, I'm about to catch them all!" Gus sounded back laughing, as he sat down in his usual spot. "It's nice out today. They should be really biting. What's the captain doing?" Gus asked.

"He's cooking supper; stew. I'm glad he's cooking today. I'm tired of cooking this week. I wish I could hire a cook, ha ha!"

"I would rather cook than cut fire wood," Gus replied.

"I cut wood *and* cook! Stop your complaining," Shay laughed.

They sat quietly for a few minutes. Then Gus came out with his news "All right, I have to tell you now: I'm enlisting in the Army as a scout. I'm going, Shay!"

"Say again?" he asked in disbelief. "Did you tell your folks yet?"

"I'm telling them tonight. It's done. I'm a grown man and I need to do what I think is right! All our friends have long since joined the fight. Some have even died, and I just sit here at home like some coward. Nope, no more. I'm going to fight and prove myself. We all need to kick in, Shay. So, I just wanted to tell you as soon as I could, because you're my best friend," he explained while observing his line for a catch.

Shay was shocked. He felt pulled apart. Gus had done what Shay dreamed of doing long ago. To do his part and prove himself.

"I can hardly believe it," Shay said somberly.

"Well, believe it, friend," Gus responded with a look of determination.

Shay continued., "You know how bad I've wanted to get into the fight."

"Well, get into fight, then! You're a grown man and can make your own decisions. I plan to pay my parents back the $300 they spent to keep me from going."

"I just don't know how I can tell Mr. Price what I want to do. He saved my life, Gus. I told you about everything. If I go and enlist, it's as if I'm ungrateful and disrespectful. And I will not disrespect him."

Gus looked over at him. "Shay, it won't be any harder for you than for me. My parents and Captain Price are the same. They did what they thought was best, but you have your own life to live. You should be your own man," he said while shaking his head.

They sat quietly for a while. Neither one was catching any fish. Gus turned to Shay. "Listen to me. We ride well, we hunt and track, and we read maps well, too. We've been doing this for years. Well, that's our skill, and the Army is always in need of good scouts. If you joined, then we would be together during the war and could depend on each other. Talk to the captain and see what he says about the idea."

"I already know what he will say. He will not accept the idea."

"I understand you're scared," Gus chided.

"I'm not scared of fighting, and you know that. I'm no coward!"

"I know you're not a coward, but you fear Captain Price, at least what he might think. That's what I mean to say," Gus said apologetically.

They fished for another hour, catching nothing. They shook hands and departed company. All the while, Gus's words continued to sting Shay's conscience. Even though Shay loved and respected the captain, he wondered if he did indeed harbor fear of him.

For Shay, the fear of disappointing him seemed worse than the fear of death itself. He picked up his pole and bait and began walking home as the sun began to set. He pondered what to say. How should he bring up the matter? The thoughts sank deep and his stomach felt as if it were tied in knots. Everything was going so well, Shay thought. He was happy though he still longed to experience the outside world. Imaginations of fantastical feats of glory and valor filled his mind, invigorating his spirit. He used these exciting thoughts as encouragement for the conversation he knew must happen. He clutched the jade amulet which still hung around his neck which always seemed to make him feel better. Only briefly did the memory of his departed mother come to mind.

Quickly he eschewed the visions, as they never failed to bring him sadness. Determined to be independent, he made up his mind. He approached the back of the hardware store.

The small building was divided into two halves, the rear being the living quarters, kitchen, and common area with a couch and chairs. Shay entered and removed his hat, leaving his pole and bucket outside. The smell of the hearty stew was in the air and Shay was famished. Captain Price was sitting on the couch reading. He stopped and took off his spectacles.

"Did you catch anything?"

"No, sir, not a single thing. Gus came up empty handed, too."

"I'm surprised at that. Gus seems to always fill his bucket. Let us eat."

They sat down and broke bread, as they had done for the past ten years, and ate supper together. They had an invisible bond which seemed more apparent to both of them during these times. Captain Price noticed the odd silence during the meal. Shay usually talked about a great many things during supper, but yet on this night he ate quietly.

"What is on your mind? You are quiet as a church mouse," Price asked.

"Well, sir, Gus told me today that he is enlisting in the Army. He is going to join the cavalry as a scout." Shay paused as the captain stopped eating and fastened his eyes upon him. Shay continued, "He wants me to go with him, so we can serve together and look out for each other."

Captain Price wiped his mouth and remained silent.

"I told him you would not approve of it, even though I want to go."

Price breathed deeply and folded his hands with his elbows on the table. He responded to Shay, "The first issue I have is with Gus. He will not be in the cavalry and will not be a scout. He will be infantry. The Twenty-ninth Colored Regiment is the next regiment being formed and he will be with them. You would most likely be assigned to the twenty-seventh regiment, and that as reinforcement, leaving before him. Gettysburg just took thousands of lives according to the reports." He looked at Shay who was listening intently. "I do not see you joining the cavalry, as the First Connecticut Cavalry have long since been deployed. It would take some planning and communication with those of high station to even have you considered for a cavalry unit."

"How do you know all this? You hate the war," Shay responded.

"The news reports, the customers who we deal with, and the officers at the tavern confirm all I have told you. Besides, why should hating the war have me remain ignorant about the war? A man should always be aware of his surroundings, near and far. Besides, you still have not told me the reason why you want to leave me and all we have built here." There was a long pause as Shay tried to collect his thoughts in response.

He replied, "Yes sir, but they also said in the news that those non-citizens who fight would have their immigration for citizenship expedited. I want to be an American citizen. I thank you for allowing me to use your last name and treating me as a son. I am grateful, sir, but all my friends have left, save Gus, and he will be gone soon, too. I just want to do my part." Shay paused. "I just want to live my own life, sir."

Captain Price was taken aback. He had never heard Shay truly speak his mind in this way. He spoke as young man would. Price accepted the fact that Shay was a grown man now.

"You are a man indeed. I have tried to protect you since the day our paths crossed. I see the danger and deception in a great many things concerning this war which others see differently, including yourself. Alas, my beliefs are not of higher value than yours. I must yield to you in this matter, but you know how I feel about it." Captain Price got up from the table and walked toward his room.

"Sir, I will repay you the $300 you spent for the—"

"No! You owe me nothing. What I did for you was done from my heart, and acts that are done from the heart require no repayment. Goodnight." Price closed his door.

Shay sat at the table alone. He felt conflicted. He was excited that the matter was now settled. He was somber due to the mood of Price. Shay had spoken the truth, and so had the captain. The fact was that the truth still hurt. It was then that Shay realized that no one ever said the truth would not hurt. He now understood what that meant.

It was high noon and not a cloud was in the sky. The Alabama sun shone down with all its majestic ferocity upon the town square. At least 200 citizens had showed up to hear the latest news, officially. Unofficially, everyone had already heard the rumor of the new income taxes that were to be implemented on the citizens of the Confederate States. None were thrilled about the extra tax which many found comparable to the sacred tithe instituted in the scriptures. With most of the men-folk going off to fight and regularly being killed or maimed, the Southern women were left to do anything and everything in order to preserve any remnants of their families. It was no wonder that the women present at the gathering outnumbered the men almost three to one.

The men there, however, were a diverse group themselves. From the wealthiest slave owner to the poorest Southern man, the distance between their respective stations in life mimicked the gap between the fairness of the new tax. While the majority of citizens were burdened with this new unjust levy, a majority of wealthy land and slave owners were exempt from it. This led to the spreading of a new Southern mantra. "Rich man's war, poor man's fight". It seemed a point that could not be debated, since most Southerners never owned slaves and were underprivileged citizens. They were humble folk, yet proud of their heritage. Many of them never took part in the politics and were only concerned with the preservation and survival of their families.

Not surprisingly, the Confederate Army was comprised mainly of the Southern common folk, as was the Union Army. Discontent was in the air, and as the temperature rose so did the tolerance of the people. The speaker departed the podium, heading straight for his carriage. He apologetically conveyed his regret that he could not detain himself any longer to answer any questions as he had to leave immediately for the next county. As the dust of the horses trailed slowly behind the party, the citizen's uproar began to increase.

"Damn that son of a bitch! Dammit!" an old man shouted out from the fervor. Colonel Walters shook his head in disgust. While many of the wealthiest were exempted from the new tax, he was not.

"Come on, Ned. I am taking leave of this place this instant!" They walked south, out of the square to side of the general store where the wagon was hitched, and climbed up.

"This thing got you powerful troubled, Massa Walters! What the devil they talkin' 'bout, Massa?" Ned asked.

Walters shook his head and then replied. "You wouldn't understand the mathematics, and don't need to understand them." Walters paused. "Just you understand that your master is not happy!" Walters shouted looking directly at Ned, who hung his head.

"Yes, Massa! Ned understand," he responded and sat quietly. A few moments later Walters patted Ned on his leg.

"Don't you worry about nothing, Ned. It's not your fault. It's them that got my temper up. You are a good boy, Ned."

"Yes, sir, Massa Walters! Ole Ned be here right by your side, Massa!" he responded gingerly, as this type of interaction was commonplace whenever the colonel was upset.

Walters looked around the area feverishly. "Where is she, Ned? Get down and find her. Hurry up!" Ned started to make his climb off the wagon, slowly and painfully.

At that moment Victoria briskly walked around the corner directly toward them. Colonel Walters visage changed from impetuousness to relief.

"Girl, what took you so long? You should have been here waiting for us," Walters asked as he climbed down to help her up onto the wagon.

"Massa, I been got the sugar and the spices Miss Elizabeth wanted, but a woman with two chaps in front of me took the longest time. Then I was leaving out, three men hindered me. They was all around me. Massa, I was scared! They was asking me who owned me? Where is my papers? I thought they was gonna take me! I was looking for you!" Victoria exclaimed while climbing up to sit in the middle. Her legs were trembling, and she was visibly shaken. Walters climbed up and took the reins.

"What then?" he asked.

"I started to cry, and one of them said, 'shit, let's go.' Then they left me. Massa, I was ready to throw the spice in their eyes!" Victoria explained. Walters laughed as he started the wagon down the street.

"Had you done that, they would have beat you, dragged you in the alley way and knew you ten times over. It's my fault. I know good and well how the men turn their heads and come to you like bees to honey," Walters stated with a smirk. They turned west, heading back home to the plantation. Just then the colonel saw three men standing across the street from the stable.

"Look over there, Victoria. Are those the men?" Walters asked.

"Yes, those men was the ones!" The colonel pulled in front of the men and slowed to a stop.

"Hey, you three! I'm putting you on notice here and now. Don't you ever detain my slave again. Look at her, and take a good look at me and remember my face. There will not be another warning." The men looked dumbfounded and puzzled.

One of them began to plea some false excuse as Walters immediately set off on his way with disregard and finality. As they made their way out of town there was silence, but Victoria grinned with satisfaction. The colonel always displayed such gestures on her behalf. Surprisingly, there were instances where the colonel seemed to take her side over the wishes of Miss Elizabeth.

"You ought to thank the Lord every night that you have a Master such as I. Most would have ravaged you long ago and even made you lay for profit as a prostitute. Yes, you should thank the Lord for me!" he exclaimed in self-righteousness.

The colonel was not entirely untrue with his statements. The once malnourished and boney black girl from western Nigeria had flourished in health and beauty. She was an extraordinarily beautiful woman. To distinguish her further, she was gifted with exceptional eyes. The type of which were rare among any race of human people. Her beauty alone increased her value nearly fourfold of any comparable Negro woman of the same age.

Now at age twenty-one Victoria was well into child bearing years. Multiple times her purchase was propositioned to the colonel by large visiting plantation owners. The answer was always the same, no matter what price was offered. Mrs. Walters could not understand why her husband refused the tremendous and occasionally outrageous offers made. At first it infuriated her. Victoria's sale could have provided revenue to purchase three or four more slaves. But Colonel Walters saw Victoria as a rare jewel. The fact that so many of his neighbors and fellow slave owners desired her made him feel a sense of importance and power, similar to the power he felt while serving as an officer in the Army.

Deep down he felt satisfaction in the envy of others. He relished in the ability to refuse the monetary offers of others who were wealthier than himself, but more so he enjoyed having Victoria in the house. She was extremely pleasant to the eye. Her addition brought a refined luster to the plantation. Whether entertaining visitors or having breakfast, her presence seemed to add the refinement of a higher station to the Walters Plantation. Being taught the basis of her role as a slave, her duties, and basic English by Maggie was just part of her early education. Further development came from her exposure to Emily.

For the past ten years Emily and Victoria were inseparable, with the exception of her servant duties. Emily cherished her new Negro playmate, and as they both grew together Victoria began to speak and take on the mannerisms of her friend. The result was a well-spoken and beautiful Negro house slave. Colonel Walters watched this unfold before his eyes. He refused to let Victoria have relations with a white man or slave. Within his deepest contemplations he knew that she should not be sullied, and in his estimation, although she was a slave, she was very different from the others. Victoria was special.

The heat on the road back home had improved due to heavy southwesterly winds.

On the front porch of the big house, Mrs. Walters sat accompanied by Emily and her suitor Nathan Treadwell. Supper time was upon the hour and Maggie had everything prepared, simmering in black iron pots and skillets.

"William should be here soon," Mrs. Walters remarked. "Unless the meeting ran long, he should be here within the hour."

Nathan stood up with his hands on his hips and stretched his back. "I hope so ma'am, because I am working up a powerful hunger. One cannot smell the sweet aroma of Ms. Maggie's culinary labor without becoming ravenous!" he exclaimed.

Mrs. Walters and Emily both chuckled. "At times, I don't know if you come calling on me, or just using me as an excuse to eat Maggie's cooking! What say you about that, Mr. Treadwell?" Emily demanded.

"Now, Miss Emily Walters, I declare right now in the presence of the honorable Mrs. Elizabeth Walters, and before God Almighty, that you are my one and only interest on this plantation."

Emily sat back in her rocking chair and responded. "So, Mr. Treadwell, should I take that statement to mean that on other plantations you have other interests? Such as Sally Mae Jackson, perhaps?" Nathan's eyes widened and he started to turn red. Emily continued. "Why so silent on the matter, Nathan? I asked a simple question. Well, I guess you answered it then, thank you." Emily enjoyed the use of sarcasm in general, but specifically with Nathan.

He responded as he walked closer to Emily's chair. "Emily, my dear, I have in no way shown interest in that young woman. Please be reasonable with your thoughts and understand that I—" Just then he was interrupted by Mrs. Walters.

"Nathan, please! Don't you see she is having fun with you? I have told her about that before. You need only answer her question with no, and then be done with it."

Emily pouted. "Mama, you shouldn't interfere."

"Well, if I have to hear all this foolishness, I am going to speak my peace. Now you mind your tongue, young lady!" Mrs. Walters sat forward suddenly with an unkind look on her face. There was an awkward silence as Nathan retreated to the corner of the porch. He took hold of the banister and used it to support himself with one hand. He used his other hand to massage the pain in his knee, which was caused by a riding accident as child; he walked with a noticeable limp. Emily saw his discomfort and walked over to him.

"Let me rub it for you, Nathan." She squatted down and began to slowly massage his knee. Nathan closed his eyes and savored the relief brought on by Emily's touch. He was also relieved that she was not truly angry with him. She would squabble with him at the oddest times, but then be sweet to him in the next instant.

Mrs. Walters glanced over at the two of them. She was partly disgusted by her daughter's behavior. Bending down so low and rubbing her suitor's infirmity in a mother's presence was a violation of social etiquette, to say the least. Notwithstanding, she knew that Nathan loved Emily and believed that Emily loved him in her own unique way. Just then a wagon could be seen at the plantation entrance. Mrs. Walters stood up.

"You both compose yourselves. William is back home!" She smiled and walked to the top step in anticipation. Nathan made his way down the steps and stood in front of the house. Emily stayed seated. All of them waited with sincere smiles. The wagon pulled up, and the colonel set the brake. He took off his hat and wiped the sweat from his brow.

"Hello, family!" he exclaimed "Greetings, Nathan." Mrs. Walters walked down the steps in front of the wagon. Mr. Walters climbed down and put his arm around his wife.

"I'm hungry dear and ready for supper."

"All is ready. Go wash up and I'll have Maggie make ready."

"Very good." He looked over at Nathan, who stood waiting in anticipation with an outstretched hand to greet the colonel.

"It's good to see you, Mr. Walters! I'm looking forward to hearing your report from the meeting, sir!"

"In due time, Nathan. Not good news at all, unless you are a rich man or a politician," Walters moaned as he and Elizabeth walked up the stairs, where Emily was now standing, waiting.

"Hello, Papa! Did you bring me back anything from town?"

"No, Emily, not this time." Emily pretended disappointment. Walters continued, "When is the last time Nathan brought you something? I mean to say something besides wild flowers and a few pieces of candy, that is."

"Papa!" Emily exclaimed in anger. Walters shook his head and walked in the house holding his wife's hand as Elizabeth looked back at Victoria.

"Come on in the house and bring those spices I had you fetch. Maggie has been asking about them."

"Yes, ma'am!" Victoria replied happily. She quickly walked up the steps and past Emily as their eyes met. As best friends, they had the seeming ability of non-verbal communication, and Victoria knew Emily was out of sorts. Furiously, Emily walked to the front banister and leaned on it with both hands, she caught Nathan's eye. She stared intensely at him in anger until she could no longer refrain.

"Well!" she shouted out loud. His eyes widened as he slowly turned away from her view, carefully contemplating his words.

Meanwhile, Ned got in the driver's seat, trying all the while to quell his laughter as the discord between the two transpired. He rode down to the stables and told Jasper to water and feed the horses. Jasper was initially uncooperative, citing that Mr. Shannon was the overseer and not Ned. However, after receiving a verbal lashing, Jasper reconsidered his position. Ned reminded him that Ned was the colonel's favorite.

Ned went back up to the big house and tried peeking in the window to catch a glimpse of Maggie, with no success. He decided to do a certain bird call that she knew as his signal. After a short time, she came to the back door and spoke to Ned in an elevated whisper.

"Hey, Ned, I knows you all are back. I'm about to serve supper. I'll come down and bring you some fixin's after a while. Now, 'bye!" She walked back inside and out of sight. Ned just smiled, nodded his head happily in agreement, then hobbled away as he smelled the savory aroma of future nourishment.

The morning sun had just started to rise as the New England dew was at its fullest. It coated the land as completely as skin clothes a man. Shay and Captain Price had long since risen, and Shay was about to leave and report for duty. Gus was assigned as foretold by Price to the Twenty-ninth Colored Regiment, which would be leaving at a later date. The farewell between best friends had taken place the night before. Concerning Shay, Captain Price had used his contacts in the War Department and those locally to secure Shay's opportunity to serve as a scout in the cavalry. Although Caleb Price was his patriarch, he had not formally adopted Shay, so a slight misrepresentation was used. Shay enlisted under the surname Price and an affidavit was signed by Caleb Price as Shay's father.

Shay was an excellent rider and hunter. He also could read maps extremely well. He was disciplined naturally, but all these traits could not reassure Price of his well-being. Nonetheless it was done. Shay gathered his satchel and turned to Captain Price

"Well, sir, I am ready."

"You look ready," Price replied. They stood silent for a moment, each looking for words.

"Well, goodbye," Shay said.

"Goodbye, Shay. Remember who you are, and come back home," Price responded sternly. Shay turned and walked out the door and onto the street, untied, and mounted his horse. Price stood at the door and watched him slowly ride off. The feeling of emptiness filled them both.

Shay suddenly stopped and turned and said: "I love you, Father."

The words hit Price unexpectedly, but he stood stoic. In acknowledgement, he nodded his head. Shay smiled and continued up the thoroughfare and out of sight. Price closed the door and paused. He walked over to the table and sat down. He took a deep breath, removed his spectacles, covered his face, and sobbed quietly.

Six

WAR OF SHADOWS

It was September 27th and the Union Army was close to completing the largest combined troop movement in history, sending 24,000 soldiers over 1,100 miles in support of the Army of the Cumberland, led by General Rosecrans at Chattanooga, Tennessee.

The arduous journey was a logistics nightmare. The days were spent marching to railway connections, loading trains with the troops, horses, and supplies with the utmost sense of urgency. Repeated short trips were made by rail as Union forces inched their way south from Virginia to their final destination of Bridgeport, Alabama.

Shay was deployed with the 1st Connecticut Cavalry, which had been assigned earlier to the XI Corps, Army of the Potomac. Shay was asleep in his seat with his head leaning against the rail car window. The rhythmic sound of the train put most of the men to slumber. Some wrote letters while others were playing cards. Faint laughter could be heard throughout the cars as many dreamt, as did Shay.

He found himself as a small child running through the grass in springtime. He saw a young woman whom he recognized as his mother. She smiled at him and glowed with the fullness of health and vitality. He ran up to her in excitement and hugged her around her waist. She looked down at him and ran her fingers tenderly through his hair. He inhaled his mother's scent and with each breath became more invigorated. Then she was gone.

He became very sad and frantically started to look for her. As he began to cry he noticed Captain Price standing behind him. He looked older and frail. Shay smiled and ran over to the him with anticipation as the captain knelt down, displaying a sad countenance. Shay stood in front of him, reached out his tiny hand, and touched the captain's bushy white beard. He slowly raised his head and caught Shay's eyes.

"My son!" Captain Price shouted with fervor, clutching Shay and picking him up. Standing tall his face now beaming with joy, he began to walk off into the field with Shay in his arms.

"Wake up, Price! Price!" the sergeant shouted. Shay opened his eyes and began to examine his surroundings.

"We are in Nashville; last stop before Bridgeport. Listen up, everybody! You got one hour to get off and stretch your legs! Do not wander off! Whorehouses in the area are off limits! I need two volunteers to accompany me and deliver some items to the Field Command!" There was a brief pause as he continued sarcastically, "Don't all volunteer at once!" He looked down at Shay. "You, sleepy head, come with me." Shay got up and followed the sergeant out the car.

"Private Woods, fall in!" the Sergeant barked at another soldier. They both trailed the sergeant down the line a bit and gathered two medium-sized chests. They each took one.

"We got no time to get a wagon, so let's be off double-quick time!" he ordered.

"What's in these?" Woods asked as they hurriedly marched.

"That is of no mind to you, Woods. These are for General Dodge. Just so you both understand this is my first time meeting him, so you two keep your mouths shut and maintain attention. I will do the talking!" Shay and Woods looked at each other in silent communication.

At last they arrived at the Field Command Post. Armed guards were posted beside the double door entrance, with two more at the stairwell. At the bottom of the steps Sergeant Hollister presented a document to them. One guard stepped forward and examined it.

"Give me the keys to these trunks and set them down." They did as instructed and stood awkwardly for a moment. The guard directed them down the steps from where they had just come, it was then that Sergeant Hollister became red faced.

"Corporal, this is meant for General Dodge! What do you think you are doing?" The corporal seemingly ignored him as he opened both chests slightly to inspect the contents. He nodded to the other guard, who went inside briefly and returned with a sergeant major and another gentleman. They walked over, picked up the chests, and carried them inside. The other man was not in a uniform and looked like a common trapper, a rugged type wearing a wide-brim hat. Hollister could take no more.

"Sergeant Major, we were given orders to deliver these to General Dodge personally. This does not sit well with me," Hollister spoke loudly but with a tempered tone. The two men stopped and turned back to look. The Sergeant Major responded firmly,

"I don't really care what sits well with you, Sergeant. You have completed your assignment and may return to your unit. Thank you." The other man, while looking at Shay, leaned over and whispered into the sergeant major's ear. Hollister was undone but maintained his bearing.

"If I might ask, would it be possible to meet the General? I never had the—"

"Are you hard of hearing, Sergeant? I am the personal aid to General Dodge! Do I have to put down this trunk and reprimand you in the field?" Hollister came to attention with snap, the position which Shay and Woods had long assumed.

"No, Sergeant Major," Hollister answered.

The sergeant major smiled and looked at Shay.

"You there, come and take this chest inside. Who knows, perhaps you will meet a general."

Shay hurried up the steps and took ahold of the chest, and all three men walked inside the building. They led Shay down a hallway into another room where a guard stood in front of double doors. The guard knocked twice and a voice inside commanded entry. The doors opened to a great room where sat a very large desk, and tables covered with maps. Behind the desk sat General Dodge who stood up with anticipation.

"Is it all there, Naron?" the General asked the civilian.

"Yes, sir, General, it is all there. Twenty bottles of the finest cognac from France." General Dodge walked over, took out a bottle, and inspected it with a smile. All this time Shay maintained the position of attention. The three men chatted for a few minutes as if Shay were non-existent.

Naron lthen ooked over at Shay as if he had unfinished business with him. He then spoke quietly to the general, who also intently looked at Shay and at times nodding in approval to the words spoken. The sergeant major ordered Shay to stand at ease.

"Private, this man would like to ask you some questions. He may not be in uniform but make no mistake, he is part of this Army and very important to us. Do you understand?"

"Yes, Sergeant Major," Shay sounded out as Naron walked over to him.

"What is your name?"

"Shay Price."

"What is your unit son?"

"1st Connecticut Cavalry XI Corp, Army of the Potomac, sir!" Shay responded. He was nervous but hid it well as his heart began pounding hard in his chest. Naron nodded in approval.

"You do much hunting growing up? Do you speak Spanish?" Naron asked.

"Yes, sir, hunting and fishing, sir. No, I speak only English," Shay answered.

"You have a different look to you. The Oriental I see, but what kind I know not. What are you?"

"Chinese and Japanese by birth, sir." Naron nodded.

"I see. It's a shame you don't speak the language of the Chinese. That would be very useful. My last question: Would you want to be scout, working under me for the Union?" Naron asked. Shay paused even though he knew the answer.

"Yes, sir, I want to be a scout." Shay stood back at attention. Naron looked at General Dodge gingerly with a smirk.

"I want him. How soon can we make the arrangements, General?"

"At once, Naron." Dodge turned to the sergeant major and instructed him to send a wire and draw up papers for the transfer to give his unit commander. After a few minutes, another man came into the room and stood by Naron, also clad in common clothing. Naron turned to Shay.

"Call me Chickasaw. No more of that 'sir' horse shit."

"Yes, sir, I mean, yes, Chickasaw." Shay was somewhat bewildered. Naron walked around Shay slowly examining him intently.

"Hmm, from here on out you don't cut your hair. Let it grow; the longer the better. Make sure you stay clean shaven, too. You can pass for Indian or Mexican easily at three paces, if you look straight ahead. Keep your mouth closed as much as possible. Lose that fancy up-North talk. Speak as few words as possible, even broken talk. You hear me?" Naron asked after firing off his litany of instructions.

Shay responded firmly.

"Yes, sir. Uh, I mean yes, Chickasaw."

Naron stopped and put his hands on his waist, shaking his head. "Dammit, son! That is what I'm talking about. Be at ease but be sharp." Naron tapped Shay's head. Shay and Naron looked in each other's eyes as Shay relaxed a bit while Naron took a step closer.

"You are gonna go with Hardy over there. He is my most dependable man in northern Alabama. You and him are gonna be like father and son. He will teach you everything. The Union is moving south, and they need more eyes in Alabama. You will survey three counties, maybe more. The general needs a fresh look at what is to come, so any changes, movements, signs, or peculiarities need to be reported. Hardy will be your superior and you best to follow his orders as you would your pappy. You follow me?" Shay nodded his head in affirmation.

"Yes, Chickasaw." Shay was resolute. Naron smiled.

"I'm just loyal to this here Union, trying to see this here thing to the end and get back to my family. Those that are left." He walked over the general's desk where sat a bottle of liquor. As Naron poured a drink and walked back his countenance changed and his smile was replaced with a blank expression.

"You lost anyone in the war yet son?"

"No," Shay responded.

"Good for you!" Naron smiled and took a drink. "I lost my wife, the mother of my six young uns. So, know my work here is vested in blood, the kind of blood that runs deep." Naron paused. "Be honest with me. Are you scared?"

Shay paused for a moment. "I'm not scared," Shay replied. Naron cocked his head to the side as he looked at Shay. "I might be a little nervous is all." Shay inhaled deeply while Naron replied.

"How about instead of saying nervous, say something like skittish?" Naron raised his eyebrows and smirked. Shay started to adjust.

"I can do that," Shay responded.

"Good! Best wishes, Private Price," Naron said as he shook his hand. "Hardy, take him and teach him properly; and do teach him how not to talk." Hardy tapped Shay on his arm, beckoning him to follow.

"Will do, boss. Come with me, partner." Hardy and Shay made their way across the room toward the entrance. They crossed through the vestibule and out the front door where Sergeant Hollister and Private Woods were still waiting. Shay looked at Hollister and Woods and then glanced at Hardy.

Hollister shouted at Shay. "Fall in Price!"

Hardy looked over at Hollister. "This soldier has new orders, so carry on without him."

The sergeant major walked out the front door and stood.

"I have orders just wired in for the transfer of Private Shay Price. We will provide him with his mount so there is no need to locate his steed for unloading and such." He walked down to Hollister who appeared befuddled and handed him the orders.

"Sergeant, you are dismissed." The sergeant major turned to walk back inside and further added without looking back. "The general sends his regards!"

Woods noticed that Hollister was turning completely flush with color. Hardy walked off with Shay following quickly at Hardy's side. Hardy turned to Shay with a grin.

"Forget about them, you are one of us now. Welcome to the war of shadows, young man." Shay thought on those words and took his comment to heart. He was nervous about the unknown, but he thought about Captain Price and what they had been through together. That gave him firm resolve and he no longer felt unsure, unsettled.

They made their way down to the tavern for food and drink as the bulk of the Union forces pressed on to Bridgeport. There were men to be relieved and battles to be fought as the tide of war had turned and the Confederate forces were starting to crumble.

It was high noon on the Walters Plantation in Alabama, and the dining area of the main house was filled with laughter, idle chatter, and the smoke of the finest tobacco grown in North Carolina. Present within the assembly were plantation owners and slave holders, which consisted of white men and freed blacks alike, beside various small business owners. Many of the guests were personally known by Colonel Walters, while others were just known to him. The September air was cool as the fall season brought forth it's change.

Victoria was busy serving while Maggie was disposed to cooking, and Mrs. Walters was overseeing every task performed. All were working in concert to serve the nearly twenty-four guests that were invited. The colonel had called the meeting to discuss the current events of the war and the current condition of the state. Everyone present had a vested interest in the affairs of the day. The war had taken a toll, and all had been affected, personally and financially. No one had been omitted and the affects of the war could be felt by each soul daily. As time passed and the alcohol flowed, the guests became somewhat emboldened and inebriated, as they shared events and told stories of glory and loss.

The hour to begin formal discussions of matters at hand had already past, as Colonel Walters stood in front of the master fireplace with Nathan Treadwell at his side; he was in halfhearted discussions with a neighboring plantation owner, Satchel Gibson. Walters checked his timepiece and, with eyebrows raised, called the meeting to order. He picked up his glass and struck it three times with a spoon.

"Everyone! Time is past, so let us begin this meeting! It is high time we addressed the condition of our dear Confederacy." The men all took seats and positions around the room. Walters gave a half minute for the room to settle and he began:

"Good sirs, friends, and dear countrymen of the Confederate States of America. I bid you all greetings and thank you for traveling to attend this meeting. A special thanks to those of you who have travelled from the counties of Marion and Dekalb. It is well-known that recently you have been personally violated and injured on your land by the Union invaders, and you take great risk in traveling this far south to attend this meeting." The majority of the room acknowledged the mentioned parties by raising glasses or nodding heads. Colonel Walters took a step forward and continued.

"At this time last year we all met here at this very place and prayed to the good Lord before the Battle of Manassas for a victory. For whatever reason, the good Lord in his eternal wisdom thought otherwise and many of our beloved sons fell defeated on that battlefield. They fell defeated in body, but not in spirit." Walters looked around the room, intently gauging the listeners.

"At that time, we knew not the result of what was to come, but the Yanks removed all ignorance from us and six months later they took Huntsville, and with that a good portion of the Tennessee River. As you all know the Devil didn't stop there but went on to take more. Florence, Gadsen, Crooked Creek and all the land surrounding Hog Mountain fell into their hands. They have commandeered most of our railroads to the north, and in doing so have further tightened their nooses around our throats, hindering our commerce and thus hindering our way of life." Heads in the room nodded in agreement and low rumblings marked their discontent. He paused briefly to let his words marinate into the minds and hearts of his audience, somewhat reminiscent of his former military station and oration experience. "Now we all have given to this war. We have given dearly, whether it be our sons or our property. Yet some Southerners have chosen a different offering to give. That is the offering of treason and treachery." More grumbling could be heard. "Unionists, they call themselves! Here at our back door they are in full concert with the enemy!" Walters became impassioned. "Spies! Traitors! Aiding the enemy with supplies and information, so much that I even heard tale of a Northern Alabama Union Cavalry Regiment! If that news is disheartening, then what of the Negro infantry regiment you hear tale of in Tennessee?" Walters asked rhetorically.

He paused and watched the men feverishly comment to one another as some stood, unable to stay seated. "I state all these happenings to prove my suspicions and yours. We have traitors among us! Maybe not in this room, but in our counties and towns. They are the primary reason that the Union has been victorious here in our own land! How can they know our own land better than we who are born from this soil? It must stop! The Confederate Home Guard does everything in their power to search out and find these criminals, so we need to support them to the utmost!" Walters stood posturing while glaring at the men in the room. "I open up the floor for discussion. Step forward and speak!" The colonel stepped back and sat down in his chair with Nathan standing at his side.

Each man took their turn in the center of the room and conveyed their thoughts and passions. Thirteen men spoke with fervor over the space of two hours, contributing to the agitation in the room. As the evening drew on Emily called Victoria to the front porch where she was seated. Victoria made her way through the crowded room, repeatedly requesting pardon.

"Excuse me, sir." Was a term repeated several times as the men would slowly step aside, seemingly memorized by Victoria's stark beauty. Victoria was always aware of the lust radiating from the onlookers, which in the close quarters of the front room began to smother her. She burst through the front doors onto the porch and inhaled the fresh air to recover. She closed the doors behind her.

"What do you need, Emily?"

Emily patted the seat next to her. "I don't need anything. You come and sit down here and rest a while."

Victoria sat down and stretched her legs out and took off her shoes. "Oh, Emily my feet are so sore from these shoes you gave me. I got two welts rising up." Victoria moaned and squinted.

"You need to use them more than once a month to get wear on them. They look very nice on you," Emily said. Victoria wiggled her toes and then put the shoes back on.

"They are fancy." Victoria smiled. Emily stood up looking through the window and searched the room until she saw Nathan. She stared at him, studying every detail of his movement and his mannerisms. Victoria noticed her.

"I know why you're smiling: Mr. Treadwell. Is he looking at you?" Emily stood with her glass of wine to her chest, never averting her gaze.

"No. He doesn't even know I'm looking at him." She paused and took sip of her wine. "I think he is going to ask Papa for my hand in marriage soon." Victoria's eyes widened with excitement.

"That be great and mighty news, Emily!" Emily smiled. Slowly, Emily's smile turned to melancholy. She looked back to Victoria and sighed.

"Believe me, I would be happier, but this war has me fearful. If the Yankees win, then everything will change for us all."

Victoria looked puzzled. What do you mean?"

Emily blinked her eyes and held them closed, and slowly opened them as if to gather her thoughts.

"You keep what I am telling you between us. I mean, don't you tell another soul what I speak of. Do you promise?"

"Yes, Emily, I promise."

"If the Yanks break through here, just know that they will have their way with you. It may be a hundred men or more, Victoria. My Papa will fight to the death but after he is gone, all of us women will be forced into relations. They will burn everything here to the ground, the big house and anything that stands." Victoria was appalled and hung her head low, her hands grasped together in sorrow. Emily watched her reaction and touched Victoria on her shoulder.

"I'm sorry to have to tell you that." Victoria could contain herself no longer and started to cry. She looked up with tears reflecting against the lantern lights, streaming down her face.

"Oh, Lord! Please save us!" Emily was surprised at her heart felt reaction and rubbed her back.

"Stop crying, Victoria, they haven't won yet!" She rubbed Victoria's back in small circles, trying to calm her. "Wipe your eyes now and go back inside. Remember, don't you tell a soul!"

Victoria nodded in agreement and stood up. She walked back into the house as if dazed and walked around the walls of the room to the kitchen, avoiding the glares and hidden touches from the men. She entered the kitchen and found Maggie busy with her tasks and Mrs. Walters helping her. Mrs. Walters saw Victoria standing there.

"Victoria, finish helping Maggie. I am retiring upstairs for the night."

"Yes, ma'am." Victoria answered as Elizabeth went upstairs and left Victoria standing next to Maggie. As Maggie was scrubbing a skillet, she noticed the silence and quiet demeanor of Victoria.

"Now what be wrong with you, girl? Why you got da long face?"

"Nothing, ma'am." Victoria answered. Maggie smirked and looked at Victoria out of the corner of her eye.

"Nuttin? Oh, I think it's sumtin! Now, what got you in this dread? Tell me ,now."

Victoria built up the courage to tell Maggie, thereby disregarding her promise and Emily's warning.

"I was thinking if the Yankees win the war, all us women here be forced to fornicates with them. Master Walters will fight until they kill him and then we all going to suffer miserably!" Victoria blurted out. Maggie stopped scrubbing and looked at Victoria.

"First thing, girl, is if dem Union win then they might have their way with you and every other split tail on this plantation. That mights be true. They be men and men do violates women-folk when it fits they pleasure. Massa Walters may fight or not, I don't know. What I do know is ain't nuttin like that happened yet, so just you no ever mind!" Victoria didn't feel any better by Maggie's words as she continued. "You keep on like this, you think yourself fool worryin about this and that. You needs to keeps prayin and truss da good lawd! Now you take these vittles down to the field hands. I made too much so they could have a taste. Go on and stop all that worryin, girl!"

"Yes, ma'am," Victoria replied begrudgingly.

Victoria took two pails of leftover food stuffs and headed out the back door. She heard Ned's loud voice and Mr. Shannon outside. There sat Ned on the steps with a bowl of food and Mr. Shannon laughing while leaning against the banister with a cup of ale.

"As soon as that boy seen that snake, he took off! Looked like a black jack rabbit without the ears!" Ned shouted out while Mr. Shannon reared back in hilarity. "I tell you, boss, t'was something to see!"

"Aye, I can take no more, Ned! Enough, I tell you!" Mr. Shannon pleaded almost in tears.

A deaf slave named Georgy stood by, also laughing himself and immersed in the jovial atmosphere. Ned noticed him.

"Even deaf Georgy heard dat boy holler!" Mr. Shannon bellowed out another howl. He turned away with tears in his eyes, no longer able to contain himself, bent over with one hand on his knee. Ned noticed Victoria and greeted her.

"Hey now, Ms. Victoria!"

"Hey, Ned." She waved hello to Georgy, who smiled and nodded his head back. "Mr. Shannon, Mrs. Walters want these vittles brought to the field hands." Mr. Shannon being red-faced, recovered himself temporarily.

"Aye, take my keys and feed them and take Georgy to tote them pails for you." He handed Victoria the keys to the locks at the field house and she motioned to Georgy to take the pails. "Hurry back now, girl. I'm needing sleep," Shannon added.

"Yes, sir," she replied as she and Georgy made their way to the field house. Mr. Shannon watched her keenly as she walked away. He yearned after her, as most men did. In his inebriated condition, he contemplated sharing his feelings with Ned but chose to withhold them. He couldn't risk any gossip getting back to Colonel Walters. He understood how he protected her and that no man could have her. He reflected on previous years and marveled at how many times Colonel Walters refused to even sell her, even turning down offers of five to six times her market value. Mr. Shannon was under the belief that Walters surely must be taking liberties with her, and he didn't fault him for doing so. Who would ever part with such a rare jewel in their possession?

Meanwhile, Victoria and Georgy arrived at the east side of the field house quarters, where there were housed twenty-two male slaves. They removed the lock and opened the door. As Victoria entered, most of the men stood up. The slave named Tom came to the door slowly and received one pail of food. He was by far the largest field hand on the plantation, a man of massive build who bowed his head in respect, as Victoria smiled back. She paused and looked throughout the room at the men and realized the room was sweltering hot, and the air filled with the sweat of manhood.

She and Georgy left and locked the door and went to the west side of the house. She removed the lock and opened it the door. Inside were the women and children. Several children ran up to Victoria, surrounding her, and several of the women came to the door, Tabby leading the way.

"What you got for us?" Tabby asked as she took the bucket and inspected the mixed contents.

"All kinds of good vittles," Victoria replied while some of the children tugged on her fancy dress. The crowd took the bucket to the center table and began dividing the contents among the mothers. They distributed it as equally as possible. Victoria walked inside as a straight-faced Georgy waited at the door. She looked at the make-shift beds and a toy made out of straw, stick and, string, which she picked up. Everyone was enthusiastic about the food as it was certainly a welcome gift.

As the women sat around to eat Victoria smiled, but her emotions pulled her heart asunder. She was happy to bring such a delight, but contrariwise also depressed by guilt for receiving such fine treatment, the likes of which these poor women deserved to partake of. She pitied them, and at the same time felt shame. As she turned to leave, someone called out.

"Victoria, see if you can get some of dem blankets. We cut and share dem," a slave named Ruth inquired.

"I will look," she answered as she and Georgy walked out, locking the door behind them. While they walked up the hill to the big house, Victoria's eyes started to water, and Georgy noticed. He tapped her on the shoulder while performing a jig, hoping to make her smile. She stopped and watched him a few moments then gave him a false smile as they walked onward.

They gave the keys back to Mr. Shannon, and Victoria went back inside to start cleaning.

———————

The night drew on and the visitors began to leave. Colonel Walters, with Nathan by his side, stood on the front porch and shook hands with the departing guests. They bade each other farewell and god speed, wishing all a safe journey back to their respective homes. God save the Confederacy and solidarity were the parting sentiments shared between all. After the last guest had departed, Colonel Walters led Nathan into the private study behind closed doors. They remained there for a short time before exiting. Emily was in her room looking out her window at the last departing wagon and was anticipating spending time with Nathan before he also left. She considered going downstairs and making herself known but decided to linger in her room and wait for the announcement of Nathan's request for her presence.

Time was passing slowly and as she stood looking, she found herself very restless and losing patience. She wondered what was taking Nathan so long to call on her. Agitation set in and she became angry very quickly.

Then she saw him walking down the front porch stairway, mount his horse, and ride off. She was livid. She stormed away from the window and started changing into her night gown. She removed her clothes and started unbuttoning her corset. One button was difficult to undo, making her more furious as she tore her corset open causing several buttons to be ripped off, falling on the wooden floor. She became enraged and removed her shoes, throwing one across the room at her bureau, which scattered several containers of perfume.

Wild thoughts raced through her mind and she was adamant that Nathan would suffer for this disrespectful act. She mentally demeaned him and mocked his infirmity, believing how unappreciative he was, and how no other woman in the county would have him because of his limp. She finished changing and was about to snuff her lantern and get into bed when she heard a knock at her door.

"Who is it?" she yelled.

"Your father. I wish to speak with you." She went to her door and opened it slowly.

"Yes, Papa?" she said looking up at him. He noticed her flushed face and the tone of her voice. Knowing his daughter well, he deduced the reason for her troubled countenance, but proceeded to inquire of the source regardless.

"Why are you out of sorts this late in the evening, pray tell?" he asked. She snapped at him.

"The so-called gentlemen Mr. Treadwell decided to leave without speaking to me! He has not respected me and insulted me! I am finished with him and he is not welcome to come calling on me ever again!" She was so angry that her lip was quivering as she spoke. William pretended to be surprised by her disclosure. He marveled at his daughter's temper and how quickly her mood could change. She had been like this since she was a child.

He responded calmly. "I believe you have answered the question I was about to put forth to you. I hope you feel better in the morning my daughter. Sleep well." He turned to walk away but Emily stopped him.

"What question, Papa?" she asked inquisitively, as her anger and tone began to subside respectively.

"I was going to ask you if you loved Nathan and if you wanted to accept his future proposal of marriage."

Emily was shocked. Becoming speechless, her entire demeanor changed as the anger and rage drained from her body.

"Just a short while ago Nathan asked my permission and blessing in proposing marriage to you. He assured me of his undying love for you and his sincerity." Emily started to cry, tears filling her eyes. "I told him that I would speak with you on the matter first and give him my answer tomorrow. I'm glad that you have expressed your true feelings and sentiments about him. I will inform him of your feelings, and that he is no longer welcome to call on you." Walters kissed Emily on her forehead and again turned to walk away. Without hesitation, she grabbed him by his arm and stopped him.

"Papa, I accept! I accept!" She exclaimed with joy, while he feigned confusion.

"I am confused, Emily. You accept my refusal of Nathan?"

"No, Papa! I love Nathan! I will accept his marriage proposal!" she reaffirmed.

"I do not understand. You just told me you did not want to see hide nor hair of the man. Now you want to marry him?" he baited her. Emily wiped the tears from her eyes and composed herself.

"Papa, it was just that he did not call on me before he left. I did not know the reason was because he asked you for my hand in marriage. You know how I can become angry at times. Please give him your permission and your blessing!" she pleaded.

Walters stood looking into his daughter's eyes. He regained his normal demeanor. He placed both hands on her shoulders. He would give any good thing to his daughter in order to secure her happiness, but he also knew that Emily was spoiled, immature and had a wavering temperament.

"I understand and want you to know that I favor Nathan. However, you must control your anger. It is quite unbecoming of a young Southern lady, and if you and Nathan are married, it will reflect upon his name and the Walters' name. If you promise me that you will strive to control your emotions and learn to exercise more patience, then I will give my permission and blessing."

Without pause she responded. "Yes, Papa, I promise! I will be a good wife to him!"

Walters narrowed his eyes in feigned contemplation. "Very well! You both have my permission and blessing!"

Emily immediately embraced her father tightly, laying her head on his chest. "Thank you, Papa! I love you so much!"

She spoke with absolute sincerity. He gently held her in a paternal embrace. They bade each other a good night and parted. Walters' walked to Elizabeth's room and opened the door, as he was eager to share the news with her. He entered slowly but saw that she was asleep. He closed the door quietly, as not to disturb her and walked down the stairs to his study. There he poured himself a spirit and stood looking at the portrait of his family. He had commissioned it several years prior when they were younger and little Emily was but seven or eight years old. He chuckled in deep recollection, recalling her early years and began to smile at the joyful memories she had brought him and Elizabeth.

Suddenly his expression became somber as he realized that she would be leaving him soon. He wondered if Nathan was truly ready and capable of handling Emily as a wife. Walters started to worry if Nathan could even protect Emily as well as he could. These thoughts subsided as he stared at her likeness in the portrait and he realized that she was a woman now. He was losing her and although no tear fell from his eye, inside he wept bitterly.

It was midnight at the Walters Plantation and all souls were asleep, but not all minds and not all hearts. Victoria and Maggie lay in their small room in the basement of the big house. Their bodies were recovering from the previous day's activities.

Victoria found herself in another place. Her mother and her father were present and had come to visit her. Both of them were always happy and smiling. Victoria was ecstatic and overwhelmed with joy whenever these rare occasions transpired even though the dream was the same. She was be filled with happiness at the appearance of her deceased parents, but she did not see her little brother Soja. When she would ask her parents about his whereabouts and why was he not with them, they would always continue to smile and remain silent. Victoria would become extremely sad and this would eventually overcome her and causing her to awake in tears.

Maggie slept lightly and would wake, and upon seeing her child grieving, would comfort her. This night was no different as Maggie held her and quietly hummed a Christian spiritual. As she swayed Victoria back to sleep, the katydids and crickets played their melodies as well, sending Maggie to join her.

Seven

THE SMELL

It was Sunday morning at the creek and the water was cold. Sunlight parted the trees and illuminated patches of water from which a hazy mist slowly rose. Shay and Hardy were washing off a week of stink at the water's edge, as it had been several weeks of constant movement for the two throughout the counties of northern Alabama. Hardy wasted no time imparting to Shay training and tactics along the way as a scout and, especially, as a spy. Shay's new identity was that of a Navajo trapper whose name was Ashkii. Hardy chose this identity because of the scarcity of Navajos in the region, meaning there was less chance of crossing paths with another Native American and possibly being called forth to speak the Navajo tongue.

Shay acted as his traveling and trapping companion from the western territories. Hardy already had an assortment of pelts and furs, which he would rearrange after he and Shay left a town or pass members of the local Confederate Home Guard. This was done in order to give the appearance of being active trappers with fresh inventory. Hardy took advantage of all measures possible not to draw curiosity or unwanted attention, and Shay also did his part by staying silent, looking calm, and riding slightly behind. Most importantly, he absorbed Hardy's instructions and embodied his new character. He had thought of Captain Price over the past weeks, wanting desperately to write him a letter and disclose his well-being, however, Hardy would not allow it. He reasoned that if they were fallen upon by the Home Guard and thoroughly searched, a well written letter in the English language by a Navajo would bring about warranted suspicion. And if beating and torture followed, it could mean death for them both. Shay was instructed to only write when in town and mail the letter when they were leaving that town. It would be at least one more week before Hardy planned their departure to the nearest Union controlled town in Tennessee, and Shay would have to wait until then. He was also instructed not to write down any details of their activities, particularly where they had been or what they had seen.

Shay had witnessed shocking things, many of which were unimaginable to him only a few months prior. As he and Hardy winded their way through northern Alabama, he was astonished at the magnitude of destruction of human life and property. The offensive and pungent smell of the dead emanated from shallow, unmarked graves which peppered the landscape throughout their route. The poverty was reminiscent of Shay's memories as a young child in China. Even though the folk in America looked different to him, the poverty looked the same. They passed countless decimated dwellings, houses and plantations. Those places which were not completely destroyed seemed to be only partially occupied by inhabitants. White women, children, and crippled men seemed be the majority of what was left of each town's population. Slaves made up the rest of the inhabitants. Sometimes they passed small bands of able-bodied men which made up each town's or county's Home Guard.

Hardy would approach these men on sight and attempt to sell or barter the furs and pelts, but no exchange was ever made due to Hardy's high asking price. It was his way of earning a friendly trust within the communities while continuing to on their objectives. Hardy called it "hiding in plain sight" and, indeed, it was effective. By day he and Shay would survey a section of a county, interact with interested parties, and keep an open ear for any pertinent information, particularly troop movements.

At night, Hardy elected which towns and plantations to scout. They would conceal themselves within nature and take turns performing reconnaissance with a spotting scope. Before daybreak they would head deep into the woods and far away from trails and crossings to make camp. Hardy would decide when they would ride back over the Tennessee line and report any significant information.

Shay finished washing up and sat down on the bank to put his clothes back on. He looked at Hardy. "Are we going back into town today?" Hardy walked out the creek to the water's edge and got dressed.

"I don't reckon we need to. I got word of a person of interest. I was told there is a Union loyalist who Chickasaw dealt with last year. He lives about twenty miles from here. I got a payment set aside for him, if he has something good for us." Shay looked off into the distance and contemplated what might lay ahead. "We gonna survey a few plantations in that same area, make camp and then set up a meeting with this loyalist fella."

"Sounds good to me," Shay responded as they packed up their camp and mounted up to begin their day.

Colonel Walters sat on his front porch in a rocking chair, inhaling the Sunday afternoon aroma of supper as Maggie was busy in the kitchen. Emily was reading in her room and Elizabeth was in bed not feeling well. She had stayed home from church, insisting to William that her coughing would disturb the entire service, so the colonel and Emily went without her. As for the slaves, they were allowed a day of rest and were permitted to sing and pray to the Lord within their own religious gathering. Infrequently, Colonel Walters would attend and read from the scriptures as a type of mock pastor then exit the proceedings and go back to the house. Not all the slaves prayed to the Christian Lord. Many older slaves held firm to their original beliefs, and underneath the loud praises emanating from the fold, they would blend their voices with the fold and proclaim the words *"Allah hu akbar."*

Victoria was among the souls who left their former belief in the god Chukwu and adopted the new way. Regardless of individual belief, all were happy and appreciative of the much-needed spiritual release. Also, this was a time that slave couples were permitted to openly stand with one another as husband and wife. Colonel Walters allowed the mating and informal family structure of certain slaves, and Sunday was his day for the field hands to pursue affections if the couple's union had been sanctioned. Those who were not paired by Master Walters were more careful and discreet with their affections. Some accepted the possible penalties for disobedience, but others, knowing that if they were caught in the act with the same gender, would receive twice the punishment meted out by the Master for what his bible deemed an "abomination to the Lord".

Notwithstanding, the slave's human passions and needs prevailed regardless of the danger, and plantation life continued. Ned left the main gathering where they were still deep in praise. Most of the grown folk had settled down, and the children were playing. He walked up the hill to the back of the big house to see Maggie and find out what kind of Sunday nourishment he would be receiving. He walked in through the back door and saw her standing over the wood stove.

"What we got here! I smell something mighty tasty!" Ned exclaimed as he walked up close behind her. She turned around to him and appeared indifferent.

"Stew chicken, rice, collard greens, bread. Ain't that what your nose tells you?" He drew closer and placed his hand on her hip and gazed into her eyes.

"I ain't talkin' 'bout the vittles. I be talkin' 'bout you," he said with a soft tone as he slowly kissed her cheek. She closed her eyes and opened them again, this time with a smile on her face.

"You be old, Ned, but you be sweet, and that never get old to me. You mine, Ned." He smiled as she brushed past him to go start on the pie.

"Shucks!" Maggie shouted. She was supposed to have one of the chaps fetch preserves from the neighboring plantation. She turned to Ned.

"Ned, I needs you get have one of dem chaps to run to Massa Johnston kitchen and get three jars of apple preserves. They be waiting for us."

"Ain't no need for chaps, I get dem for you, don't fret."

"Thank you." She walked up to him and gave him a kiss on his cheek.

"Old Ned getting all kinds of sweets today! Sugar from you and sweet apple pie later! I must done gone to heaven!"

Maggie laughed. "Hurry back now."

Ned left and went down to Mr. Shannon's one room dwelling where he was out front in a chair with his legs propped up, and his hat covering his eyes. Ned hobbled up to him.

"Mr. Shannon. You be wake?" Ned inquired. Shannon sat motionless but answered.

"If I wasn't, I am now. What do you want?"

"Needs to go fetch three jars of preserves from Massa Johnston. Maggie need to get da pie made."

Mr. Shannon replied sarcastically. "You ain't back already?"

Ned grimaced as Shannon chuckled at his own humor. He limped away down to the path leading to the Johnston plantation. Victoria, who was at the gathering, saw Ned across the way and called out to him.

"Ned! Where you going?"

"Gone to the Johnston plantation and fetch preserves for Maggie!"

"Want me to walk with you?!" She hollered back.

"No, child! I be back right directly!"

Victoria nodded and smiled. She was glad to spend more time with the folk before having to work the rest of the day serving and cleaning. She cherished Sundays and disliked being closed up inside the mansion. There would be three more hours of light before nightfall arrived.

As Ned walked down the path, the sound of the children playing could be heard echoing through the trees.

Hardy and Shay had ridden for several hours until finally arriving in the area that was to be scouted. They chose where to make camp and were waiting until nightfall in order to survey at two adjoining plantations. They gathered their firewood and consumed a few morsels and water. As they lay back against a tree, waiting, they conversed about fishing and became drowsy during their respite.

Suddenly Hardy stood up. "I can't lay around waiting no more, I'm about fall asleep." He took a deep breath while stretching his arms and yawned. "Let's mount up and set up at the first plantation. It's Sunday, and I don't expect too many folks are moving around hunting and foraging. We will set up near the tree-line to the southeast."

"Aye, aye," Shay responded as Hardy laughed.

"There you go with that sailor talk again."

Shay mounted his steed and retorted with a smile. "Aye, aye, sir!"

They both chuckled and set off through the forest. As they approached the tree line, the landscape opened up to a beautiful view of tall wild grass set upon rolling hills. They trotted past a second cluster of trees and the flat fields of a plantation. After leaving their horses in the woods, they ran on foot toward the tree-line. They lay on the ground just within the tall grass for a while, taking turns with the spotting scope. Hardy grew impatient as the vantage was not adequate.

He turned to Shay. "You stay here. I'm moving up to the next tree-line. We can't see a damn thing here."

"We only have a couple more hours until dark. Why not just wait a little longer?"

"Just stay here. That grass is tall enough to hide me and I got ample range of sight," Hardy responded as he slowly crawled to a small tree cluster. After a few minutes, he was in position. Shay could barely make out his form in the grass as Hardy was an expert in concealment. After ten minutes Shay's mind began to drift from boredom. The various sounds of the birds and a good breeze brought him a peaceful feeling. He marveled at how he would feel relaxed at certain times while deep in enemy territory. He reflected on how the war had changed him in such a short period of time.

While recollecting memories of home with Captain Price, he imagined the captain would be proud to see how he was helping to preserve the Union. The thought caused him to smile.

Unexpectedly, he caught movement out the corner of his eye. It was about forty yards to his left, stirring beyond the trees. He thought it might be a deer and checked Hardy's position, who appeared to be unaware of the disturbance. Shay slowly brought up his rifle and laid it in front of him as a precaution. He watched intently as his heart started to beat heavily. The form became clear. It was a slave. He appeared to be an unarmed old man with white hair, carrying some items with his arms across his chest. The man limped out from the main trees toward the second tree-line. He was humming a melody and completely unaware of both men. Shay watched as the old man's course appeared to lead ten yards left of Hardy.

As Hardy lay in the tall grass looking through his scope, he started to hear someone humming. As it became louder, he carefully and quietly set the scope down and eased his revolver out his holster. He made himself ready and lay completely still while listening. Deciphering the sounds and cadence of the steps, he knew there were no more than two men. As the loudness of the humming declined, Hardy knew the direction of the men and also that he remained undetected. He removed his hat and slowly pushed up until his eyes reached the edge of the grass.

He saw old Ned walking away, humming while carrying something in his arms. A feeling of relief came over Hardy. From afar Shay watched as Ned passed by Hardy and he breathed a sigh of relief. Hardy began to slowly lower himself back to the ground, but just then Ned stopped humming. Hardy remained still, with his eyes steadfast upon Ned.

The passing seconds felt like minutes and Hardy unintentionally exhaled loudly. Ned turned and momentarily glanced in Hardy's direction but kept walking. Hardy remained still, never flinching, with his eyes fixed on Ned who continued on his way.

Ned began to hum again, but a different melody. Hardy stood up and started walking toward Ned, who could hear the man walking somewhere behind him. He knew he had to get back and tell Colonel Walters about this strange man. He decided to move as fast as he could while clutching the preserves tightly and attempt to get within shouting range of the plantation where someone might hear him.

Shay watched as Hardy chased down the old man with ease and pulled him down to the ground. Hardy untied the long kerchief he kept around his neck and then knelt down on top of Ned.

He turned him over and wrapped the kerchief around Ned's neck and began strangling him, as Ned frantically clutched at the ligature around his throat. Hardy kept a tight hold for several minutes after Ned's lifeless body stopped twitching. Shay was in disbelief and found himself in shock, even numb. Hardy carefully removed the ligature and turned Ned over on his back. He dusted Ned off and left the jars of preserves where they lay, one having broken. After brushing the grass back into place and covering the nature of his movement, he made his way back to Shay, who sat expressionless.

"Whoa! I didn't expect that! You did good kid, really good!" Hardy was trembling slightly. "You stayed calm, and I see you got your rifle ready to cover me! Hot damn! We had to do this one quiet, no gunfire but that was close! Let's get back to camp. They will come looking for the old bastard after a while. That one was so black they won't be able to tell what happened to him. I made my kerchief nice and wide so it wouldn't cut in to his skin or mark him up. They should figure he fell dead from old age." Shay just stared at him and listened.

Hardy continued. "Hell, I couldn't pull that off on a white man, you can't hide them marks!" he said laughingly. Shay started walking into the woods toward the horses, with Hardy trailing him and talking steadily.

"We're finished for tonight, but we' come back tomorrow. I have to go into town and meet with that loyalist and I'll need you to keep your eyes on that plantation." Shay stayed silent. Hardy walked up behind him and grabbed his arm. "You got a problem with me kid? You got a problem 'bout what I did?" Hardy sneered through his clenched teeth.

Shay pulled away from his grasp. "Get your damn hands off of me!" Hardy took a step back in surprise as Shay turned to him. "It's done! I understand that! Maybe he would have compromised us, I don't know. Seems like there had to be a better way! Still, it doesn't mean I have to like it! You're all happy and excited that you just killed a man!"

Hardy answered. "I didn't kill a man! I killed a slave! An old washed up slave who had a limp! There's a difference kid!" Shay stared at him as Hardy's tone intensified. "Listen up dammit! I have no problems in sending you back to Chickasaw with a letter explaining that you can't handle your station! So, tell me now, do you want to go on?" He stared at Shay intently, waiting for his answer. Shay stood silent for a few moments.

"I'm staying. Let's get on with it." Hardy lowered his tone and walked up to Shay and rested his hand on his shoulder.

"You're gonna see this type of thing all over. This is the first war I been in, but I suspect they are all the same. You do best to get used to it, 'cause this is what it is. You think killing him makes me happy? It don't, because killing him was work. What would make me happy is if I could take one of them jars of preserves off his dead body to have with our supper, but I can't." Hardy walked past Shay and added. "Just so you know how I feel about it, young man."

Shay looked at him and responded. "Why don't you just shut your mouth. I'm tired of hearing you talk about it."

They made it back to their camp site and ate, keeping the fire suppressed to that of hot embers.

Mr. Shannon found Ned's body later that evening. After nightfall Maggie made inquiry to him concerning his whereabouts. After a brief search of the plantation, Mr. Shannon decided to search along the path that led to the Johnston plantation. He walked up upon Ned's dead body slowly and bent down to check if Ned had breath. He surveyed the area, noticing the preserves scattered about and the broken jar. He went back to the house to inform Colonel Walters, who was having supper with Emily. After removing his hat, he told the colonel, who immediately stood up and followed Mr. Shannon out. Emily was shocked and Victoria covered her face and wept. Maggie heard the commotion and came out of the kitchen. Emily walked over and told her that Ned had been found dead.

"No, Lord! Please, sweet Jesus, help me! Please, sir!" She cried out as she bent over in pain as if receiving a blow to her stomach. Victoria, who was sobbing intensely, ran to her aid and embraced her. Emily started to cry and consoled Maggie as well.

Meanwhile, Colonel Walters and Mr. Shannon arrived at Ned's body. William Walters walked up slowly, removed his hat, and knelt down beside Ned. The lantern light flickered across Ned's face. His eyes were slightly open, and his mouth closed. The deep wrinkles and lines of his weathered face sat upon the backdrop of a proud and regal expression, one rarely shown by Ned just hours ago when he walked among the quick. He put his hand on Ned's chest as Mr. Shannon stood behind him holding the lantern. William closed his eyes and whispered a prayer for Ned as he began to sob.

"He belonged to my father. He raised me from a chap. He was no common field hand. I trusted him more than any friend." He stood up and looked at Mr. Shannon. "He was part of my family."

Mr. Shannon's eyebrows raised. "Ye,s sir, old Ned will surely be missed. There be no doubt," Mr. Shannon replied as he made a sign of the cross, after which he fetched a three field hands to lay Ned upon the wagon. They would bury him in the slave cemetery the next day at sunset, after the field work had been completed. The colonel directed that Ned's grave to be marked with a wooden marker reading "Ned. A Faithful Servant".

That night, as the news spread through the slave quarters, a great cloud of emotion and sadness spread throughout field house. The reactions were varied from the youngest to the eldest. Most of the men sat in silence, but after a short while they began talking about their experiences with Ned. Soon laughter began to erupt at the telling of the stories and then digressed back into silence and thought.

The women had mixed emotions. Many of the women and children were crying, but the majority were heavy in song and praising their Lord. The spirituals echoed throughout the building as they rejoiced in the home-going of Ned. They celebrated the fact that his pain and suffering in this life were over as he crossed the spiritual river of Jordan into the Promised Land. No more toiling. No more suffering.

Contrariwise in the big house, the love of Ned's life continued to grieve. Victoria spent the night laying in bed with Maggie until she fell asleep, the same Maggie who had done the same for her throughout the years.

Hardy went into town for his meeting and instructed Shay to scout all activities on the Walters Plantation until sunset before rendezvousing at their camp. Shay began his work and observed the plantation from two perspectives. He clearly saw Mr. Shannon was the overseer and witnessed movements of Colonel Walters. The majority of activity was from the slaves, who were farming the land for fall and winter crops.

As Shay lay in hiding and watched the slaves, he wondered which of them were related to the old man Hardy had killed. The hours passed on and sunset was soon upon the land. The overseer had called off all hands from work and they slowly started to leave the field and head back toward the houses. A short spell later Shay spotted a wagon slowly being driven out with the master of the plantation at the reins and a young white woman next to him.

In the bed of the wagon was a body wrapped and tied in linen. Behind the wagon followed a procession of slaves, all singing. The wagon rode to patch of open ground within a clearing of trees near a cultivated field. Shay watched in silence with his scope as slaves removed Ned's body and lowered it into a deep grave. They began to cover it up as the slaves gathered around and the colonel read words from a book, which Shay concluded was a Bible.

After a several minutes the grave was covered and the master mounted the wagon, helping the young woman onboard first, and headed back to the plantation house. The overseer remained with the slaves and Shay was surprised to hear the slaves erupt in unison into lively song. It wasn't the singing that amazed him, but more so how they were singing. They were full of emotion and passion. He didn't understand why they were so happy about the death of their loved one. He pondered the notion that perhaps their lives there were so insufferable, that death was a better alternative in some sense. He watched on as they ended the song and the mass of folk started walking back to the slave quarters with the overseer following.

Shay was about to pack up and head back to camp when he saw her. She was at the front of the group with her arm around an old woman. Shay pulled back the scope from his eye to reposition. She was still there, and as his chest tightened he felt uneasy. It was sunset, and although she was distant and moving away from him, her beauty and form reached out and took hold of him. Her form seemed to radiate an essence of familiarity to him. He never experienced such feelings before. He immediately attempted to bury the foreign feelings deep within him as he thought himself possibly mentally ill. Living in the field for months with constant anxiety must be the cause, he surmised, yet still he watched her until the slaves departed the area.

He finally packed up and withdrew back to camp. He didn't make a fire, but instead waited for Hardy. A half hour later Shay heard movement in the woods and the call, which he echoed twice back to confirm. It was Hardy.

"There he is! Let's get that fire started, partner!" Hardy exclaimed.

"Aye, aye. I'm hungry and cold." They started the fire, and after a time began to eat. Hardy recounted his day's travels and the meeting.

"All right now, let me tell you what needs to happen. This fella tells me that the county meets at that Walters Plantation to discuss goings-on and that the owner is some sort of old colonel, been in wars and so forth. I need you to keep an eye on the Walters Plantation for me. I need to ride back and give my report and requisition more demand notes from Chickasaw at headquarters. I paid that gimp nearly the last hundred I had."

"Gimp? What do you mean?" Shay asked.

"Son of a bitch has a bad leg is what I mean. So, you see anything today?"

"I spotted the owner, who must be that colonel, the overseer, and maybe the colonel's daughter. The slaves worked all day, and then they buried the old man. They had a funeral of sorts and then were led back, probably locked down for the night. That's about all I saw."

"Good. They don't seem to be suspicious as far as I can tell. I want you to scout that place from sun up till sunset. Keep a good remembrance and write nothing down. If you get pickled, I want you to mount up and get your ass back to headquarters. Take your time, be like a ghost and you just might make it. Remember, if they catch you, you are done for. Probably peel you like an apple until you talk, and you will talk after a while."

"I don't plan on ever being taken alive. They would have to kill me," Shay responded resolutely.

Hardy smiled. "I hope so, hero, for your sake and mine. Tomorrow we'll find another camp site to meet at before I set off."

"Sounds good to me," Shay affirmed.

They stayed up for a bit before going to sleep. The woods were cold, and the hot embers that gave its frugal warmth were waning. Shay couldn't sleep and felt as if his chest was on fire. He turned on his back, looking up at the visible stars above the tree tops. "Why?" he asked himself while desperately searching for the answer to this question. Each passing moment would bring her in sight within his mind's eye, and each time he would try to dismiss her.

He did not know who she was, but he knew what she was, just a slave. Or was she? He hated these intrusive thoughts and feelings, as they were out of his control. Shay lay this way for hours until finally giving into the impulse to see her one more time. Perhaps the scope lens had been dusty or fatigue had set in after laying in one position for hours. These final thoughts gave Shay enough mental relief to allow himself drift off into a deep sleep. An owl's call echoed into the cold Southern night, and the countryside was still.

––––––––––––––––––

After returning to the house, Victoria began to serve the supper which had been prepared earlier. Out in the back yard hung two great pots over the fire pit, containing supper for the field hands. Victoria would serve both today, as Colonel Walters had instructed Maggie to rest for evening. He had observed her looking sickly, lethargic even.

He went upstairs to change his clothes from the funeral and to check on Elizabeth, who was too sick to attend the burial and disappointed she would be absent. He slowly opened the door and quietly entered the bedroom. She was laying on her side, seemingly asleep. He crept over to his bureau and quietly removed his shirt, when he heard his wife's small voice whisper.

"You needn't be quiet, William. I'm awake." She paused. "I'm only resting."

He walked over to her and sat down on the edge of the bed, placing his hand on her shoulder.

"How are you feeling my dear?" he asked. She remained silent for a few moments.

"I just feel tired. So tired," she whispered.

He began to slowly rub her back and was concerned because she had been this way for over one week with no improvement.

"Turn toward me, dear, and let me feel you for fever." He gently turned her over on her back as she quietly grunted in discomfort. When on her back she started coughing, mildly at first and then violently. He gently rolled her onto her side, while using his shirt to catch her dribble, and while he continued to rub her back she coughed up even more fluid.

"There, there my dear, get it up and out of you." He looked at his shirt and saw that the fluid was discolored. He folded it up as Elizabeth turned onto her back and looked at her husband. He smiled and placed his hand on her forehead and cheeks.

"You don't feel to have a bad fever, but the issue from your lungs is not right. You are sore and your body aches. Your cough is weak and comes too often. Tomorrow I am going into town and retain the doctor. A tonic or some remedy will surely be needed."

"I will be fine. We don't need to spend money on a doctor. A few more days and I will be better," she quietly pleaded as fluid rattled in her chest. He caressed her hair, from her crown to her neck.

"Nonsense, it is settled. What do you want at this moment to feel comfortable?"

She looked at him and thought. "Call Maggie up here for me please. I haven't spoken to her since Ned passed away."

Walters stood up. "You are in no condition to carry on conversations. There will be time later to have words with Maggie."

Elizabeth narrowed her eyes. "William, I know how much Ned meant to you. He's been with you all your life and he will be missed. If Maggie had passed and you were laying in this bed ill, would you agree with me denying you words with Ned?" She paused and then answered for him, "No, you would not." The colonel held his prepared response in light of the spoken truth.

"Once again, you speak reason to this old foolish soldier. Forgive me. Let me summon her," he responded with a smile.

"Thank you, my love."

He went downstairs into the basement, calling out for Maggie to come to the master's bedroom to see Elizabeth. Maggie walked upstairs past Colonel Walters and into the master bedroom.

"Yes, ma'am, what you needs Maggie do for you?"

"Come closer to me, Maggie." Maggie walked over to her bedside. Mrs. Walters took both of Maggie's hands in hers. She beheld Maggie's eyes without breaking her gaze and addressed the colonel. "William, please give us a moment alone."

He was curious as to why but conceded to her request. He stepped out and closed the door. Only minutes later, Maggie came out of the room and went back downstairs. William went back inside the room to find Elizabeth laying on her side resting.

"What did you say to her?" He asked out of nosiness.

She paused and without moving answered, "William, need you know everything? Had I wanted you to know, I would have asked you to remain in the room."

Colonel Walters became slightly irritated but smiled anyhow. "Once again dear you speak truth. I'll have Victoria bring supper up to you. Also, Nathan will be arriving soon and supping with us downstairs. Do you have any words for him?"

After a few moments, she said, "Yes, I do. Tell him we expect our Emily to be cared for when she is ill, just as you care for me in sickness and in health." She coughed.

"I shall surely express the sound advice given by his soon-to-be mother-in-law." Elizabeth closed her eyes and nodded in approval.

He finished changing clothes and retired to the front porch, and shortly after Emily came outside to sit with him. They talked while waiting for Nathan to arrive. Victoria had finished feeding the field hands and also went out onto the front porch to join them. He smiled as she stepped out.

"There you are, gal. I know you have had a long and dreadful day. It's almost over with and would be even sooner if Nathan was punctual!"

Emily whipped her head around. "Papa, please! I can hear your stomach churning with hunger. Nathan will be here directly."

Victoria walked down the front steps, squinting out into the darkness at the road leading to the plantation.

"I see a light. It must be his lantern. He's coming, colonel!"

The light grew brighter until Nathan could be seen on horseback. He rode up and dismounted, tying off to the fence post.

"I apologize for my tardiness, colonel, sir." He turned his attention to his fiancée. "Hello, Emily, how are you fairing this fine night?"

She began to answer but was interrupted.

"She's fairing the same as me, Nathan, hungry." The colonel stood up and went into the house while Nathan appeared baffled. He turned around to Victoria and Emily.

"Emily, why does he treat me like a son one moment, then turn on me like a cottonmouth the next?" She walked down the stairs and led him up, chuckling.

"He's just like his daughter, he gets out of sorts when he is hungry." He smiled, and Victoria laughed as Nathan and Emily walked inside to the dining room. Victoria was following them when she stopped and turned around. She crossed her arms and looked into the darkness as a cold breeze chilled her further and her thoughts turned toward Ned. She felt a sense of loss and the same lonely feelings which she had had as a child. Her heart brimmed with sadness as she started to sniffle. She missed Ned terribly and began to daydream, imagining Ned would walk right out from the darkness or from around the side of the house. He felt near to her, but also far away. It was as if he was watching her every movement. Then a shout came from the dining room.

"Victoria! What are you doing? Serve us!" Colonel Walters barked.

"I'm coming, Colonel!" She ran into the house shivering, and began to serve, as Colonel Walters expounded his expectations to his future son in law.

———————————

In the darkness, Shay watched Victoria scamper back inside the house, and as the door closed, he lay down his scope. He turned onto his back and looked up into the night sky. Butterflies and stomach knots returned to him. He now regretted remaining with Hardy and not leaving when he had the chance, that way he would have never seen her that day. Who was she? It was as if an unforeseen force had grabbed hold of him and woken him from his sleep. Even at this very moment, Shay felt as if he were changing.

He packed up and went back to his camp site where he started a small fire. He gazed into the flames and decided that he would have to cross her path and pondered ways to put himself in her presence yet remain uncompromised. His intention was only to know her name, or so he kept telling himself, as he bedded down and slept effortlessly.

In Connecticut, Captain Price was laying in bed, reading the scriptures by lantern-light with his spectacles sitting on the end of his nose. He could not find peace this night within the ancient words as he searched through different verses. There was no remedy found within its cover to cure his depression. Shay had not written him in months, which meant he could be alive or dead. He would give his entire livelihood in exchange for one letter from his son. The reports proclaimed that the Union was winning the war soundly, with only a short wait of time before absolute victory was achieved.

The nature of time was the issue, he being very aware that waiting during war-time feels opposite of waiting during peace-time. Price retrieved his locket from the night stand, which also held Shay's picture. While looking at it, he regretted never telling Shay that he loved him, blaming himself for not being the loving father to Shay that he should have been. He shut away the thoughts of regret and disappointment, knowing that deep regret could consume him wholly with self-contempt. He had always accepted his wrongs in life, and so now he dismissed any further notions of paternal neglect. He removed his spectacles and extinguished his lamp. It was in the still darkness when the silence became deafening.

"Write me, son. Write me," he whispered as he went off to sleep and dreamed.

WINDS OF CHANGE

It was late in the fall of November 1863 on the Walters Plantation. The Friday afternoon sun was hiding briefly behind the transient clouds as Nathan and Emily sat together on the front porch discussing wedding plans and their forthcoming life. Although both were enthusiastic, they hadn't taken the latest events of the war into consideration. News was known to travel at a snail's pace, and no person in the county knew that the Union Army had just won a decisive battle at Chattanooga, Tennessee. Although this victory exposed the Confederate heartland to assault, the majority of the state was still reading about President Lincoln's address at Gettysburg.

"I want the porch to face west. The summer sun is just too hot, so there is nothing else we need discuss about that." Emily continued as she finalized her list of requirements for the building of the house after the wedding. Nathan nodded in approval.

"That sounds perfectly fine to me. There is one thing that we don't truly need, and that is the second well. I don't see a reason to have two wells, but with that aside, I'm in agreement with everything."

Emily frowned. "I don't want the coloreds pulling water from the same well as us! We will have ours and they will use the other. I always wanted that." She smiled and stood up to stretch while Nathan started to fidget in his chair, pondering an adequate response.

"But darling, we are not going to have any slaves. I run a store, and don't plan to do any farming or such. We just won't need any," he replied nervously.

She spun around quickly. "What about cooking? What about cleaning? Do you think I'm going to do all that?"

He began to plead with her.

"We can just hire some local folks to cook and clean. There are plenty of white folks who need work. They can cook and clean as well as any colored, except Maggie." He chuckled. "Slaves are very costly dear." He stood up with his hands on his hips and walked down the front porch steps. "You want everything: a house, new carriage, slaves, and two wells. I aim to provide you everything you want in this life, but it takes time." She walked to the other side of the steps and faced away from him.

"I didn't know you had such troubles with your earnings, Nathan. I apologize. I believe I have put too much weight on you. You are simply not able to provide what I need. I understand completely." He came toward her and grabbed her arm, pulling her close. He looked in her wandering eyes, trying to get her attention.

"I promise to provide everything you need, and after the war I will provide everything you want. Trust me." She rolled her eyes and was unimpressed with his gaze, but eventually succumbed to his determination.

"I will hold you to your promise," she said sternly. He leaned closer.

"If you do that, I will give you a special gift. I've decided that you may retain your dowry, which should give you more assurance of my word as a man." Her mood and expression brightened.

"Oh, Nathan! I love you!" She exclaimed before kissing him deeply and sealing that with a tight embrace. Just then Victoria came out the front door and witnessed their affection, waiting until Emily looked at her.

"Don't just stand their cow-eyed, Victoria. What do you want?" She asked while still in Nathan's arms.

"We need corn meal and sugar. The colonel is upstairs with Miss Elizabeth and I weren't sure to bother him or not. Would you please ask him what to do?"

"There's no need to bother Papa with this. Have Georgy take you into town with the wagon and tell Mr. Shannon I said so." Victoria looked puzzled.

"But what about our papers? I don't wish no one to trouble me and Georgy."

"Girl, everybody in town knows who Georgy is, and especially who you are! No one dares question you or him lest they feel my Papa's wrath. I know how frightful you get around the men in town. Just go on now, and don't fret," Emily responded and returned to Nathan's attentions as Victoria walked into the house to tell Maggie.

Shay took another bite of a sweet apple while looking through the scope, intently observing all the activity on the front porch. It was his first time today seeing her, but well worth the wait. The sight of her now brought him relief. The surprise of the couple kissing on the porch triggered a wide-eyed reaction on an otherwise cool and uneventful day. Shay had noticed some peculiarities during the past two weeks.

Mrs. Walters hadn't been seen and Colonel Walters had scarcely been outside the house. Also, there were several visits from whom he presumed was a doctor. Shay deduced that the wife must be very ill. He began to daydream about his deceased mother and wondered if the colonel was experiencing the same desperation as Shay had, a decade prior. He awakened himself back into the present and focused on movement at the back of the house. He saw Victoria walk from the back of the house down to a field. The overseer was there on his horse. She walked back from the field with a male slave, headed to the stable, and rode off in a wagon toward the main road.

Immediately, Shay thought to make his way back through the woods to the east and intercept them on the main road without suspicion and feign he was heading toward town. He watched the wagon travel to the intersecting crossroad outside the plantation entrance. He paused and inhaled deeply, then packed up quickly and headed toward the forest. Once he was within ten yards of the tree line he began to sprint through the forest toward his horse. He jumped over a fallen tree and navigated his way while increasing his pace. After seventy-five yards he arrived at his horse, stowed his scope and rifle, and set out to intersect them at the main road. Five minutes later, he arrived at the other side of the forest and next to the main road. While recovering his wind, he lingered some distance away to catch a glimpse of the wagon.

He wondered if he had missed them, but then, through the trees, he saw the wagon slowly approaching. His heart raced with vigor as he found himself impetuous with desire.

He questioned what he was doing. He was a Union soldier assigned and tasked to observe and report, not to interfere. Shay knew he could be making a dangerous decision which held deadly ramifications.

As the wagon approached, he trotted out onto the main road. He looked over at the driver and then at Victoria, who was looking directly at him. For only a moment their eyes met. Shay nervously tipped his hat at her and galloped ahead of them, remaining ten yards in front. He slowed his gallop down to a walk, flushed with excitement. He walked his horse its slowest, intending for the wagon to pass, but the driver would not.

After travelling a few miles, they approached the town. It was agonizing for Shay not being able to turn around to look at her again without causing suspicion. He decided to go into the general store, which he had frequented before with Hardy, and find something to purchase. He figured he could watch their departure from the store window and ride back the same direction with them.

He trotted to the general store and went inside. There were several customers inside, looking around and purchasing goods. Shay lingered in the background, examining items with his hands behind his back. Hardy had instructed him to put his hands behind his back when inspecting items in any store. It was to dissuade suspicions of thievery and to not draw the unwanted and attentive eye of a store owner.

While looking through one of the front windows he caught a glimpse of the wagon passing. A short while later, Victoria walked in the front door and stood behind a mother and her small child. She hadn't noticed Shay, as she was looking forward, but he noticed her.

Within the close quarters of the store, he found himself mesmerized. She stood elegantly tall with square shoulders, and her peach colored dress was clean and fit perfectly. It contrasted her smooth, dark skin, which glistened and accentuated the contour of her shoulder line as it ran up the base of her slender neck. Her hair was pulled up and hidden away under a wide brim bonnet, which exposed her facial profile. Her face embodied duality, as it appeared to be chiseled out of the smoothest of black opal and polished to perfection, but simultaneously exuded softness. The angelic eyes he had seen earlier were not wholly visible from his present viewpoint, only the edges of her exquisite eyebrows.

As the customer concluded her business, Victoria stepped up to the counter. "Sir, Colonel Walters needs two pounds of sugar and five pounds of corn meal."

The clerk ceased wiping off the counter and smiled at her while slowly looking at her up and down.

"Well, is that right, little Miss Victoria? Is that all the colonel will be needing?" he asked.

"Yes, sir, that is all. Thank you, sir." The clerk stepped backward and reached into a glass jar and pulled out a piece of hard candy. He leaned over the counter with it in his hand, waving it back and forth.

"Well, how about you? Would you like this candy?" She stood silent, thinking about what she should say while he continued his impropriety.

"Don't you worry, now, you don't owe nothing for this, it's free!" He smiled. "It tastes really good. The more you lick on it, the better it tastes! I can see your mouth watering for it right now. I tell you what, why don't you come around here and we go in the back room for just a few minutes? That's all, and I'll give you here this piece of candy." Victoria became frightened and stepped back.

"Wait, wait! Listen, this here will be a secret and the colonel won't know nothing about it. Hmm? Come on, gal, don't be afraid! I won't hurt you," he pleaded with constraint.

Victoria became weak but mustered the strength to take a deep breath. "Sir! Colonel Walters needs two pounds of sugar and five pounds of corn meal, please! Thank you, sir!" She would not look into his eyes, and instead looked at the counter. The clerk sighed and put the candy back in the large jar. He went into the back for a few minutes and came back with two small sacks. He continued to glare at her as she gathered them and turned to leave.

"Now don't you go lying to the colonel about what we talked about. If he asks me about anything, all I know is you came in here begging for some candy without any money. I would keep your mouth shut. Next time you best to mind your goddamn tone with me, bitch. You understand me?" She nodded to him and walked out the door, almost in tears. It seemed she was totally unaware of Shay during the entire episode.

Shay walked to the counter and stood as the clerk looked up at him.

"What can I do you for?" After looking at the different types of candy, Shay pointed to a jar and held up four fingers. The clerk grabbed a piece of cloth and wrapped up the four large pieces of hard candy.

"That'll be eight cents." Shay paid him and walked out to see Victoria and the driver leaving. He mounted up and followed behind them at a distance. He kept thinking about how the clerk had behaved and it infuriated him.

After a few miles, Shay increased his trot, gradually advancing on the wagon.

While driving, Georgy became concerned about Victoria and wondered what had happened in the store that would make her sad with watery eyes. She had come directly out of the store, so he was sure nobody had troubled her. He concluded that somebody inside had been hurtful to her, the same way people had been hurtful to him most of his life.

He continued peeking at her, then commenced in making contorted facial expressions, attempting to make her laugh. Suddenly, there was a man on horseback trotting up next him.

"Hello, friend, I'm a trapper. You see foxes near here?" Shay asked Georgy in a simplistic, dull voice, void of any particular accent. Georgy looked at him fearfully and then back to Victoria, who was surprised as well.

"Mister, he can't hear you. He is a mute," she answered and then faced forward, while wondering who he was. She knew it was the same man from earlier, but where was he from? Victoria had never seen anyone who vaguely resembled him. He was a man of average height, lean and muscular. His skin was not white, but tan like the mulatto. He was clean shaven and had long black hair. Above all, his unique eyes that raised her curiosity. She also had strange sense that he wouldn't do harm to them.

"I see. Have you seen any foxes near this place?" he asked. She thought about it and she couldn't remember the last time she saw one, since being in the house most of the day.

"I work in the big house on the Walters Plantation. I don't know, sir," she answered and faced forward again. Shay was at a loss for words, not knowing what he should say after this point. He had left that part out of his plan. He was about to thank her and ride off into the woods when she turned to him.

"The plantation is a short spell up the road. Mr. Shannon is our overseer, and he would know about foxes and such. You might talk with him." This was unexpected for Shay as he became sweaty, somewhat perplexed as what to say.

"Thank you, but I don't want to trouble anyone. Folks around here might not take kindly to my kind of people. I'm just a simple fur trapper."

"What kind of people are you? You have a different look to you," she asked inquisitively.

"I am what the white man calls Indian. I am Navajo, and my people and land are many days travel west of this place." She became thrilled at the thought of a different race of people. "What is your name?" Shay asked.

"My name is Victoria, and this is Georgy," she answered patting Georgy on the leg, who continued looking nervous during the exchange, not knowing what words were transpiring.

"Thank you, Miss Victoria," Shay said with a smile.

"Goodbye, mister."

He began to gallop away before turning back. "Miss, if you could not speak of me to anyone, I would be much obliged. I am a stranger in this land waiting for my partner. I don't want any trouble."

"I won't say nothing about you and I promise poor Georgy here won't either."

Shay reached down and pulled out the small cloth-wrapped parcel and handed it over to her.

"Please take this, and thank you," he said. Victoria hesitated momentarily before accepting it. He tipped his hat and rode off into the woods. Georgy looked at her with wide eyes, clutching at the parcel as they pulled away.

"It could be a bunch of dead frogs for all you know, but you go steadily grabbing for it!" she yelled while he gave her a boyish grin. She unwrapped it on her lap and saw that it was sweet candy, the same kind Colonel Walters would sometimes give her during holidays. Georgy tried to take a piece and quickly got his hand smacked.

"Wait." She broke a small piece off and gave it to him. He began to suck on it, while she broke off a small piece for herself and tasted it, moaning with satisfaction.

"It's so good!" she exclaimed, while Georgy shook his head vigorously in affirmation. "I'm going to hide this and share it with just you and Maggie. The others would be asking too many questions." They continued on to the plantation while enjoying their treats.

Meanwhile, Shay was exhilarated, but started to settle down and think about what he had just done. Why had he given her the candy? If she told anyone about meeting him or if it were found, it could bring more questions and unwanted attention to the area. His exhilaration turned anger at himself as he began to sulk. He condemned his own actions and accounted them as foolishness, vowing to never have contact with her again. Shay felt that he was back in control of this potentially volatile situation. He ate a few pieces of jerky and left his camp to continue his reconnaissance of the plantation.

———————

Emily and Nathan were still sitting on the front porch when they saw the wagon returning, and they watched it make its way onto the plantation and toward the stables.

"Oh my, time has passed by so quickly. I need to check on Mama," Emily said, as she stood up and headed for the door.

"Please, give her my love," Nathan asked.

"I will." She went inside and up to the master bedroom and stood outside the door. There she knocked quietly on the door before letting herself inside. Her mother was laying on her back, sleeping. Her breathing was strained and raspy. Colonel Walters sat in a chair next to the bed, having just been woken by Emily's knocking. He mustered a smile as she walked over to him.

"Papa, how is she?" He sighed.

"I'm sorry to say that her condition has not improved. Doctor Jenkins told me all that can be done, has been done. The pneumonia must run its course now." Emily looked to her mother and placed her hand on her forehead.

"Is she going to die?" Emily asked in a trancelike state.

"It is in the good Lord's hands now." He stood up and put his arm around her.

"We must have faith in God and in the prayers that we have sent up to him. I am assured that he will deliver us and that he will raise Mother from this bed of infirmity." She looked at him in admiration and for the solace he provided during this time of anguish. She embraced him firmly as he held her close, while they turned their attentions to Elizabeth.

William Walters could only hope that his words would come true. Emily began to walk out the room when she felt as if something was missing. She walked back over to her mother and kissed her on the cheek.

"You will be better soon, Mama," she whispered and then exited. Colonel Walters sat back down in his chair beholding his wife until no longer possible, and then closed his eyes and returned to prayer.

Emily returned to Nathan on the front porch, but as the cold air fell upon them, they retired inside. Supper would be served in a few hours.

The evening had been spent as all souls on the plantation were fed and bedded for the night. Victoria and Maggie had put on their bed clothes and were laying down, with one small lantern burning. Maggie was still not herself on account of Ned's passing. She lay on her side and turned away from Victoria, who was deciding when she would surprise Maggie with the candy.

She decided now was as good a time as any. She sat up and lifted up her bedding, reaching deep inside and retrieving the small package and walked over to Maggie.

"Maggie. Maggie, look what I got for you," she whispered. Maggie turned over partially to see as Victoria pulled out a piece of the hard candy and showed it to her.

"Is that candy?" Maggie asked.

"Yes, it is, and it tastes so good!" Victoria tried to contain herself while Maggie looked up at her.

"Where did you get it?"

Victoria attempted to deviate from the whole truth. "I helped a man in town and he gave it to me. Have some." Maggie looked at her and then took the piece and tasted it. Victoria went back and sat down on her bed and started sucking on a piece herself. A few minutes passed by.

"So, do Massa Walters know you got this candy?" Victoria never lied and always told the truth, even when it was uncomfortable.

"No, ma'am. He was busy tending to Mrs. Walters, and I didn't trouble him about it."

"So, Miss Emily know 'bout it then?" Maggie asked. Victoria sighed with displeasure.

"No, ma'am. Miss Emily and Mr. Nathan was busy together courting and such. Why are you asking me all this? I ain't done anything wrong. The man gave it to me," she answered defensively as Maggie sat up and looked at her.

"Well, how did you help the man?"

Victoria stood up. "We was heading back from the store and a man on the road asked us about some foxes around here and had we ever saw any. The man said he was a trapper. I told him no I hadn't and then told him he should ask Mr. Shannon at the plantation. I know the colonel is tending to Miss Elizabeth. That's all! He said thank you and gave us this candy, then he went off in the woods."

"Hmm, so what this man look like? A man from town?" she asked as Victoria sat back down.

"He's not from around here. He said he was an Indian man. A trapper from far away. He had long black hair, and his skin was colored bright pecan. Oh, and he was a young man, too!"

Maggie thought for a few moments.

"Here, you take this back." She slowly stood up and walked over to hand Victoria the candy. "Take it."

"Why?"

"'Cause I don't want no parts of your foolishness! You know you ain't posed to take nuthin from nobody!" Maggie scolded. "The colonel be jealous of you and Miss Emily. He find dis out whilst Miss Elizabeth be sick, he'll act a fool! You best dig a hole and tossed dat candy in and let the critters have they fill. Now take it." Hesitantly, but obediently, Victoria took the piece of candy and put it back in the cloth. She wrapped it up while Maggie lay down again.

Victoria's feelings were hurt as she hid the candy back under her bedding and she got back into bed. Maggie snuffed the lantern while Victoria started to cry silently.

She was merely trying to comfort Maggie during her mourning and got fussed at. After a minute, Victoria's sadness turned to anger as she became restless, tossing and turning in bed. Finally, she could hold it no longer.

"I don't care, I'm keeping it. It's mine!" she blurted out. There was no verbal response, only the wisdom of silence. Victoria lay worrying that she may have indeed done something mistakenly but would keep the candy whether it be wrong or right. She settled the matter in her mind and went to sleep.

In a tavern in Connecticut, Captain Price sat at his usual chair at the counter facing the door as the nightly patrons entered and left. He was mindful of each one, as he sat and drank his last cup of ale before walking home. The establishment had a piano, which would be put to use depending if a customer had the ability and courage to play before the crowd. Price began to feel slightly nauseated, primarily because he hadn't eaten supper and it was past his bed time.

He had begun to frequent the tavern more as he began to miss the presence of Shay exceedingly. It seemed to be impossible to remain in the house at certain times, as the foreboding loneliness appeared to transform it into a tomb. Just then the bar's keep walked up to Price.

"Another one, Captain? The bartender asked.

"No, Shawn, this will be my last. It's time for this old man to head home."

The bartender laughed. "Aye, it may be time for you to head home, but you are far from an old man, Captain. You're like a marble statue, sir! You never seem to age," he complimented in a heavy Irish accent.

"A fine accolade, young man, and gratuity is in order. I will give you what remains in balance after settling my bill! You are one fine bartender!" he exclaimed as they both laughed.

"That's the first time you've hooted tonight." Shawn began wiping the counter. "Have you received word from Shay as of yet?"

"Not as of yet." He drank deeply from his mug.

Shawn sighed. "He will be writing you soon, Captain. You can rest assured. I feel it in me bones."

Price nodded while raising his mug. "Aye, Shawn."

While the bartender assisted another patron, Price observed one good swallow of ale remaining. Feeling nauseated and well drunken, he decided to leave. He paid his charge and left ample recompense for Shawn's gain. He attempted to make his way to the door, navigating the aisles filled with boisterous drunken folk. Just then he was grabbed by the arm. Price turned about and broke the grasp quickly, and directly faced the young man who had handled him.

"What say, young man?" Price yelled in anger.

The young man's demeanor changed, and he ceased laughing, while his expression appeared remorseful. After realizing his thoughtless behavior, he apologized.

"I apologize, mister! I ain't mean nothing by that, I promise! I only wanted to hear your opinion." The drunken young man pleaded while Price stood expressionless, and so he composed himself as his friends behind him laughed.

"You see my friends here and I have what some might call opposite opinions. In fact, some might even call it a dilemma. Charlie, there, says he loves his lady friend more than I love my lady friend. Both ladies shall remain nameless for the sake of this discussion. Now, I visit my lady friend twice a week, and he only once. I give mine flowers once a month, and he gives candy twice during the month. We both write letters regularly. We ask for your opinion. Who loves their sweetheart more, him or me?" The group continued to chuckle as they looked intently to Price. He straightened his coat and wobbled slightly as the alcohol pulsed through his veins, and he responded vehemently.

"Who knows the depth of one's love? It must be proven to be truly illuminated. How else can one know its dimensions? Understand that you won't find the answer in the giving of flowers and candy, or other trinkets that would-be lovers exchange. No, lads, you will only discover the true magnitude of your love through sacrifice. This is true for all who profess to love someone. Any and all other claims are just mere words spoken to tickle the fancy, while some claims are made to shackle a soul with unforeseen obligations." Price paused to measure the young men, who appeared to be dumbfounded by his words. He shook his head in disgust and put on his hat.

"I will leave you with sound advice. Be wary of love and its promises. Never be prideful about love, and at no time boast as to its depths. One day you may be required to prove your bold claims. Take heart, lads, and know that if you continue to seek the answer as you travel the road of life, you will find it." Price turned and steadied himself with chair backs as he headed toward the door.

"Hey, mister! Find what?" The young man shouted. Price got to the door and walked into the night.

"Truth," he murmured, as he staggered home through the cold damp air.

———————

It was the next morning just before sunrise on the Walters Plantation. The silver, shadowed landscape shimmered along its contours from the half-frozen dew. All was peacefully still and quiet in the big house, with exception of the occasional creak from within its wooden timbers. All the inhabitants started to open their eyes in preparation to rise and make ready for the day.

"No!"

The cry was heard throughout the house. Emily woke up immediately and realized it was her father. She rushed out of bed and ran into the hallway to the master bedroom. She saw her father laying next to her mother, holding her lifeless body.

Elizabeth looked as if she was sleeping, but Emily knew she was dead. She covered her tearful face and walked over to the other side of the bed where she fell to her knees. Emily reached out and grasped her mother's hand and held it to her cheek.

"Mama!" she cried out in grief as her father wept bitterly. Victoria led Maggie by the hand as they rushed upstairs.

"Oh, my Lord!" Victoria exclaimed. She folded her arms across her stomach and began to cry as Maggie walked into the room and stopped in the center. She looked up at the ceiling and clutched her hands together as she began to pray. It seemed that time had stopped. The room grieved and mourned the passing of Elizabeth Walters.

The colonel's countenance was unrecognizable.

"I kissed her as I was about to rise from bed." he said, sobbing. "But she was gone." His sobs escalated as he slowly released his embrace and gently laid his wife down. He tried to find the strength to stand, and Maggie walked over to and took him by the arm. She remained silent and looked up at him with tears in her eyes. He looked at her and fell into her arms weeping uncontrollably.

The old woman struggled to keep him upright. She received his overflow of grief to help bear his burden. Despite the depths of his despair, he was comforted because of it.

Victoria walked over to Emily, who was still on the floor next to the bed with her mother's hand held fast to her cheek. She laid her hand on Emily's shoulder, who then became aware of her surroundings and looked up at Victoria as if surprised. Not letting go of her mother, she took her other hand and clutched Victoria's robe and pulled her down onto the floor. She embraced her tightly around her neck as they both continued to weep. The reverberations of the event would soon be felt across the Plantation and the county. The cocks stopped crowing as the sunlight broke through from the horizon to shed its warmth among the living souls within its path.

Shay lay at his camp site for a short while after sunrise. He started a small fire which was just hot enough to heat his water for coffee. After he had eaten, he packed up and set out for the Walters Plantation. A half hour later he made it to one of his three usual surveilling spots. They were well hidden in shallow grass-laden burrows which had surrounding foliage for concealment. He began his usual day of observation.

After a short while he realized that something was wrong. There were no slaves working and no field work was being done. He watched as the overseer mounted a horse and rode off toward town. An hour later he returned accompanied by the undertaker and the doctor. Shay surmised that the illness must have overtaken the lady of the house. Within the same hour, after both men had departed the estate grounds, Shay observed a steady stream of visitors coming to pay their respects. This lasted throughout the day and into the early evening. He kept meticulous mental notes of the activity, which he purposed for self-recitation and recollection at the appointed time.

After making his way back to camp he started a small fire to warm up some beans and recounted the day's events, attempting to classify the visitors, particularly their occupations and social status. Any and all details could be relevant.

Being tired and ready for sleep, he set more wood on the fire and bundled up in his small tent. He inhaled the cold air as he slowly began to drift off. He opened his eyes suddenly and realized something didn't feel right. He couldn't determine what at first, and then he realized that he had not seen her today. He wondered what she had been doing all day, as he fell asleep and dreamed about her. Had a mirror been present, he would have seen the smile on his face.

The next day at noon, the funeral visitors began to arrive in droves. Shay watched intently as people from all over the county made their entrance into the house and out the back door, assembling at a small plot which sat on a hill. Two headstones and a freshly dug grave were set within a picket fence. The masses totaled over two hundred folk, which surrounded the small burial plot and hill which it sat on. Among them were a group of nearly forty armed men who rode in column formation onto the estate. They weren't wearing uniforms but clearly a leader rode in front. They were local volunteers of the Confederate Home Guard who had assembled at the burial site and remained in a semi-orderly group. Shay saw the casket carried out the back door by six men, followed by the colonel with his daughter and her suitor.

Trailing several yards behind were Maggie and Victoria. Shay focused on Victoria as they gradually made their way to the gravesite. The pastor of the town church stepped into the fenced area as the men lowered the casket into the ground. The ceremony lasted roughly fifteen minutes but felt like hours to Shay. He could not help thinking of the passing of his own mother. His memories were persistent, and painful. As the funeral ended and the masses began to disperse, he was relieved to turn over and lay down his scope. While looking up at the sky, he mentally composed himself for a moment before continuing. He noticed that most of the visitors had left, but none of the

Confederate Home Guard, so Shay watched as their leader went inside the house behind the others.

"The colonel will be down to see you shortly, sir." Victoria said to Jeff Davey, leader of the Guard. Davey nodded in acknowledgement while never making eye contact with Victoria, but closely observed her as she turned and walked away. After a few minutes Colonel Walters came into the main vestibule.

"Thank you for your support in these most grievous of times, Jeffrey."

Jeff Davey stood up and shook his hand. "Colonel, you have not only my sympathy and condolences, but those of all the Guard. We are truly sorry for your loss."

Colonel Walters nodded. "Thank you. So, what do you wish to speak about?"

Davey hung his head for a moment. "Sir, I know this is not the best time." He paused. "Gosh, I feel terrible about coming to you at a time like this. It is about the war and new information. Maybe I should come back tomorrow?"

"No, Jeff, it's alright. Let us continue this discussion in my study, behind closed doors." Colonel Walters led him into his study and closed the doors behind him. "Now, what is it you need to tell me?" he asked.

"Right. Then I'll be direct, Colonel. The Yanks are knocking on our door. I know you are aware of that, but what you might not be aware of is the number of deserters we are catching every day. All across the county, a lot of our boys are turning tail, even as we speak, and with no end in sight. We are making a request to property owners asking to leave a small detachment of men at each plantation.

Walters appeared unaffected by the news. "How many men exactly?"

"Five to six men, who will bring their own tents and set up in whatever area you deem desirable. They will also bring their own rations and be no burden on you and yours. The Guard will only be patrolling for deserters."

Colonel Walters took a moment for thought. "I have but one rule for your men. Do not trouble my field hands, especially the wenches. If once such incident occurs, then they all will be removed. Are we in agreement?"

"Yes, indeed, Colonel. You have my word," Davey replied while saluting. "I will choose five of the most loyal out of our company and leave them here tonight, if that is acceptable with you."

"Indeed, that will be fine," the colonel responded as he opened the study door, leading Davey through the house to the front door. Davey stopped for a moment before exiting.

"Colonel, I can let Mr. Shannon know of our agreement, if it pleases you. There is no need to trouble yourself in doing so."

"No, Jeffrey, I need to discuss some matters with him at the present. If you will, fetch him for me?"

"Yes, sir! The Confederacy thanks you."

"Good day, Jeffrey." Walters let him out and returned to his study. Shortly, Mr. Shannon came into the house and found Colonel Walters at his desk in the study.

"You wanted to see me, Colonel? What can I do for you?" Shannon asked.

"Mr. Shannon, you have been on this plantation for over a decade providing me with loyal service and hard work. I thank you." Shannon blushed at the recognition.

"No, Colonel, it is I who thank you!" he responded cheerfully.

"However, now it is time for us to part ways. I would like you to gather your belongings and be gone by tomorrow afternoon. I will give you a suitable severance for your service and wish you good fortune in your future endeavors," Walters said while sorting papers on his desk.

Mr. Shannon was taken aback, livid with confusion and anger. He stepped closer to the desk. "Sir, I understand today is a most grievous and sorrowful day for everyone. I don't know what I have done to deserve this as I have been loyal to you and your family." Shannon pleaded with restraint as Colonel Walters continued shuffling through bills of lading and other papers, never looking up at Mr. Shannon.

"It is not a matter of your loyalty, but of finances. There is not enough money to pay for your service, it is that simple."

Shannon was dumbfounded and searched for a rebuttal. "Sir, I understand the cost this war has brought. I've seen it and experienced it with you all and I am willing to forego payment for a few months. We can revisit this notion at that time." Mr. Shannon pleaded as Colonel Walters looked up at him.

"This is not a notion, this is my word. Your reasoning is not my reasoning, Mr. Shannon. If it were, you would make better decisions. Respect my word and cease from this course of debate. I have spoken." Shannon could barely restrain himself at this point and raised his tone.

"Better decisions? Name one decision I made that was dubious!" Colonel Walters slammed his hands on the desk and stood.

"You allowed an old slave with a limp to walk over two miles and back carrying a load! That's a bad decision, sir! It cost Ned his life and you are to blame for that!" Walters was seething with anger and Mr. Shannon stepped backward.

"Is this about Ned? I loved me old Ned! Aye, and you know this! Ned wanted to go fetch those preserves himself! I didn't pick him out to do it, he came to me!"

"Yes, indeed he did come to you, and you let him do what he wanted to! Any of the young bucks could have done that task ten times over while running, and still have good breath! You should have had better judgment. Do you let a young child do what they want if it will kill them? No! Ned was like a child in an old man's body, and he knew no better!" Walters' face was red with color. With nothing else to say, Mr. Shannon nodded his head and walked out of the room.

Victoria was listening to the shouting as she dusted the dining room furniture, and watched Mr. Shannon storm out the study, briefly glancing as he passed. She looked down the hallway and could see the colonel, now sitting down at his desk. She walked to the study entrance.

"Colonel, do you need anything?"

He stopped his fumbling for a moment. "Mr. Shannon is no longer with us and will be leaving tomorrow. I will be handling all the overseeing," he said calmly.

"Yes, Colonel." She started to walk out to spread the news to Maggie, but Walters continued.

"Also, there will be men from the Guard staying on the plantation. I will show them where to set up their tents. I am telling you to stay away from these men. Do not speak to them beyond a greeting, and do not let yourself be found alone with them. If any of them touch you or trouble you in any way, I want you to tell me at once! Do you understand me, Victoria?"

"Yes, Colonel, I understand." She left the room trembling and could feel a change in the man. He had a look in his eyes which she had never seen, but in light of the present circumstances, allowed that his change was due to grief.

Victoria closed the study doors behind her and carried on with her cleaning.

Shay watched with trepidation as he saw the men of the Guard set up tents on the eastern side of the plantation and start a fire. He noted their weapons and realized that he could make no mistakes, as he was alone and in harm's way. The enemy was here.

He packed up and went to his camp site. He would need to move camp and cover up the area as best he could in the dark. Shay filled in the fire pit and tent post holes with dirt and then covered them with leaves. Another site would have to be scouted, further away from the plantation. As he made his way through the mist and deeper into the dark forest, he wondered when Hardy would return.

An hour later he came upon one of his alternate locations. After starting his small fire, he sat and made plans as the night drew on but began to feel the effects of his isolation.

He took out his jade amulet and looked at it against the backdrop of the fire. Its jade majesty was illuminated by the flames which caused it to radiate in the darkness. He found himself staring into it. It told the story of his life experiences and those of his deceased family. Shay thought about each person who it belonged to, his mother and father. It made him think about the day Captain Price first saw it and how he recovered it for Shay. Feeling comforted and encouraged by these memories, Shay brought the amulet to his lips and kissed it.

"Hoo-dee-ay," he whispered in the Chinese tongue and put it back in his shirt. He could remember very little of his native language, but he would never forget that.

Shay sat for hours as his thoughts drowned out the sporadic crackling from the fiery embers, which echoed into the night.

Nine

THE QUIET BEFORE

A week had passed since the funeral, during which Shay observed many changes at the Walters Plantation. The departure of the overseer and the embedding of the Home Guard were among the most important events. He also noticed that the young Miss Walters was spending more time in town in the company of her suitor. The Home Guard's activities remained constant and amounted to getting drunk on the front porch with the colonel, and walking around the grounds, pestering the field hands.

Surprisingly, Colonel Walters did not spend much time overseeing the field work; rather, at his behest, the Guard would take turns and scrutinize their progress.

Shay walked out of his tent with his blanket on his back into the cold morning air. He drank water from one of his canteens and soaked a kerchief to clean his face and teeth. One of his molars had been aching for the past few days and as he looked around camp, he spotted a lone dogwood tree. Shay walked to it and broke a small green twig off a branch, chewed one end until it became soft and fibrous before cleaning his teeth with it. After finishing, he ate two boiled eggs out of his lot, and began his work. It was the appointed time to check the rally area and see if Hardy had returned.

While casually navigating through the forest, Shay took in the sights, sounds, and fragrances of the land, just as the morning dew started to vanish. After crossing the last stream, he saw the hidden markers which brought him closer to the rendezvous area. He sounded out two different bird calls and listened until he heard the call returned.

It was Hardy.

Shay dismounted and walked his horse through the tall brush and could see Hardy sitting in front of his tent on a log. He walked over to him and they shook his hands.

"Looking like a savage done turned trapper! It's good to see you partner!" Hardy exclaimed.

"Same here. I wasn't sure you would be coming this week, but I'm glad you're back! I have information for you," Shay responded.

"Good, I have some for you, too. First, we are definitely winning! It seems Gettysburg caused a whole lot more trouble than the Rebs counted on. Right now, they are like dogs scattering from a pack of wolves. We breached the Alabama border, and elsewhere it's going the same. I met with Chickasaw and have orders to take a gander around the counties west of here. The Rebel Home Guard has been on the move, too, increasing patrols and capturing deserters everywhere. So be careful and be sharp. I'll return at the end of the month and we'll meet right here."

"All right, we meet here and then what? Why can't I go west with you?" Shay asked.

"No, I need you to continue surveilling this area. When I come back, we are going to meet with Chickasaw in Tennessee. He asked about you and I told him you were working out fine, no problems." Shay looked at Hardy, squinting eyes.

"Why are you eyeballing me like that? He wants to check on you for himself and might have plans for you elsewhere. Georgia, I think." Shay nodded his head with raised eyebrows.

"I guess I'm trained up and ready now."

"There's always more to learn every day for a willing mind. You'll never know it all, but I told him you know enough and you have the steel in you to do this kind of work. Besides, I thought you would be happy, seeing as you want to mail off letters to your Pa and such. You'll get a hot bath, a drink, and a whore!" Hardy replied with a wink. "Now what have you got for me?"

"The Walters plantation has had plenty of activity. The wife of the colonel died last week, and on the same day the Home Guard left five men embedded on the plantation grounds. They are mounted; three of them have rifles and two of them pistols and one shotgun. They haven't patrolled and seem to drink all day with the colonel. To my surprise the overseer packed up his cabin and left the day after the funeral. The suitor of the colonel's daughter was present. They have been spending a lot of time in town together." Hardy listened intently.

"I see you haven't been just hiding out here napping all day!" Hardy laughed. "How things can change so quickly. I need to have another meeting with the gimp in town before we leave the region. I'll do that when I come back to get you at month's end. Anything else you got for me?"

"I'm just beginning my report. I've been repeating it in my head every day, and I'm ready to get it off my mind so I can fit more inside!" Shay proceeded to recount the funeral and the particulars of his observations about the visitors. After comparing their observations and information they both realized that the "gimp" and "suitor" were the same person, Nathan Treadwell. They talked for half an hour or so before parting ways again, bidding each other safe travels.

Shay made his rounds of reconnaissance points before settling in between the Johnston and the Walters plantation. It was the same infamous field where the old slave had been killed. It was a beautiful vantage point but ambivalent feelings reverberated through his core. Lying prone with his scope in hand and concealed from view, he counted the days until he might return from enemy territory. He needed to send word of his well-being to his father, and a hot bath wouldn't hurt him either.

————————————

"When are they going to leave? I'm dreading even the sound of them!" Victoria told Maggie as she set down a bucket of water in the pantry.

"Hush yo' mouth girl!" Maggie responded. "'Fore Massa hear you, come askin' what troublin' you!"

Victoria lowered her tone.

"Yes, ma'am. But all them men are just drinking all day. They are stumbling around drunk, clumsy, and doing nothing but making a mess everywhere. I've done cleaned up two of their messes on this day. They got the colonel drinking, too! They done run off Miss Emily, who don't want to be bothered with their foolishness and left. Now it's just us here to fool with them!"

"Victoria! I told you to quiet yourself, now I ain't gonna tell you again. You want Maggie go upside yo' head?" Maggie turned to her and raised her hand. Victoria went still and hung her head.

"No ma'am," she responded with her hands folded in front, while Maggie stared at her.

"Massa is plum full of sorrow. He do what he needs to, but them mens ain't got no hold on him. Massa is a most great man. More great then all them pups out there, so don't you mind 'bout that. Beside that, Miss Emily gone be wit her Mr. Nathan as she should do. Wedding be comin' soon, don't you figure?" Maggie asked rhetorically. "You, you just mind yo' work and keep yo' mouth shut. What wrong wit' you? Did one them men touch you?"

"No, ma'am, but they look at me and whisper to each other. Just a matter of time before they try to put hands on me." She bent down and picked up the bucket as Maggie laughed and walked out of the pantry into the kitchen. Victoria followed her, puzzled because of her laughter.

"Why are you laughing at me?" Maggie stopped and turned.

"Girl! Mens been looking at you all your life and ain't nobody ever laid hands on you, because theys know'd Massa Walters would kill them dead. You is a blessed child. Very blessed!" Maggie exclaimed while raising her hands and closing her eyes, briefly praising her god. Victoria was still confused.

"Blessed? What do you mean?"

Maggie put her hands on her hips. "You been blessed wit a powerful beauty. On the inside and outside. You a slave, don't you know? All these years the good Lord done kept you! Kept you clean from a man's nature. There ain't no such woman I ever heard of. Massa guard you like you his child and you fretting over a man's eyes. Dat's why I laugh, 'cause you blessed and don't even know it." Victoria stared at her for a moment before leaving to empty the bucket then came back inside.

Maggie called out. "Victoria, find someone to go fetch eggs from Massa Johnston. We in need."

"Who do I ask? Mr. Shannon is gone. I don't want to bother the colonel and his drinking friends."

Maggie turned to her. "You just never mind the smart talk, go'n tell Massa what I said." Maggie said.

Victoria sighed and abruptly left out toward the front porch, where Colonel Walters and the five men from the Guard sat. She walked onto the front porch and watched all the men bellowing in laughter after the colonel's last tale, waiting until the laughter died down.

"Colonel, Maggie said we need eggs from the Johnston plantation. Who do you want me to send to fetch?" Colonel Walters sat in his rocking chair looking at her, while the rest of the Guard undressed her with their eyes.

"I would have one of the young bucks fetch the eggs, but by the looks of you it seems that you have been fattening up." Victoria's eyes widened. "You go and fetch them yourself. I don't wish for you to get too plump so you can't fit into that dress my daughter gave you." The men chuckled at his disparaging comment, and although Victoria was hurt, she didn't respond.

She turned and went back inside, through the kitchen, and out the back door. She walked toward the path that led to the Johnston Plantation and watched the slaves working in the fields. There was no overseer present, and their pace was slow. The field was full of chatter with folk taking time to stretch. As she walked past, someone in the south field saw her gazing and waved to her. She couldn't recognize who it was, but she threw her arm up overhead and waved back as she walked down to the path.

Feeling unhappy, she wondered why the colonel had shamed her. She tapped the tips of the small brush leaves as she walked, daydreaming and becoming lost in a moment of thought, within nature.

The path ended at an open parcel of land with tall grass, which was divided by a small tree line. This was the path that Ned had taken, and when she realized it, she stopped and took a deep breath. A smile parted her lips as she thought about him and continued on to the Johnston Plantation. She imagined Ned's final walk along this way.

"What was he thinking? Did he feel pain and suffer? Did he think about Maggie?" She began to feel sad again and took her mind off those thoughts, realizing how long it had been since she had last walked to the Johnston's. The landscape had changed and grown up.

She looked about to get her bearings, trying to make sure that she was heading in the right direction as she approached the second tree line. She stopped and looked around. Then she saw something move in the tall grass about twenty yards away, and became frightened, fearing it was a wild animal. While looking around on the ground for a stick or a rock, she looked back at the tall grass and wondered if she should run back home, or to the Johnston's. While debating, she steadily grew curious about what else might be in the tall grass.

Finally, curiosity overwhelmed her judgment. She slowly walked toward the area, maintaining a watchful eye of her surroundings. Still, Victoria was intensely nervous and on the verge of panic. She could barely see the outline of a form through the tall, tan rye, but it became apparent that it was a man lying on the ground, apparently asleep. Relieved, she exhaled her anxiety and inhaled a breath of intrigue, wondering who this man could be.

She stopped ten feet from him. After noticing his long black hair and tan skin, she immediately recognized him as the man who gave her and Georgy the candy. Victoria became excited and didn't want to wake him from his slumber but called out to him anyway.

"Mister? Are you all right?" She watched him intently. Shay slowly opened his eyes and turned his head to look. When he saw her, a wave of emotion pulsed through him. He stood up.

"Yes, I am. I was tracking some game and sat down, then fell asleep." He responded calmly while brushing himself. Victoria didn't realize that she was smiling profusely.

"Mister, I remember you. You gave me and Georgy candy that day, not long ago."

"Victoria." He smiled. She couldn't believe he said her name, that he even remembered it. Her heart started to pound in her chest, as her breathing became rapid.

"I remember you, too. I hope all is well with you." Victoria blushed and stood with her hands behind her back, looking at the ground.

"What are you doing out here, Victoria?" She looked up.

"I'm on my way to bring back eggs from the Johnston Plantation, just up the way from here."

"I see. How did you like the candy?"

Victoria became even more flush. "I liked it very much and Georgy did, too. We thank you again." Shay was lost within her gaze and disregarded his former vows he had made to himself.

"If you would like, I can walk with you a short way," he inquired, but her smile suddenly dissipated.

"No, sir, it would not be a good thing if someone was to see us walking together. I remember you asked me to keep silent about you and that you didn't want any trouble. Remember? How folks around here might not want your kind around here." She said apologetically, and Shay smiled.

"You are right, Miss Victoria, but you don't have to call me sir. You can call me Ashkii." She repeated it and they stood looking at each other in silence. Victoria broke it.

"I best be off, Mr. Ashkii." Victoria said.

"No, not Mr. Ashkii, just Ashkii."

Victoria smiled and waved goodbye to him. He watched her walk off into the distance, beyond the tree line, and felt his insides ablaze with desire. Although she stood ten feet away, he felt as though they stood face to face. Her soothing voice and brief words comforted him. He lay back down and looked over the area with his scope, ascertaining if any witnesses were present during the encounter.

After finding no one, he headed to a different location and realized every other thought was of her. As for Victoria, she was in awe of this kind stranger, and sensed her heart beating faster when thinking of him. This scared her.

On her way back home, Victoria was curious and went to see if Shay was where she had found him, but he was not. She continued to the plantation and arrived at the kitchen, and put the eggs away. Maggie noticed her smiling.

"I see that walk did you good, calm yourself from all that fussin'."

"Yes, ma'am, it did. I need to take more walks." Maggie nodded in affirmation.

"Yep."

Suddenly, Colonel Walters voice could be heard.

"Victoria! Emily and Nathan are back!" he shouted.

Victoria made her way to the front of the house and onto the front porch as Emily and Nathan rolled to a stop. The men lusted after Emily as they watched the beautiful, blonde Southern belle descend from the wagon with the help of her fiancé. He held her arm as he limped to the porch and up the stairs. One of the men whispered to his friend.

"What the hell?" he mumbled, showing disdain for Treadwell. In his estimation, his money had gotten him this woman, not his manhood.

"I am tired, Papa, and hungry." She left Nathan's arm and went to her father. "How are you feeling today?" she asked.

"As well as can be expected. Go inside and rest yourself."

"Nathan bought me some chocolate sticks! I think I shall go indulge myself. Don't stay out here in the cold too long, Papa," she admonished, causing him to smile.

"I'll be in shortly, dear," he replied as Emily turned her attention to the men.

"Don't you all do anything else besides drink and talk loud?" she sniped. The colonel looked up at her.

"Emily! Don't disrespect our guests. These men are welcome here," he said, sitting up in his chair. She simply rolled her eyes and went inside, followed by Nathan. Once alone on the porch, one of the men teased.

"Aw, Nathan purchased some chocolate sticks. Ain't that so sweet of him." They all laughed while the colonel took another sip of whiskey, ill content with his daughter's attitude.

As Emily went upstairs to her room, Nathan waited until she closed her door and then went into the kitchen and whispered,

"Maggie. Victoria. Come here quickly!" Maggie and Victoria walked to him and stood.

"Yes sir, Mr. Nathan?" Maggie asked.

"Oh, do I have something for you!" He seethed with excitement, and they with anticipation. "Now, this is a secret, so don't say anything to anyone. I bought Miss Emily something called chocolate sticks. It's a sweet candy and a taste of heaven. I've set aside two of them; one for each of you!" He took out a folded piece of brown paper from his coat pocket and unwrapped it. With a smile, he presented it to them. They had looks of wonder on their faces and were almost afraid to accept.

"What are you all waiting for? Taste!" he encouraged them. They each took one and bit into it. They looked at each other with eyes widened in amazement at the flavors they were experiencing.

"Good? Hmm?" he asked, and they both nodded their heads, continuing to devour the remaining portions while he grinned. "I'm glad you like it. And remember not to tell." He left them and returned to the great room, while they quickly consumed the remaining delicacies amid moans of gratification. Maggie walked back to the table jesting.

"Secret? I know that's right! If Miss Emily find out, she liable to go fool!" They both laughed and returned to peeling potatoes. Laughter could also be heard on the front porch, along with boisterous and offensive language which disturbed the usual peace.

Emily had gone up to her room in order to refresh herself, after which she looked at her reflection in the mirror as memories of her departed mother flooded her mind. She began to sob as a wave of grief surfaced, crashing on the shores of her peace.

"Victoria! Victoria!" she cried out. In less than a minute Victoria was in the room inquiring as to what was needed.

"Yes, Emily, what's wrong?"

Emily turned to her sobbing. "Tell Nathan I am not feeling well and that he should leave." Her eyes were bloodshot, and as Victoria was about to comply, Emily continued. "I just can't let him see me like this!" She wiped her eyes and attempted to fan them dry with her hands, but tears continued to flood her cheeks.

Victoria looked at her childhood friend and could feel her pain, then also started to tear. They embraced each other and wept together. Their physical bodies were touching externally, more so their souls coalesced within the pure and mysterious nature of love. In that brief moment they experienced something greater than themselves. They released their embrace, seemingly whisked back to the present.

"I'll tell him, Emily," Victoria said before she walked out. Emily went over to her bed, lay down, and curled up with her pillow to her chest. From the day's events, it was evident that the Plantation was in subtle disarray.

The next day began as most, with the sunlight peering over the horizon and illuminating the land. The slaves had already awakened and started their day as Colonel Walters unlocked the field houses. After giving direction to all, he subsequently went back to bed, his head throbbing from the previous days' drinking. He had no fear of mischief from them, such as running away or the like. The plantation once again became alive with its tedious activity and became even livelier due to the recent guests. Colonel Walters allowed each man to eat breakfast with him in the house.

Dinner and supper were their responsibilities solely, but the drinking on the front porch became a daily obligation and a way to pass time for all the men. They consumed spirits for various reasons, but each shared the same fear. The destruction of their way of life was almost unfathomable, but they knew that the Union Army would soon be in their homeland, and they attempted to drink away the advancing dread.

The day drew on to high noon, as Victoria and Maggie set down for a rest in the living room. The grandfather clock chimed as they listened to the ruckus on the front porch. Maggie sat humming a song and tapping her foot with her arms folded. Victoria was leaning to one side with her hands on her lap. Maggie muttered while never altering her rhythm.

"You best go see about them."

"Yes, ma'am," Victoria sighed as she walked out onto the porch into the revelry. She remained unnoticed while one of the group simulated erotic exploits on an imaginary female. Being ashamed by their conduct, she turned to go back inside but was hindered by the Colonel.

"Wait! Where are you going?" Walters slurred.

"Colonel, do you all need anything?" she asked as the men stopped their clamor, and a brief uncomfortable silence passed. Colonel Walters looked around at everyone for their request, and with none given, he responded.

"No."

However, one man stood. "Wait, I am in need of something, Colonel. In fact, truthfully speaking, we all are." He looked around at his comrades nervously and continued. "We need some relief, sir. Maybe your wench could provide that for us," he boldly spouted. The men looked about at each other as if to rally, as the spokesman became edgy.

"I mean to say, we can recompense you the cost, whatever that would be. At your pleasure, of course, Colonel." He looked around eagerly, while Walters paused for a moment of thought.

"Not at this time, young man. Perhaps if she becomes too unruly I will consider such an offer." He smiled and took another drink, looking at Victoria.

"That will be all," he replied as she began to feel nauseous.

"Yes, Colonel." She began to walk inside when he stopped her again.

"Wait! Come here!" He shouted. The group went silent as she stood in front of his chair.

"Yes, Colonel?"

He glared at her, seething with indifference. "You are the only Negro I own, that addresses me as Colonel. Why is that?"

She remained silent with her head bowed, while he answered his own rhetorical.

"You have become somewhat unruly."

She was afraid but answered. "I'm sorry, Colonel," she pleaded.

"No! I am your master! Now, say it again correctly!"

She became terrified and obeyed his command. "Yes, Master," she said with a loud and clear voice.

He turned his attention from her and shouted. "Now get!" He hollered as if addressing a stubborn horse.

She immediately hurried inside, while someone remarked jokingly. "Damn, Colonel! She liked to get her colored feelings hurt!" The group erupted into laughter. Colonel Walters smirked at the comment and drank another sip of whiskey.

She walked up to Maggie. "Mama Maggie! I need to walk!" Victoria said with watery eyes.

"Go on, but don't be long," she responded sympathetically as Victoria wasted no time in abruptly marching through the house and out the back door. Her stride was long, and with each step her pace increased. She didn't know where to walk, only that she needed to be alone. She walked down the path that led to the Johnston Plantation. The sun was bright, but it was cold, and Victoria crossed her arms to shield her body as a breeze whipped around her.

Tears streamed down her cheeks as she wandered on, her stomach in knots. Wild thoughts raced through her mind, followed by the fleeting remnants of emotion. She was confused and almost disoriented, she trudged on until arriving at the opening of the path. She looked at the trees and the tall grass beyond while the wind blew hard against her and she contemplated walking back. Aimlessly, she wandered through the tall grass, near the location where she had previously found the stranger, Ashkii. While imagining what she would say to him if they ever met again, she arrived at the place where she had first found him.

He was not there, only the flattened grass within a small burrow where he had slept. As the wind continued to whip across her body, she lay down on her side within the shallow indentation. The gusts passed over her as she lay there, and after a short while the natural bedding became more comfortable. Her anger and pain subsided as she began to feel the peace within her solace.

Shay completed his reconnaissance of the neighboring plantations and began to make his way to the Walters'. This day had been colder than in weeks past due to the high winds. His ears were the most vulnerable it seemed, no matter how far he pulled his hat down on his head.

He tied up his horse to a tree and started on foot toward his frequent observation spot and thought about his upcoming meeting with Chickasaw. Shay wondered what exactly the purpose of the meeting was, suspicious of the reason that Hardy had given him. Shay respected and trusted Hardy, in fact he depended on him for his life, but did not like him as a person. There was a quiet feeling of discontent in his company, very subtle and just under the surface of recognition. The thoughts of moving to another territory such as Georgia brought Shay mixed feelings.

He walked through the forest and approached the tree line with caution, casting his sight across the tall grass and the open terrain beyond. Seeing that all was well, he proceeded up the small embankment and onto his hands and knees to crawl. The ground was cold as he made his way, and the tall grass brushed across his face.

Suddenly, he stopped. Through the grass he could see the form of a person. He quietly reached down to his left side and unsheathed his knife, gripping it tightly. His hair stood up on the nape of his neck as his survival instincts awoke. He controlled his breathing, the same as when he hunted.

Although afraid, he was determined to kill the enemy immediately, being charged by his fear and fury. The person seemed to be laying on their side, very still, with their back to him. Shay began to slowly crawl forward in preparation to cut the throat of his first human being. As he came within reach, he suddenly became still. Even though she was facing away from him, he could recognize that it was *her*. He was relieved to such a degree he felt that his heart skip a beat, but contrariwise he was in wondrous bewilderment. He sheathed his blade and began to crawl backward, slowly and silently, while Victoria was completely unaware of his presence.

He stopped after a few yards and raised into a crouch and wondered if he should call to her; instead he whistled.

Startled, she whimpered in fear and quickly turned over to sit upright.

"Victoria. Don't be afraid! It's Ashkii." He approached within a few yards as she paused for a moment to collect herself after recognizing him. He saw the relief in her expression and was relieved himself.

"Why are you out here?" he asked. She stood up with her arms folded across her chest as the wind cut through her thin cotton dress, chilling her to the bone. She didn't know what to say and instead started to shiver. Shay saw how exposed she was to the winds.

"Victoria, why don't you sit back down and stay out of the breeze?" She looked at him and sat back down on the ground while he entered the burrow and did likewise.

"I came out here to walk, and then the wind got so bad. I laid down here to keep it off me. I'm sorry, I'm in your hunting place."

"You don't have to say you're sorry to me, this isn't my land. You don't have to call me sir either, unless you forgot my name?"

She looked at him curiously. "I remember your name, but I don't think I can say it to your liking."

Shay was baffled by the meaning of her comment. Against his better judgment he offered another alternative.

"Well if it's easier, you can call me Shay if you want to."

"Shay?" she asked loudly and clearly. He nodded his head and smiled, feeling as if she had called his name a thousand times previously.

"Yes!" he exclaimed. Victoria smiled as Shay's expression changed to one of concern. "Are you in danger? Are you hurt?" he asked. Her eyes narrowed as she seemed to look through him.

"Since you asked me, Shay, I'll tell. I hurt on the inside." She smiled disingenuously. "Just my feelings, they don't mean nothing." She shook her head. He moved a bit closer in order to hear better.

"Your feelings do mean something. They matter." She looked at him in amazement. He added, "I'm sorry you feel hurt. I wish it wasn't so." She was speechless and could only utter two words.

"Thank you," she said, smiling.

"You are very welcome."

They sat together for nearly half of the hour, both of them seemingly lost in simple conversation. The harsh wind lessened in bite and howl, but neither noticed, as they both were nourished by each other's uncomplicated sincerity.

Suddenly, Victoria jumped to her feet. "I have to go back! I've been gone a long while now, and the colonel might be asking about me!"

Shay rose to one knee. "Yes, I understand. Go back, please!" She stood there and brushed her dress off, then waved nervously.

"'Bye, Shay!" she said smiling.

He smiled and waved back.

"Farewell, Miss Victoria."

She turned and walked off slowly. After ten paces, she stopped and turned around to him with her hands behind her back.

"If you are going to be here tonight, I can come back and give you some vittles if you want."

Shay was taken aback. "Yes, I would like that, but I don't wish you get into mischief on my account. I told you that I'd rather not be known for hunting and trapping around these parts.

If people start looking for you it will cause trouble for you and me," he responded reluctantly, wearing a half-smile.

Victoria's smile faded as her eyes widened. "Don't fret about that. I can come back late when everybody in the house is asleep. There are men from the Guard on the plantation now, but they sleep hard because they stay drunk all day." She paused and waited for his answer, but his face was expressionless. "Do you want me to come back?" she asked.

His mind was still working out the potential risks and danger as he blurted out his answer. "Yes, come back and I'll be here and waiting for you. Thank you." Again, she was amazed at his speech and his giving of thanks to a slave.

"If you're not here tonight, I'll just leave it in your little burrow. 'Bye." She turned and started walking back to the plantation at full stride.

Shay's eyes remained fastened on her until she disappeared beyond the trees. He went back to his camp and began to worry about what had just been arranged. He had promised himself to not place interest in this woman but was failing miserably. He contemplated a retreat from the rendezvous, reasoning that nothing good could come of this foolhardy behavior. He resurrected his resolve and decided to forego the impending engagement. He arrived at camp and started his fire in preparation for his meal while the sun began to set. Looking into the flames, he began to daydream and realized that he felt terrible about not meeting her tonight.

"Dammit!" He stood and removed his hat in anger and threw it to the ground. He began pacing and kicked a small rock into the fire, which caught his attention. He stopped and gazed into the flames, which calmed him. He picked up his hat and dusted it off before sitting back down and taking a deep breath.

While looking at the fire, he took out the amulet from beneath his shirt. With his eyes closed, he kissed it and exhaled. This brought an emotional relief, but still no escape from his quandary.

Victoria returned to the big house through the back door without being noticed. The colonel had retired to his study, and the other men to their camp site on the west side of the house. Maggie was making supper when she heard Victoria.

"'Bout time you showed yourself. If you tarried much longer, Massa would be asking 'bout you!"

Victoria walked to the cupboard. "Yes, ma'am," she responded, unaffected.

The two of them began their rhythmic preparation and serving of supper to the Walters family. Young Emily and Colonel Walters sat in their usual chairs, while leaving the chair of the dearly departed present but empty. It was a constant reminder of their missing matriarch. The evening's events continued as accustomed, and few hours later all were in bed and the house stood quiet. Maggie and Victoria were in their basement room, under their blankets. A half hour passed since Maggie had extinguished their lamp, and hearing her short bouts of snoring, Victoria was certain that she was sound asleep. Victoria slowly and quietly moved back her covers and stepped out of bed. She grabbed her shawl and draped it around her and headed for the door.

"Where you going?" Maggie asked. Her words broke the silence of the room and startled Victoria.

"My stomach is wrenched and I'm going to the privy to do my business."

"Watch for them snakes," Maggie grunted as she turned over and returned to slumber. Victoria watched her until she was still and crept out the door and upstairs to the pantry. She stopped and listened for any activity. Satisfied, she opened a bottom cabinet door and reached her arm deep inside. She withdrew a bundle of cloth containing uneaten food and quietly made her way outside.

She stepped out onto the back porch and surveyed the grounds, and seeing no one, she walked toward the path to the Johnston Plantation. It was extremely cold, and she pulled her shawl even tighter while walking along the dark path. One hand remained raised in front of her for fear of walking into a tree. There was an uneasiness in her stomach as her heart pounded profusely, but different than the familiar feeling of fear.

Upon arriving at the location, she saw that it was empty. She looked around for Shay but couldn't see more than a few yards in front of her. She was disappointed but laid the food in the center of the burrow and walked off. After a few steps, she heard a distinct whistle and stopped to peer into the darkness, trying to find where the sound came from. She perceived a dark figure approaching quickly.

"Victoria, it's Shay." She felt a sense of relief and walked back, coming face to face with him at the burrow.

"I brought you something to eat. It's wrapped tight there on the ground," she said while shivering. He looked down and retrieved the small bundle.

"Thank you, I appreciate this." Victoria understood his thanks, but the other word was foreign to her. Due to the murky darkness, they were unaware of the smiles on each other's faces.

"I hope you like it. Mama Maggie cooked all of it," Victoria replied.

"I will, I'm sure of it." He noticed Victoria trembling.

"I'm going back now. 'Bye." She began to walk off, but Shay stepped forward and stopped her.

"Victoria, if you want to a sit for a short spell, I have a small fire kindling in the woods. We can sit around and warm ourselves."

She thought about for a moment.

"I don't know. I feel skittish out here, and I don't want no harm to come to me. I only wanted to bring you something to eat."

Shay stepped closer. "Listen to me. I promise to do you no harm. You came out here in the cold to feed me and I have a fire close by and out of the sight of anyone. If you want to talk, we will at least be warm." Victoria thought for a moment, and since she didn't feel threatened by Shay, conceded and nodded in agreement. Shay walked slowly and ensured she was close behind, as they made way into the forest. A few minutes later, they had arrived in front of a small fire pit, partially covered by stones. Beside the fire were two large logs, which Shay motioned toward.

"Sit here if you would like." She sat down on a log in front of the fire, and immediately started vigorously rubbing her hands together. Shay sat down on the other log and unfolded the cloth, exposing the food inside. He was happily surprised to find a portion of chicken, a sweet potato, and two biscuits. He partook of the gift immediately and ate quietly while looking at the fire. He had never tasted food such as this or cooked in this manner. The flavors and spices astonished him.

Victoria watched him intently as he ate, observing every detail that the fire light exposed.

"Do you like it?" she asked.

He raced to chew and swallow his food before responding. He swallowed and took a deep breath.

"Yes, very much so. It's been a long time since I ate this well." He continued to devour the last remaining morsels as she smiled, being content that he was pleased and satisfied. After finishing his meal, he wiped his hands on his kerchief, and returned her cloth to her.

They sat for a time without any conversation. The two were content with looking into the fire and receiving its warmth, while searching for words to exchange. Suddenly, both began speaking at once, and after realizing it, they yielded to each other. Victoria and Shay looked at each other and chuckled, which led to them talking for nearly an hour. They chatted about simple things which were common to them both.

There was no awkwardness or uneasiness during the moments that passed, or the emotions which passed between them. It was natural for both of them. When they bade each other farewell, neither thought about the world around them, only what had just transpired.

Shay bade her to meet with him again and she assured him that it would be so. It was midnight as both returned to their respective dwellings in a euphoric state. They didn't consider the next day to come, rather their hearts dwelled only in the present. Victoria quietly got back into bed and experienced familiar feelings, akin to those of her joyful years in Nigeria. While she slept, visions of her childhood abounded in her mind. Willingly she entered the world of dreams, temporarily freeing herself from the bonds of her present life.

Nearly three weeks had passed, and love was alive on the Walters Plantation. Emily and Nathan Treadwell had finalized their wedding plans for the upcoming month, and now only waited for the seamstress in town to complete her dress. They found themselves together every other day and coming closer to the terms of endearment which would bond them in Holy matrimony. Nathan was surprised that Emily had insisted on such an immediate wedding date, considering the passing of her mother. He wondered if it might be too soon, but with the acknowledgement and consent of the colonel, his question was answered. Nathan was delighted in the happiness of Emily and encouraged himself with optimism that she would remain this way after they married.

He pondered that if she reverted back to her unpredictable ways, it would never change the fact that he loved her dearly. He had known her since his youth and had always been fascinated with her. Even during those youthful days, Nathan believed that he loved her, and that finally he would have her. The pair yearned for one another when apart, constantly daydreaming about the other, and absorbing the deep feelings and emotions which rained down on them relentlessly.

Likewise, Victoria and Shay were victims of the same. Though they were not betrothed to one another and hadn't made confessions of deep affection, they were caught in a web of intimate uncertainty. Both burned inside to see each other, and every other thought lent itself to that intent. Victoria would make every reasonable excuse in order to visit the Johnston Plantation and meet secretly with Shay. To avoid suspicion, she would alternate their meetings at night, feigning late night visits to the privy. The two would meet in the woods at an agreed upon location in the woods. They would eat, talk, and laugh during the short interludes, avoiding thoughts of the outside world. The conversation never overreached into long-past memories of family, and they intuitively avoided asking each other questions that might bring up grievous recollections of their own personal calamities. At times, there were brief periods of comfortable silence between them, the two finding a perfect solace in each other's presence.

Shay had not told Victoria that he needed to leave at the end of the month. He had purposed himself in disclosing it to her forthwith, but could not bring himself to tell her, fearing her reaction and anticipating her disappointment. It was the same disappointment he was presently experiencing.

Meanwhile, Colonel Walters was not his usual self, and was digressing rapidly. While continuing to grieve the loss of his wife, he was overwhelmed with his self-appointed overseer duties and became harsh, even brutal in his handling of his slaves. The members of the Guard endeavored to assist him with those tasks but lacked the skill and sobriety to be effectual. There were instances of abuse by their hands, sometimes hidden from the colonel's unsuspecting eye, but also in his presence. Colonel Walters seemed uninterested with such episodes for the most part, with the exception of any instances involving Victoria. The men had a very clear understanding as to the limits of their folly, understanding Maggie and, especially, Victoria were not to be troubled in any fashion. Subsequently, the slaves began to feel a deep resentment of the new treatment by Colonel Walters and his new friends. They increased the pace of their work with all their might, and also the pace of their prayers, hoping and believing for deliverance from the tribulation that ensued.

It was the end of the month. The colonel and Emily had finished eating supper when he was called away into town and the field hands were fed and quartered. Meanwhile, Shay and Victoria sat in the forest near a small fire. They had not eaten on this night and had not laughed very much either. Shay was solemnly quiet, while Victoria noticed but did not mind. For her, just to be in his presence was enough. Suddenly, he broke the stillness with the troubling news.

"I have to tell you something," Shay said.

"What?" Victoria asked smiling.

He sighed and stood up. "I have to leave here, tonight. I don't want to leave, but I must. It's not my pleasure." He spoke clearly and firmly. Victoria stared at him with a troubled expression. Her eyes became watery, but she made an effort to suppress the tears that wanted to follow.

She stood up and faced him. "Why? You said you don't have a wife, so it must be another woman."

"No!" he shouted. "I told you, I've never even had a lady friend!" Victoria shrunk back slightly, her eyebrows raised, never seeing him so emotional or hearing him shout. At once he realized his tone and the effect it had on her.

"Please, forgive me," he said calmly. "I shouldn't raise my voice at you. I have to meet my partner and travel for a spell. I should have told you already." She listened intently to him.

"When are you coming back?" Shay searched for a response, as she continued her inquiry. "Are you coming back at all?" she asked anxiously.

He honestly didn't know the answer, but determination filled his heart and compelled him to make a commitment to her.

"I know where you are, and I promise to give my very best effort to come back to you," he responded earnestly, while she gazed on him without expression.

"Then, be careful, Shay," she said softly. He stepped closer and extended his hand, which she held.

"I will, Victoria. I want you to be strong and keep yourself safe from harm." He shook her hand as she smiled halfheartedly, while her eyes silently pleaded with him. Shay tried to release her hand and turn away, but her grasp prevented him. Their eyes were locked in an embrace, but neither spoke a word. Shay deliberately pulled her hand to his lips and kissed it. She closed her eyes momentarily, lost in emotion, and clung to the brief respite from the anguish of the unknown.

"Goodbye." He slowly withdrew himself and began walking into the forest as she watched. Uncontrollable tears filled her eyes as she could no longer contain her feelings.

"Shay!" she screamed and ran toward him. He turned around to see her crying and running to him. He remained still and tried to silence the voices within his heart but surrendered as she ran up to him and embraced him tightly. They embraced and he released himself from the emotions which had held him captive his entire life. He inherently knew and believed that this moment in time was meant to happen yet did not understand why. They embraced for what seemed an eternity, and experienced a change within themselves and the world around them.

As Victoria walked back down the path to the house under the moonlight, everything she saw appeared different.

While Shay rode off to meet with Hardy, he accepted the truth that nothing mattered more to him than this woman. He also accepted his duty to his country, sworn as he was by oath and honor, which was his primary obligation. Their paths had crossed, and his duty to his homeland had now met on the battlefield against the duty to his heart. Unlike the current war, Shay purposed in his mind to somehow make peace with both sides and at all costs to reconcile them both.

He arrived at the designated meeting location, but there was no sign of Hardy. He started a small fire and waited. An hour had passed, when he heard the rustling through the fallen leaves. Shay hid in the woods, just beyond the fire light with his revolver drawn, and watched as Hardy walked hurriedly into the clearing with his horse in tow. Shay holstered his pistol and walked out.

"Hey." Shay greeted Hardy as he turned toward him.

"Leave the fire burning and come on! We got to move!" Hardy was sweating profusely as Shay hustled to his horse.

"What's wrong, Hardy?"

"I'll tell you later when we get a chance. Right now let's go and be ready to shoot. We may get in a tangle, so stay right on me!" Hardy implored as he made his way out of the clearing with purpose.

Shay kicked dirt over the fire, mounted his horse and followed, while preparing himself for whatever might come.

———————————

Victoria walked into the house through the back door, passing by Maggie to see what service might be needed. Victoria checked through the first floor and then went upstairs. She saw that Emily's door was closed and knocked.

"Who is it?" Emily asked.

"It's me."

"Come in, Victoria." Emily sat in front of her mirror, deciding which fragrance to wear.

"Is Mr. Nathan still coming tonight?" Victoria asked.

"Of course. You heard me tell Papa at supper, silly. I wouldn't be putting on perfume if it wasn't so, now would I?" she smirked, while looking at Victoria's reflection in the mirror.

"Yes, you're right. Just getting late is why I asked." They both heard the heavy footsteps of Colonel Walters walking up the stairs. Victoria became tense and excused herself from the room, hoping to look busy and avoid his attention. He arrived at the second floor and walked toward Emily's room, passing by Victoria, seemingly oblivious to her presence. Victoria was relieved and returned downstairs to the kitchen. He stood in Emily's door way and remained silent. She glanced at him before putting her perfume away and stood up to meet him.

"I know the night is late, Papa, but Nathan will be here shortly. I promise to not let him stay long." She walked up to her father with a grin.

He had an expression on his face that she found peculiar, but he also reeked of whiskey, which she surmised was the cause of it. He paused for a moment.

"My love, Nathan will not be coming."

Ten

COCOON

Hardy and Shay rode all night and into the next morning, until they were safely out of the county. They had avoided several patrols during their retreat, and now found themselves exhausted and hungry. They approached the Tennessee line and knew that only a half day of riding remained. Finally, they decided to stop and rest beside a creek as both men and horses desperately needed recuperation. After they ate and settled themselves, they lay on a cold creek bank and were further nourished by the heat of the sun. Shay began his inquiry into their hasty departure.

"All right, so let me know what went on back there."

Hardy breathed deeply.

"Well, it kind of goes like this. I met up with Treadwell the gimp, and we always meet in his store, but this time he closed early. It seemed he was on his way to meet his sweetheart, the Walters gal. I saw him through the window and he looked at me all frog eyed, like he forgot we was to be meeting. He pointed to the back of the store. Big mistake right there 'cause there was a few fellas around could have been Guard. I don't know, but, anyways, it looked of suspicion. I went to the back of the store; mind you my horse is tied up out front. So he comes out the back and leads me about ten yards away from the door. His back was to the store but I stood facing it so I could watch the thoroughfare. Well, he starts rambling on and tells me about a new route for shipments of black powder headed for General Lee himself! I pay him three hundred dollars in greenbacks, and hope to God that his story is true. All of a sudden, I see two men walking down the way. They noticed us and started walking in our direction. Well, right there I know it was trouble, and as they passed to the right of the store, I began to walk away to the left. Treadwell got skittish and started to limp his way to the back door, but his house was on fire! I could hear the men pick up their pace and one called out for him to wait. I was already in my saddle and starting to mosey out of town when one of the fellas ran out into the thoroughfare shouting, 'Hey you! Stop!' Well, that's when I hightailed it out of town, hit the woods, and circled back behind to make my way to you."

Shay was surprised by the news.

"So, you don't know what became of Treadwell?"

"Hell no, and that worries me a bit. The report he gave might not be worth two bits if they found him out. I'm kinda suspecting he's been caught. If so, by the time they finish torturing him, he would have told them everything." Shay paused for a few moments in thought.

"How do you know he would have talked? How can you be sure of that?"

"Dammit!" Hardy replied angrily. "I know because I know, smart ass! Him, me, you, it doesn't matter who! After they beat you, burn and peel you, son, anyone would talk!" Hardy yelled and sat up.

Shay thought about it for a while and concluded Hardy was right. All men had physical boundaries, and pain was the surveyor.

They stayed another hour before packing up and heading back to headquarters for their meeting with Chickasaw.

The Walters Plantation was bustling with activity as the slaves labored intensely under the oversight of the colonel. He had recently ordered that all work be done absent of song. For the field hands, this made their toil feel twice as difficult and the days twice as long.

Inside the house, Emily remained inside her room. Her eyes and face were swollen, and her nose beet red in color from crying all night and day. She was in disarray and in shock upon hearing the news about her fiancé. She didn't want to believe or accept the fact that Nathan Treadwell was a traitor and working with a Union Spy, but her father's report was detailed. Nathan had been apprehended, searched, and after three hundred dollars of Union greenbacks were discovered on his person, he was taken into custody and questioned.

Colonel Walters told her that he confessed to being paid by a Union spy and giving information in order to aid the North. He signed a confession and was now awaiting his formal sentencing.

Regardless of the accusations and charges against him, Emily felt a dire need to talk to him. She rose up and walked outside to search the fields for her father. After locating him mounted on his horse, she walked out to meet him. He noticed her coming and trotted over to meet her.

"Why are you out here in this cold, Emily? You should be resting."

"Papa, I need to go into town and talk with Nathan. I'm tired of crying and wondering. I would like to talk to him, please."

"I know this betrayal is difficult for you to fathom, but rest is the best thing for you. There is nothing to wonder, only to accept. The truth has come forward. I would rather you not go see him. You know how upset and disagreeable you can become, and I do not want an episode like that to happen while he is under guard. There is no place for feelings in this matter. Nathan has confessed to treason in writing, and by his own hand, no less. There is no pardon for a crime such as this; something will have to be done," he explained firmly.

Emily took control of all her faculties and remained calm, feigning composure in order to convince her father.

"I understand, Papa, but may I speak with him briefly, please?" she inquired again as Colonel Walters looked off into the distance.

"You may go and speak with him briefly but return back here promptly. Am I understood?"

"Yes Papa. I will have Georgy take me and bring me back, directly."

"No. I will have two men of the Guard accompany you, with instructions to ensure you don't unknowingly tarry long," he responded, and hailed two men. They came over, and after receiving their instructions, they loaded up a wagon and set off toward town.

Victoria and Maggie watched curiously through the front window as Emily left with the men.

"Poor Miss Emily," Maggie uttered, as she closed her eyes and whispered a prayer. Victoria watched her with a worried expression.

"What's going to become of Mr. Nathan?" Victoria asked, while they walked back to the kitchen.

"Only God knows dat," Maggie replied, and began humming a song.

———————————

Emily arrived in town at a warehouse off the main thoroughfare. Standing at the entrance were two large, heavily-armed men. Emily and her escorts dismounted the wagon and approached the guards.

"Colonel Walters gives his permission for his daughter to see Treadwell, being as they are engaged and all. She is only allowed a few minutes with him, and then we will be on our way," the wagon driver said.

"We got no problem with that. He's over in the corner chained to the post. You'll see him," the guard replied.

Emily's eyes widened as she looked at the man with contempt and pushed her way past the two guards, with her escorts following behind. She walked into the cold and dimly lit warehouse and looked around feverishly until she saw Nathan.

He was chained to a post, sitting on the floor with his back to her. She ran over to him, but then slowed as she came nearer. He had been beaten badly. He was bleeding through his mouth and broken nose, while both his eyes were nearly swollen shut. She gasped and dropped to her knees. She covered her mouth and reached out to touch him carefully as tears of pain streamed down her face.

"Oh my, dear Nathan! What have they done to you!" she cried, and placed her hands on his shoulders, then kissed him on the top of his sweat-soaked head. He woke at the sound of her voice and attempted to raise his head.

"Emily. I can't see you," he said in a low raspy voice and started to sob. The two escorts stood in the background a few yards away, trying to refrain from laughter. Emily tried to regain composure.

"Nathan, did you do what they said? Did you work for the Union?" she asked him quietly, and after a few moments he responded.

"Yes. It's true," he croaked. She started sobbing again and he joined her as the escorts started to become restless.

"Just a minute more, Miss Emily, and we got to go!" She looked over at him and nodded, then returned her attention to Nathan. He was still, but suddenly, with a pitiful show of vigor, he began to mutter.

"I love my homeland and my people. Above all, I love you, Emily. I did it to help bring an end to this war," he sighed. "I took the money for us." Emily remained quiet as she coddled him and closed her eyes. "I just wanted the killing to end and our life to begin," he mumbled.

he escorts walked over to the couple.

"That all the time there is, Miss Emily," one of them told her. She put her forehead against Nathan's.

"I love you so much, Nathan. I'm going to talk to Papa, so try not to worry my love." She kissed his forehead and stood up, wiping the tears from her eyes as the three headed toward the entrance.

"I love you!" Nathan screeched, trying to force sound out of his lungs, but hampered by several broken ribs.

She hurried out the door and climbed aboard the wagon, as the other men joined her and rode back to the Plantation. She was filled with anger and rage at the treatment of her fiancé, and mentally she prepared herself for the upcoming debate with her father. In her opinion, Nathan's treatment was unacceptable and needed to be rectified immediately. Emily wondered if Papa would allow her dowry to be used for the acquisition of a lawyer in Nathan's defense.

The sun began to set, and only time would tell.

It was late evening at Headquarters, and Shay was reclining in a chair. He and Hardy had arrived an hour earlier. Both of them were ready for much needed rest and relaxation.

Shay was pondering the letter he would write to Captain Price, while waiting in the vestibule for Hardy, who was meeting first with Chickasaw. Shay looked around the room at the fine furniture and carpet. It seemed a lifetime since he saw the normal décor of civilization, and it was a drastic contrast from the daily rugged terrain of which he lived. He heard the door open and watched as Hardy walked out with Chickasaw's hand on his shoulder. He patted Hardy on the back.

"Good luck, don't drink too much!" Chickasaw said with a smile. As Hardy exited the building, Chickasaw turned his attention to Shay.

"Private Price! It's good to see you, son!" He walked over to Shay who stood at attention and shook his hand. "Come on inside, I want to talk to you for spell." They walked into the room and shut the door.

"Have a drink with me," Chickasaw prompted.

"I don't drink spirits but thank you." Shay stood rigid.

"Well, guess what? You sure as hell are going to have your first tonight! That's an order!" Chickasaw was excited as he poured two shots of whiskey and handed one to Shay. He raised his glass, as did Shay.

"To victory!" he shouted.

"To victory," Shay echoed, and they both emptied their glasses. Shay started breathing hard, as the burning alcohol set his chest ablaze.

"Another!" Chickasaw shouted. Shay, who was trying to catch his breath attempted to protest.

"You just be quiet and drink" Chickasaw told him as he poured another shot. They both drank and then sat down beside each other. Chickasaw observed Shay's appearance closely.

"You look good. A little on the skinny side, but you look the part of a Navajo. How are you these days?" he asked, as Shay was trying to bridle the foreign effects of the spirit.

"I feel good, but I haven't written my father since I've been in the field. I don't want him to worry about me." Chickasaw had reclined in his chair with his legs outstretched, and his hands folded on his stomach.

"You will have all night to write your Pa. I suspect you want to soak in a hot bath for a few hours to boot as well, so I won't keep you long. Firstly, the business at hand. Hardy has reported to me the location of certain Confederate black powder routes. He also reported that this Union sympathizer may have been compromised. Are you aware of any other information Hardy may have overlooked, or just plain forgot?"

Shay thought and reflected. "I really don't know anything different from what he told you, but I did survey the Plantation of the man's fiancé. He visits frequently."

Chickasaw's eyebrows rose with interest. "Good. Hardy has been seen and compromised, but he knows more of that terrain than you. I would have him go back alone to see if, in fact, the sympathizer has been found out. I want you to leave out tomorrow and head back and see if he comes a calling on his sweetheart. I will have Hardy come down a day or two later to scout the town from the hills. On the third day, you both will rendezvous and return here. I have some other work for you both in Georgia. Do have any questions?"

Shay wondered how long he would be away but felt that it was futile to inquire about what things might be certain during the uncertainty of war.

"No. No, I don't have any questions."

Chickasaw smiled and held up his empty glass. "Do you want another drink?"

"You bet, I'll have another one."

Chickasaw laughed and poured two more shots of whiskey. "That's my boy!"

He handed Shay the glass and took his seat once again, as they drank in silence. As the whiskey settled inside Shay, his inhibitions to speak freely began to dissipate.

"This is only the second time we've met, and it seems you're always happy."

Chickasaw looked at him, appreciating his unpretentiousness. "Life is a strange thing, Shay. You note my happiness and rightly so, I can't hide it. But I can, and do, hide the pain. My dear wife died this past March. She was the mother of our six children. Well, the Rebs seized our property and forced them to flee north. It was all too much for her and, in the end, she got very sick and perished. I was almost destroyed by the grief. Life felt almost meaningless and would have been if it weren't for my six darlings. They didn't ask for none of it and sure enough didn't deserve it. That's life. The common folk from north to south didn't ask for this war and don't deserve it, but once again that's life. It's personal for me now, and there will be a just recompense for those responsible, along with their associates." Chickasaw breathed deeply, Shay felt kinship with him, bonded by mutual past pain and suffrage.

"My condolences about your wife. It must be hard for you, but I still don't know how you show a smile," Shay replied.

"If you would let me finish telling you, youngling!" Chickasaw barked, before returning to his pleasant demeanor. "Now, a few months ago I was out scouting alone and got caught betwixt two troop movements and had to stay hidden in a field for days. I mean, I couldn't budge more than a hundred yards, or I would have been spotted for sure. There I was starving and my water 'bout gone. I was well hidden, but somehow, she saw me! Like an angel sent from on high, she fed me and brought me a blanket. That woman put her own life in jeopardy to help me!" Chickasaw chuckled and shook his head. "Me," he repeated with a look of astonishment. "That's when I knew that there is a reason why everything happens. I don't know how or why, but that is a fact. So, life is a strange thing. In fact! I'm going to marry her! That's life!" he exclaimed in excitement, now well drunk from sum total of the day's whiskey. Shay was caught up in the excitement.

"Congratulations!" Shay raised his empty glass in celebration.

"Indeed! We will have to drink to that!" Chickasaw replied as he went to the table and retrieved the entire bottle and came back. He filled both small glasses again, and they drank.

Both had become intoxicated, but Shay more so, as he spoke his thoughts, unbridled of bashfulness.

"I can't see myself falling in love during these times," Shay said unapologetically.

"Why is that?"

"Well, you most likely will lose them some way, whether through sickness or maybe even killed. In these past months, I've seen all of that. We are all walking in it."

Chickasaw leaned over close to him. "Listen to me. You say 'these times' meaning the war. I tell you that these times are no different from any other time. Life is made of love and hate, war and peace, happiness and sadness. If you turn away from love, you turn away from life!"

Shay looked confused, and so Chickasaw leaned closer.

"What else is there to live for but love? This world is full of suffering and hard times, we agree. I'm convinced you know this because I saw it in your eyes the first time we met! Some folks love country, family, and friends, hell even their animals! Whatever it is, so be it. That which they love is what makes life worth living!" Shay remained silent, internally debating the spoken knowledge. "You yourself have loved and lost, haven't you?" Chickasaw asked.

Shay nodded. "I lost my mother and father."

Chickasaw nodded and patted his leg. "My last word of advice to you, son, is this: don't give up on love. Love is worth living for, and love is worth dying for. Remember that."

Shay nodded. Chickasaw stood up from his chair.

"I've kept you long enough, young man. Go on and take care of your business and I will see you both back here within a week. Take care and Godspeed."

Shay stood and shook his hand. "Thank you," he replied before leaving the room and exited the building. He walked down the front steps and noticed Hardy standing by his horse.

"Did everything go good in there, partner?" Hardy asked. Shay walked up to him.

"Yep. We had drinks—whiskey. He's having me go back in the morning to check for Treadwell at the plantation. He said you will be coming a day or two later and scout for him in town." Shay was slurring his words.

"That's right. I will have to lay back in the brush, seeing as a few folks got a look at me. Go on and get washed up and we'll head to the whorehouse," Hardy said with anticipation.

"No. I can't drink no more. Besides, I need to write my Pa and get some sleep. I can't wait to get into a real bed."

"All right then, I'll see you in a few days partner." Hardy patted Shay on the shoulder before walking down the street. Shay untied his horse and walked to the hotel, where a room was waiting. He ordered a bath and began to write a letter to Captain Price as he waited. He attempted to start writing but could not remember his chosen words from earlier. It seemed that all he had purposed to write had been lost to the whiskey.

As he pondered for the right words to ink, his bath was readied, so he set aside the ink and paper. He soaked in the hot water and relaxed until the point of sleep. His mind became clear and without worry as the water cleansed the filth of his body and thoughts. The room was silent, save the sound of splashing water as he washed. After finishing his bath and drying himself, he fetched the ink and paper. Again, he sat down at the table in his room, and without pause wrote his letter.

The next morning brought in the first of December, and Emily lay in bed looking out her window. She had not slept well the night before. When she returned from visiting Nathan the previous day, she had looked for her father, but he was nowhere to be found. All night she waited for him, but eventually succumbed to fatigue and retired for the evening.

After getting dressed, she searched and found him on his horse overseeing field work. She walked out to meet him with her arms folded, shielding herself from the cold breeze. He saw her approaching and trotted over to meet her.

"Good morning. You shouldn't be out here again in this cold, Emily."

"Good morning, Papa. I was looking for you when I came home last night but couldn't find you. I want to talk to you about Nathan. The way he has been beaten and treated just isn't right.

He admitted to me that he did wrong, but he should be given fair treatment until the trial. I'm asking you to help him."

The colonel's expression transformed as he dismounted and stood in front of her.

"I want you to listen to me closely. Nathan was accepted into this family with open arms, gaining not just your hand in marriage, but also the full weight of my patronage and the respect which the Walters name holds. He decided to betray himself, our family, and the Confederacy. For that, there is no forgiveness on this earth. I will never help Nathan. I allowed you visitation yesterday to say goodbye and expel him from your mind, thereby gaining closure."

Emily was confused and didn't understand what was truly being said. She became angry.

"I asked you for permission yesterday, Papa. But I can go see him on my own. In fact, I've decided to see him right now! No one has to take me, I will walk to town!"

The colonel looked at her.

"Emily, we hung Nathan last night. I will let you know where he has been buried so you may visit his grave if you so desire." He was unapologetic. Emily's mouth fell open in disbelief as her legs started shaking and she began to tremble.

Upon seeing her reaction, he attempted to embrace her out of genuine concern. She backed away from him and shouted:

"No! How could you? You could have stopped it!"

He stopped walking and appeared confused.

"Why would I have stopped it? My sweet child, I consented to it." His words were firm.

Emily broke down in tears and walked away. She desperately wanted to run but was drained of all stamina. She hobbled into the house and returned upstairs to her room.

Victoria had been watching her through a window. Maggie and Victoria had both been made aware of the news about Nathan the previous night, as Georgy and several other field hands had been procured by Colonel Walters to dig Nathan's grave.

Victoria walked the stairs to comfort Emily. The two childhood friends loved one another, although this appeared more evident when they were children. As they both became young women and lead dissimilar lives, their affections, at times, appeared to wane, though the love between them was always present.

Victoria entered the room, and, tearful, Emily looked up at her in silence. Victoria sat in her usual place on Emily's bed and embraced her friend, stroking her hair while she wept. Victoria began crying as was typical, empathetic to her friend's grief, but she also wept for Nathan, who she knew to be a very kind man. Her sorrowful feelings converged with those for the absent Shay, as she wondered if he would ever come back. Her ignorance of his wellbeing made her anxious, adding to her outpouring of sadness.

Maggie was downstairs in the kitchen and well aware of the scene transpiring upstairs. As dinner was being prepared, she whispered a prayer.

The next day brought with it a quiet calm which was shattered by the sounds of violence.

A field hand was being whipped for a minor oversight at the hands of the Guard. This beating was sanctioned at the behest of Colonel Walters. It was evident that after his brief hiatus from drunkenness, he had returned to his cruel devices. Victoria was among those who could not endure the sound of a person crying out in pain and winced at the sound of the lash. She desperately needed an escape, and quickly made an excuse to get out of the house.

While walking the path to the Johnston's, she imagined Shay was waiting for her, and so her excitement grew with every step. She marched past the tree line and the burrow, entering the forest. He was nowhere to be found. Victoria accepted the fact that he was never coming back, so she returned to the big house feeling dejected and miserable.

She walked through the house and found Emily asleep, still shut up in her room. Victoria went downstairs to her room and reached under her mattress, retrieving the candy which Shay had given her. She broke off a piece and tasted iy. It made her feel better as she recalled the first time they met. The thoughts turned her smile into a frown followed by unrelenting tears.

The hours lingered until the day had turned to night, but there was no change in the dread that filled the air. Everyone on the plantation inhaled it and was affected by it in their own way.

The next day began no different from the previous one. Victoria was extremely anxious. The house was absent of talk, and so were the fields, as the sound of work steadily echoed throughout. The colonel was seated on the front porch entertaining the men, who now rotated overseer duties between themselves.

Victoria walked into the kitchen where Maggie was sitting down, patting herself. "Mama Maggie, I'll be right back."

Maggie looked up at her. "Don't you tarry now! You come back from whence right directly, you hear?"

"Yes, ma'am," Victoria answered as she walked out the back door.

———————

Shay lay near the edge of the woods, just beyond the tall grass with his scope in hand. He had been waiting all morning and into the afternoon with no sight of Nathan Treadwell, or Victoria. He put down his scope and turned over on his back and looked up. He could only stay a few days, and then he needed to leave. He wondered how he could tell her that he would have to leave again, and he dreaded the thought of never returning.

Shay decided to pack up and go back to his camp, knowing a storm was approaching. He rubbed his throbbing temples with both hands, as thunder rolled across the landscape and the winds increased. As he walked to his horse, he considered the possibility of never seeing her again. The thunder bellowed, and it started to rain as a faint voice was heard.

"Shay!"

Shay turned to see Victoria standing at the edge of the forest. He dropped his scope to the ground and started walking toward her. She ran toward him with her arms outstretched, and as they embraced, the world around them was dissolved. There were no questions or answers in that moment, only solace and the shared sentiment of understanding each other. They pulled back slightly from their embrace, and Shay noticed her tears.

"Why are you crying?"

She wiped the tears from her eyes. "Because I'm happy to see you! Now I know you are safe!" She sniffled. He handed her the kerchief from around his neck to wipe her face.

"Thank you." She gazed deep into his eyes as the rain poured down, the forest seemingly echoing with applause as the drops hit the trees.

"Has any harm come to you?" he asked.

"No, but it's a sorrowful time for everyone here. Mr. Nathan has been put to death. Hung. Colonel…I mean Master Walters has become a down right terror to all of us. Miss Emily is grieving something terrible." She was noticeably distraught upon her recollection, while Shay took note of all the happenings.

"I don't like it, and I'm sorry for you suffering. Why did they hang Mr. Nathan? Do you know?" he asked.

"They said he was a spy for the Yankees. He confessed to the devilment. Still, he was a good man. Good to all of us." Shay noticed the rain increasing and lightning flashing more often..

"Let's go to my tent and get out of the rain. It's not very far. We can talk and stay dry." he urged.

"I can't, Shay, I have to get back. Mama Maggie has her eye on me and supper still has to be served." Shay sighed in frustration. "Shay, let me go and finish my work and I will come back here tonight to see you, I promise." She smiled.

"Yes, please do that. I will be waiting here for you." He was excited as she hugged him once more before hurriedly walking away out of the forest.

He went back to his camp and ate some dried beef while relaxing against a tree. He was consumed by a range of emotions, but none entangled him. Above the chaotic thoughts there remained the source of his absolute peace, and that was hope. The following hours did not pass quickly, as he became restless and nearly impetuous during his wait.

It was midnight and a steady drizzle fell on the roof of the house.

Victoria opened her eyes and quietly eased out of bed, donning her robe over her night clothes. She left the house carefully, ensuring no one was stirring about. All was in good order as she trotted through the back yard and down the path. While not even half the way there, she found herself soaking wet from the rain. The cold started to sink into her bones, which caused her to shiver.

After finally making it to the field, Shay walked out and covered her with his coat. She followed him into the forest while tightly holding on to his arm. Her heart raced wildly, as she was conflicted between fear and another force which she didn't understand. They arrived at his camp and went into his tent. Inside, a lantern was burning to provide light and meager warmth. She sat down, shivering uncontrollably as he unfolded a thick cotton blanket and placed it around her.

"This will keep you warm and dry. Are you hungry?" he asked.

"No, I don't want to eat. I'm so cold," she said amidst her chattering teeth. He took off his shirt, replaced it with a dry one and sat down beside her. She leaned into his chest as he held her in his arms, both staring into the light of the lantern. There was silence and mutual contentment, until she blurted out.

"What is to become of us, Shay?" Her breathing grew faster.

"I don't know. I just don't know." The answer was insufficient for her and she began to sob quietly.

"I have to leave again…tomorrow," he added. She stopped sobbing and looked up at him.

"When are you coming back?" she asked with watery eyes.

"Victoria, I don't know. I don't like it either. I missed you dearly and wish that things were different. I wish that I could make things different."

"Will you take me with you?" she eagerly awaited his response.

"I want to, but you can't go with me. Please try to understand," he pleaded.

"Don't leave me here Shay! Please don't!" she cried, as he pulled her closer.

"Don't cry, Victoria, please!" he implored, but she wouldn't stop crying and turned away from him, breaking his hold. She lay on her side, feeling alone and afraid like when she was a child. Shay could not no longer hold back his emotions; he made up his mind and liberated himself. He grabbed her by the shoulder and turned her over to her back. Now, facing each other, he moved her hands away from her face.

"I won't leave you, Victoria! You're coming with me!"

She looked up at him in disbelief.

"You mean it?" she asked.

He closed his eyes and nodded. "Yes! I will take you north to Tennessee and put you in a hotel for the time being, until I can think of what else to do."

"Shay, what is a hotel?"

"I will pay them money and you will live there. No more slaving in this living hell! In Tennessee, I will still have to leave for a while, but I will come back. This is the only way I can make sure you are protected." She stared at him and smiled. He was secure in the decision decreed by his heart, and truly believed it a righteous mandate.

Together their smiles faded, and both sensed a force drawing them together. They did not resist or acknowledge the invisible power which seem to possess them. They kissed once and looked at each other, and then kissed again. Instantly, they were entangled in an intimate frenzy of kissing, touching, and loving each other. Their lips remained locked together as they removed each other's clothes with haste. The two became one and their fate was sealed, underwritten by love. Afterward they lay together, immersed in the timeless moments of bliss that passed. The rain stopped shortly after, and both knew that they must leave each other out of necessity. Shay took her in his arms.

"We will leave tomorrow night after supper is served and you are finished with your tasks. Don't bring anything with you,save a warm coat," he admonished.

"Yes," she nodded.

He escorted her back from whence she came, and they parted with one final kiss.

Victoria went back to the house and downstairs to the basement. She removed her wet clothes and quietly got into bed. Her insides ached from her intimate encounter, but her newfound emotions helped to dull her discomfort. Maggie's voice broke the silence.

"Whatever devilment you getting into, or whoever you been seeing, you need to quit. I done told you now. You best heed me, child."

"Yes, ma'am," Victoria answered. She thought to herself how she would miss Mama Maggie when she left with Shay. She didn't want to leave Maggie and hoped there would be a way to send for her later. Surely Shay wouldn't mind coming back to fetch Mama Maggie, even if it were after a while.

With these thoughts, Victoria drifted off to sleep.

———————————

The next day, Victoria felt like a different woman. As the day transpired, she was filled with incredible fantasies of a life with Shay, as thoughts of him dominated her mind. She was beside herself, ecstatic that Shay was the first man she had lain with. Victoria had never loved a man before in this way, and patiently waited for the hours to pass to finally be with him.

Supper had been served and the house cleaned, while the colonel and the Guard sat around a fire near their tents. One of them played a fiddle as all shared songs reminiscent of former times. This went on for hours, and with every passing moment Victoria became more frustrated while looking out the window at the group. Usually, all would be sleep, but on this night, they decided to stay awake and howl into the darkness. A bottle of whiskey was passed around the circle of men, as a minute hand would pass along a clock.

The colonel had a deep appreciation for the men. He had been long removed from soldiering but related to them individually and respected them wholly. There was a pause in song as a man named Heberden, who they called Heb, spoke up.

"Colonel, I can speak for all the Guard and say that we loves ya! You are one of our fathers, and we look to you as a leader."

"I appreciate you all as well and treat you all as would-be sons," he replied, and consumed another drink of from the bottle.

Heb continued. "We see the pain you been through. Forgive me, sir, but who could stand losing a great woman like Miss Elizabeth and not be wrenched in two!" Heb looked around at the group as they nodded amen. "Time heals all wounds they say, but you have comfort at your fingertips. Only you need whisper the

word to receive the pleasure you desire at a moment's notice."
Colonel Walters was puzzled and looked at him curiously.

"What do you mean lad? Make it plain." His disposition became serious.

"Make it plain? Yes, sir, I will. You own a colored wench, desired by every white man across the county that ever cast an eye upon her! We all noticed when we came here, that you guarded her as your own, but soon we all realized that you weren't partaking of her, and that's a fact. Now I don't intend to be out of order, sir, but with all due respect, we think you should consider easing your troubles with her help. You need the comfort, and you need the release, sir."

Colonel Walters looked at him and remained silent. He looked around the campfire at the other men, as they all seemed to know his most secret desires. He paused for a moment.

"You have spoken the truth young man," Walters said. He got up and started walking toward the house and stopped half way. "Victoria!" Victoria looked outside the window at him.

She went outside and walked up to him. "Yes, Master?"

"Go into Mr. Shannon's old cabin and light a lantern. Wait for me and I will be there shortly," he slurred as he swayed from drunkenness. She stood there motionless, trying to understand what his request was about.

"What's wrong, Master?"

He became enraged.

"Get your ass moving and do as you are told! Right now!" He yelled. She remembered that Mr. Shannon had left his lamp in his former cabin. She walked into the house upset and retrieved the oil and matches, while Maggie came into the room and took notice.

"What he wants you for?" Maggie asked.

"I don't know! He is acting all out of sorts! He wants me to wait for him in Mr. Shannon's cabin." She paused. "Mama Maggie, I'm scared!"

Maggie walked up to her. "Now, child, for sure he ain't gonna whip you, and he sure enough ain't gonna kill you. You gone be all right, just don't make no fuss about what he do, that's all."

Victoria felt no consolation from her words and left out of the house and toward the cabin. She glanced at the grinning men sitting around the fire, who watched her intently. She went inside and brought the lantern from outside on the small porch and filled it with oil. She struck a match and ignited it, then entered the dusty room.

After setting the lantern on the table, she walked to the near window which was covered by a piece of cloth. She peeked out and saw the men sitting around the fire laughing as the colonel expounded in their midst. She was worried and began to pace around the room. Victoria contemplated running away and finding Shay but wasn't sure what she should do. A few minutes later, Colonel Walters opened the front door and came inside, replacing the wooden latch behind him. He looked around the room and squinted.

"It smells like an Irishman's ass in here," he said as he walked over to an old chest and removed his hat and heavy coat. Victoria watched him cautiously, with trepidation.

"Master, can I go back to the house now? I'm cold." Walters looked at her expressionless.

"No, you're not going anywhere. Now take off your clothes and get in that bed," he said firmly. She was shocked and angry, but also weak and nauseated.

"It's cold in here! Why do you want me to do that!" Her tone resounded with insolence.

Walter's face became noticeably red, and he became furious. He stood in front of her. "Damn you bitch! You will do as you are told! Now take your clothes off!"

"Please, Master! It's cold in here! I'm sorry, Master, please!" she screamed. Outside the men sat around the fire and could hear the faint beginnings of the struggle to come.

Heb spoke up: "Play a lively one! Loud mind you, while the colonel takes his pleasure," he instructed the fiddle player. The music of the fiddle cut through the midnight air while the men laughed and rejoiced to a melody of old. Inside the cabin, the colonel's assault continued, as he bullied her to comply with his command.

"Do it!" he yelled, as she stood still.

Suddenly she ran to the door and unlatched it in an attempt to escape but was pulled back and flung on top of the bed. She tried to imagine herself in another place, removed from the reality of the situation. She sensed a blow to her head, which caused her to nearly lose consciousness. He had struck her, and although dazed and disoriented, she could feel her undergarments being removed. Victoria tried to struggle against what she knew was to come, but her body would not respond properly. She could vaguely hear men outside singing to the cadence of a fiddle, until the sounds drifted off into oblivion.

Shay had been waiting a long time for Victoria, but she had not come as promised. It was nearly two hours after the appointed time, yet there was no sign of her. He wondered if she had reconsidered coming with him, but after thinking about it, he dismissed that notion. Something must have happened.

He left the forest and made his way closer to the plantation. After arriving, he looked through his scope and saw a fire burning. He watched the four men sitting around the fire, noted one was asleep, and another was playing the fiddle. To his surprise, he observed Victoria walk to the overseer's old cabin, and a few moments later, light illuminated the window coverings. He was perplexed. What was she doing?

His questions were partially answered as he saw the colonel stand by the fire for short spell before entering the cabin. Shay put his scope away and gathered himself.

Under the cover of darkness, he ran out into the field, through the tall grass. Knowing that he was running toward unknown peril, he didn't falter nor waiver in his determination. He approached the entrance to the path and negotiated it quickly, arriving at the opening to the backyard. Hidden, he closely observed the layout of the landscape. The Guard were sitting around a fire on the opposite side of the cabin, distracted in song.

Shay crept through the dense brush along the perimeter of the yard and arrived near the cabin, which lay between him and the men. He ran up to the side of the cabin undetected and crouched near the window. He heard Victoria resist the orders of the colonel until he heard a loud *thud*, and all became quiet. Sweat dripped down from his brow as he carefully peered across the front of the cabin. He could see the radiance of the fire, but not the men. He took heart and a deep breath, before slowly climbing over the raling.

Finally, Shay stood in front of the door, and understood that this decision could not be undone. He gently nudged the door and determined that it wasn't locked. After removing his knife from its sheath, he was prepared to enter, but paused. He sheathed his blade and removed the kerchief from around his neck. Quickly, he opened the door slightly and slid inside while closing it behind him. He saw Victoria on the bed, while Colonel Walters fumbled to loosen his belt buckle. For a moment, Shay was undetected. Then the colonel turned his eyes toward the uninvited figure in the room. Instantly, Shay was upon the him and his kerchief was wrapped around Walters' neck. Shay crossed his hands tightly and began to choke the life out of him.

Colonel Walters was awakened by his will to survive and attempted to struggle, grasping futilely at the ligature. Shay pulled him violently to the floor and mounted his back as he pulled Walter's head nearly upright. Shay clenched his teeth and held his breath, while completing the task of strangulation. He trembled as his grasp loosened, realizing that he had now taken a life. He looked over to Victoria who was sitting up on the bed, awestruck. Shay left the kerchief and stood, looking at her, and then at the dead colonel. She straightened her undergarments and pulled the hem of her dress down. She got off the bed and embraced him tightly.

"Oh, my God. Oh, my God. Shay, what are we to do?" she whispered in desperation while pulling him closer.

He stood still, conflicted. Shay had killed a man for the first time. A man who was deserving, in his opinion. However, there was an emptiness inside which followed, a hollow feeling with no satisfaction in it.

She whispered again in panic. "Shay! What are we to do?"

Shay woke himself and looked at her. "We are leaving, my Victoria. Please, stay by my side."

He led her to the door and peeked out. One man was urinating, standing only a few yards away from the fire. Shay slowly closed the door, but the man looked at the cabin and saw him. Shay listened and heard the man shout "What the hell?" Believing that all had been lost, Shay grabbed Victoria by the shoulders and whispered frantically.

"I have been seen! You can't go with me now! I've failed you!" She didn't know what to say or do. Shay quickly took the amulet off his neck and placed it around hers, tucking it beneath the neckline of her dress. He held her head with both hands and stared into her eyes. "Listen to me! When they question you, tell them you never saw me before! Tell them I killed him and tried to steal you away! Just remember, I will come back to you. I promise! Victoria, I love you!" He kissed her.

"I love you, Shay! What are you going to do?" The tears ran down her cheeks. He looked at her and smiled.

"I'm going to save you."

He opened the door and screamed a Native American war cry, while bolting from the doorway and down the front steps, shocking the man who saw him. The two other men around the fire stood up with their pistols drawn and began running toward the cabin as Shay ran toward the path.

Hardy had spent the whole day on the outskirts of town, looking for any signs of Nathan Treadwell. Treadwell's store had been closed all day, which gave him some indication.

He decided to seek out Shay who should have finished scouting the Walters Plantation. The night had been well spent, as Hardy made his way toward Shay's known camp sites. As he arrived at Shay's main camp, he was surprised that it was empty, his tent removed and his fire long extinguished. Hardy moved closer to Shay's known scouting positions, but as he arrived at the field of tall grass between the tree lines, he could not locate Shay.

He produced his scope and directed it toward the light in the distance. He observed movement and decided to get closer for a better vantage. After locating a small tree set aside a hill top, he was surprised to see men sitting around a fire. There were three men sitting and one asleep on his back. He noticed a figure lurking near a window on the near side of the house.

It was Shay! Hardy watched in astonishment as Shay crept stealthily into the cabin, with no idea why. Hardy didn't delay and unbuttoned his rifle case, producing his Whitworth with a mounted scope. He wiped off the face of the scope and took aim at the men in the camp. After a few minutes, Hardy saw a man get up from the campfire and walk toward the dirt road, caddy-corner to the cabin. The man exposed his privates and began to urinate. Hardy set his sights on the man's chest. Out of the corner of the scope, he watched the cabin door open and saw Shay look out with someone standing behind him. The man urinating looked his way and shouted something, which caused the other two around the fire to take notice.

The music stopped as the men exchanged words and stood up with their pistols drawn. Hardy seethed with anticipation from the danger. Suddenly, he saw Shay open the door and yell out a war cry. Hardy was in disbelief as Shay ran down the porch looking at the men and began running toward the path. The two men immediately ran after Shay while the first went inside the cabin. Hardy brought his scope down on the enemy.

"The colonel is dead! He done killed the colonel!" the man shouted from the doorway. Shay ran with all his might, his breath and stride keeping time.

"Hit him in the legs!" one of the men shouted, as they both fired a barrage of bullets toward Shay. The ground unfolded around him, so he changed his course and attempted to weave back and forth to avoid the lead projectiles. They continued to miss their target but were gaining on Shay and steadily closing the distance in between. Shay approached the path quickly, knowing he was nearly free from the immediate threat. Suddenly, Shay felt a jolt to his shoulder. He stumbled for a moment but regained his stride.

"I clipped him!" Heb shouted.

Hardy, witnessing the entire event as it unfolded, took aim at the pursuers, following them through his scope as they gained on his comrade. He sighed and leveled his scope on Shay. He fired but missed him and then he reloaded. Shay saw the muzzle flash to his forward left and knew it must be Hardy. He thanked God for it and was encouraged. Shay was nearly to the entrance of the path and heading toward his escape when the next shot rang out, hitting him in the chest.

Hardy put his rifle back in its case and slowly began his retreat from the hill. Shay fell back with his arms outstretched. The pursuers saw the muzzle flashes in the woods and stopped their pursuit as Shay fell.

"Who is that?" One man shouted.

"I don't know," the other replied.

They walked to up to Shay and saw he was dead, and focused their attention toward the path.

"Declare yourself!" one of the men shouted. There was no response, only silence.

"Hit the bluff!" Heb shouted as all three men started firing toward the hill beyond the path. They focused a barrage of gunfire toward it, and ran to the path, eventually exiting out the opening. Momentarily, they saw a silhouette disappear into the forest.

The three men walked back to Shay's body and stood around it. Heb took Shay's gun from his holster and inspected it.

"Damn fool. He had a loaded gun and didn't even try to shoot back."

"All right, now which one of us are we going to say shot him?" He looked around as another spoke up.

"Hell! All of us got him! You ain't the only one gonna get the applause for this. No! All of us should have equal part! It only be right," the man exclaimed, and Heb agreed.

"Okay then, make sure every man's lead is in him." They all fired into Shay's lifeless body, save one man.

"Dammit! I'm out of slugs!" he complained.

"That's fine, there's a hole in him for you already. Now, is everybody satisfied?" Heb asked the group. The two men nodded and walked back to the cabin.

Victoria stood on the porch, horrified at the events which had just unfolded. She slowly backed up against the door. She was on the verge of fainting and couldn't breathe. The strength left her legs and she slid down the door onto the floor. She clutched her chest and screamed.

"No! No! No!" She lay grief-stricken and crying uncontrollably as the men walked up the steps and approached the doorway.

"Move out the way wench!" one of them ordered. Her wailing drowned out his demand. He waited for a moment and then proceeded to step over her, followed by the other two. They inspected the colonel's body.

"He's dead all right," Heb said. "That other fella looks like some kind of Injun. Damn, he snuck right in there under our nose and killed him. God damn savage!" They stood around looking at each other.

"Jake, you go and search that other fella and see who he is," Heb ordered.

"Will do, Heb."

Heb and the other man knelt to examine Colonel Walters corpse. They glanced at Victoria as she wept on the floor. Heb shook his head in disappointment.

"All that ruckus going on and I thought—or rather we thought—that the colonel was pleasing himself. Instead, him and the wench was fighting for their lives. Shit!" He paused and looked at his comrade. "I want you to ride and get Jeffrey. I'll go tell Miss Emily."

"I'm on my way!" the man replied as he left.

While two men lay dead, Victoria's weeping was the only sound that could be heard in the cold December night.

———————————

Three days had passed and the #13 Nashville General Hospital was filled past capacity. Levi "Chickasaw" Naron walked through the double doors and up to the front desk.

"Good day, ma'am. I've just received a wire. I'm trying to locate one of my men who should be bedded here. Would you look up D. Hardy for me, please? Wound by gunshot," Chickasaw said politely.

"Yes, sir, I will. If you would give me a just a moment, please. I'm covering for my friend who is the clerk. She's at dinner," the nurse responded nervously while searching the admissions book.

"Here he is—D. Hardy. Bay eight, bed thirty-two."

"Thank you, kindly, ma'am." He tipped his hat and made his way down the corridor. He remarked to himself how large this hospital was, and how many wounded were abed. There were a hundred he had passed only within a few corridors. He walked down the middle of the bay, looking to the left at the even numbers until he saw him.

Chickasaw walked to his bedside, as Hardy noticed him.

"Chick!" Hardy muttered, as morphine coursed through his veins. Chickasaw smiled as he stood over him.

"How are you feeling?"

"Right about now, I'm feeling good! Wanted laudanum, but they said the morphine would keep me from coughing so much. Hell, I ain't complaining. Got one caught in my back right side. They got the lead out, but still hurts like hell," Hardy replied, wincing sporadically from pain.

Chickasaw stood close to the bed.

"I want you to take your time and tell me what happened. And where is Shay?"

Hardy closed his eyes for a moment and nodded.

"Chick, I surveyed the town on the first day I got there. Treadwell's store was closed. At nightfall, I went to check on Shay, but found his camp empty. I searched for him until I came up on the Walters Plantation." Hardy stopped and grunted for a moment, as Chickasaw looked on.

"Now, Chick, what I'm about to tell you might sound crazy, but I swear it's the God's honest truth. I saw a cabin door open and Shay came out yelling like a wild man. I don't how he managed to get in there, but there was about six Rebel Guards sitting around a fire not twenty yards from him. A fella was even taking a piss out front and Shay just about ran into him! He tried to make it down a path and out of there. Well, they all started chasing him, so I get out my Whitfield and commenced to provide covering fire on the enemy," Hardy paused, wincing in pain.

"Slow down, but go on," Chickasaw prompted.

Hardy nodded his head.

"Yes sir. I hear one of the men yell 'The colonel is dead' or something like that. I keep firing and reloading. I hit two of them, but the other four gained on Shay. It wasn't a second or two past that when they cut him down. I couldn't believe it. I fired and reloaded faster, but they located my position and opened up on me. That's when I got out of there. One of 'em got lucky and his slug found me. I barely made it back, losin' so much blood and all." Chickasaw let his words marinate.

"So, you saw Shay fall?" he asked.

"Yes, sir, he dropped like a rock."

"So, he was killed on the Walters Plantation?" Chickasaw inquired.

"Yes, sir."

Chickasaw remained silent, trying to fathom the events as they were recounted. The news of Shay's death had shocked him, and he stared out the window, shaking his head with a tempered sadness forged from his many years of personal tragedy.

Hardy watched him from the corner of his eye and feigned anger.

"Those Rebel bastards killed my partner! But Shay put himself in that predicament. He was a good kid, like I told you last week, but he didn't need to be out there." Hardy was staring at Levi, who glanced back him momentarily, before returning to his thoughts.

Hardy continued. "I must admit though, I was a tad surprised that you didn't bring Shay up on charges for killing that old slave. Yes, sir, that was a sign indeed. It showed us that he just wasn't right in the head." Chickasaw's disposition changed dramatically. He turned around and grabbed the head rail of the bed, while leaning over Hardy.

"What are you trying to tell me?" he asked calmly.

Hardy suddenly felt suffocated, even intimidated as he changed his tone. "I ain't smartin' off at you Chickasaw, I wouldn't do it. I'm just sayin', Shay got spooked by an old colored man and strangled him. He wasn't cut out for this work. I told you, but you sent him back there without me. Now you and I both know, only God fixes a man's breaking point. It ain't nobody's fault he went and done them things, or that you forgot about my report for that matter. I'm saying, don't no one need to know nothing 'bout this affair at all. There it is, I said my piece. I'm just wanting to heal up right directly and get back to the work," Hardy replied.

They stared at each other in silence until Chickasaw spoke.

"Hardy, I didn't believe you then, and I sure as hell don't believe you now. The fact is that only you and the Almighty already know the truth. So you see, there is no secret. I will put in the report what I see fit and proper. The first order of business is relieving you of your service. Your work is done. You have no enlistment or obligation to the Union Army, and I will have your last pay voucher sent here within a few days. If there is something else you are owed, let the Almighty recompense to you what is just."

Chickasaw stood up and walked out of the bay. He was apathetic as he thought on the truth behind Shay's death. There were so many things in life that Levi had no control over.

From the many injustices he had witnessed, to the wrongs that he couldn't right, it weighed on him and drained him.

He walked out the front doors of the hospital into a cold December breeze and walked back to Headquarters while preparing a mental report of the events.

He remembered Shay had mentioned his father only a week earlier, and wanted to write to him that night. It was heartbreaking, as Chickasaw knew Shay's father would be overjoyed to receive a letter from his son, which would be followed by a notice of death.

It was repeated all too often, and in Levi's opinion, "A damn shame." This was war, but he understood that war was only a reason, not an excuse.

Eleven

THROUGH THE FOGGY MIST

THREE YEARS LATER

The sound of the front door closing resounded through the small wood building. Caleb Price woke from his sleep and winced at the daylight as he sat upright on the bed. He began a bout of coughing, as he did every morning, and rubbed the sleep from his eyes. He couldn't recollect returning home from the tavern the night prior, nor could he for the last three years. He wondered what hour it was.

"What time is it, Gus?" His head was throbbing from dehydration. Gus walked through the curtains to the back room and stopped in the doorway.

"Good afternoon, Mr. Price, it's right about noon. I heard you coughing and figured you might be waking soon. How are you feeling, sir?"

"Excuse my manners, Gus. Good afternoon to you as well. I feel fine, but I apologize for my condition this morning. So, how many orders have been made today?" he asked, while attempting to stand up, his arthritic knees forbidding him. Gus rushed over to support him.

"Why don't you sit down while I bring you some hot coffee and a biscuit from out front? Let your bones warm up a little."

Price looked at him and nodded as he sat down. "Thank you, Gus. I appreciate you. Please, bring me some water, too."

"Yes, sir!" Gus smiled as he prepared a tray and handed it to Price. He left the room and continued to work in the front of the store while Price nourished himself and began to recover his meager strength. He had a deep appreciation for the young man in many ways.

Gus had survived the war and showed no limp after losing three toes from frostbite. He was considered one of the fortunate ones. He came back and took a wife, who immediately became pregnant and gave birth to a baby girl. Price recalled how the young man had grown up, and how he and Shay had been inseparable.

As happy as Price was for the return of Gus, that happiness didn't relieve any grief from the news of Shay's death. He had not survived even one year of the war, and so the town grieved with Captain Price, as they did for all the lives the war claimed.

Gus took the news as hard as the captain, which may have been the primary reason he took Shay's place at the store. Whatever the reason, Gus was indeed a godsend. Price finished his water and biscuit, and then started on his hot coffee. He sipped and closed his eyes, savoring its invigorating effects.

His mind wandered off its usual course as he began to think about memories he was desperately trying to forget. The first letter from Shay was read a hundred times over with joy. Then the second letter arrived, sent from a Mr. Levi Naron, who was Shay's superior. He informed the captain of Shay's assignment as a scout and the danger of his work. Mr. Naron recognized Shay for serving with honor and courage, citing the location of his death on the Walters Plantation in northern Alabama.

The news was unbearable for him and tore his grip from the world which he had known. Although he was a man experienced and well-seasoned in the immersion of shock and grief, he now found himself unprepared to withstand the internal emotional onslaught.

All his hopes and dreams for Shay's future were extinguished in an instant and with finality. He knew that no emotion, thought, or promise could change his present reality. His son would never return. So, Price withdrew himself from meaningful human contact and searched for any form of solace from his nightmare. The tavern presented a brief respite from the thoughts and the sadness that haunted him. He abhorred the path which he had chosen, detesting his own behavior and struggling to keep his personal promises of abstinence from whiskey. Soon, even Price counted himself as a drunkard and began to loathe himself.

After finishing his coffee and getting dressed, he went to help Gus in the front. They worked until six o'clock and began closing up. Gus finished sweeping the floor as Price put on a coat and walked to the front door.

"All is in order Gus, thank you. I would ask that you lock up for me. I have some errands at hand."

"Yes, sir, Mr. Price. By the way, would you like to come and sup with us tonight? Sarah always makes more than enough, and our little Rebekah would be tickled to see you again. You know she is going to want to touch your beard."

Price smiled. "Thank you, Gus. I think I will head to bed early tonight but give my regards to Sarah and the little one."

"Yes, sir," Gus responded, and watched him walk down the street, knowing that his errands were at the tavern. Gus worried about him but understood his pain. He had seen many tragedies during the war, and witnessed the bravest men curl up and cry like newborn babies after receiving news about the death of their loved ones. He didn't judge Price for his behavior because he also missed Shay dearly and understood every person handled heartache in their own way. Gus wiped a tear from his eye and blew his nose.

"Boy, I wish you were here," he whispered, as he locked up the store and went home to his family.

It was near midnight and the tavern was calm, with only a few patrons present. Price sat at the counter of the bar on his regular stool and drank another shot of whiskey. Shawny stood nearby, cleaning glasses and preparing to close. Price looked at the bottle that his drink was being poured from.

"How much for what's left in the bottle? I want to take it with me," he told the barkeep.

"Three dollars, Captain."

Price paid him and set the bottle in front of him. Shawny finished cleaning the counter, ready to close. He leaned over the bar. "We are closing for the night, Captain, be safe now. I'll see you tomorrow."

Price looked up. "Yes, my good man. I'll see you tomorrow."

Price step down off his stool, and Shawny stopped him.

"Captain, we have known each other many years now, and I consider us to be friends. Do you agree?"

Price looked at him strangely. "Yes, I do. Why do you ask?"

Shawny sighed. "Aye. As a friend, Captain, I know the grief you have over losing your son. A bitter herb to chew on for any man. Have you considered taking your burdens and pain to God?" Captain Price looked at him with surprise, as Shawny continued. "This tavern can be a hall of great celebration or a den of sorrow, and rightfully so, that is its purpose. But, Captain, the church is only right down the road, and folk such as you go there to lay down their heavy burdens. I attend myself, for that matter. Why not visit such a place, and receive some comfort from the Almighty?"

Price grabbed the bottle off the counter and responded. "There was a time when I believed the way you do, but no more. Throughout the ages, people of every race and creed have tried to lay their claim on the 'Almighty,' but who can prove that such a being exists? I require more to believe. I need more than ancient words written by the hand of mere men to sway me. Don't misunderstand me, I am not completely indifferent to religious texts. Within them I do find illustrations of morality, equity, and, at times, justice, but like I separate the bones from my fish before I eat, I must do the same with those books, lest I choke to death. Alas, there lies plenty of poison within the pages," Price responded coherently, although nearly drunk.

Shawny turned red and challenged him. "What poison do ye speak of, Captain?"

"The poison written which makes the 'Almighty' into a creation that is worse than any wretched man known! One that is full of jealousy, hatred, and injustice!" Price bellowed. He realized the escalation of his tone and abated, before calmly continuing. "The writers say they were inspired, but for the love of God, how can that be inspirational?" Price asked, as Shawny showed signs of irritation.

"You should watch your words, Captain, and mind your respect. You tread foolishly close to blasphemy as set forth in the Holy Scriptures!" he exclaimed resolutely.

Price looked at him and drew close to the counter. "The scriptures are only as holy as the corruptible men that penned them. So, if there be an Almighty God, I do not know him. Goodnight, my friend."

He turned and walked out of the tavern. Shawny watched him leave and shook his head in disgust, regretting that he offered an invitation to worship.

"Old fool." Shawny then looked up at the ceiling. "Lord, you warned me not to throw my pearls to the swine. Now I know why. Please, forgive me."

While standing outside, Price turned and drank the remainder of the whiskey and dropped it on the ground. He staggered home while thinking about spending another Christmas without his son as December was soon approaching. It would be three years since Shay's death, and he pondered how long much longer he wanted to live, questioning the purpose of existing this way.

After arriving home safely, he put a log on top of the few red coals which remained in the stove before falling into bed. His mind slowed as he drifted into sleep, but not before he whispered his final daily bedtime words.

"I love you Shay."

―――――――

The next day at sunrise, the light showed through the curtains in Emily's room. She stretched her limbs and yawned, while kicking her quilt off. She cleared her mind, though still groggy from her drunken state the night before, she looked over at the other side of the bed. The man who formerly lay there the night before was gone.

"Son of a bitch."

She climbed out of bed and retrieved her chamber pot to relieve herself. Life had drastically changed on the former plantation since her father's death, and the end of the war. Over one hundred acres was sold off before the war's end as the taxes and debts rose exponentially. Most of the freed slaves left the plantation, adopting the Walters surname as their own. Those that stayed had arranged to sharecrop the land which they had worked all their lives. A few white folks also bartered sharecropping arrangements with Emily, which helped sustain what remained of the estate's wealth.

During the years which followed, Emily searched for love in the company of several suitors. All the men were willing to take liberties with her sexually, but none wanted to fulfill their promises of matrimony and the responsibilities that came with it, namely the debt of the estate. Regardless, there were other reasons the men ran off. She had extreme outbursts of anger and unexpected mood swings. Individually these traits could be accepted by the men, but the combination of both usually caused their hasty retreat in search of more peaceful affairs. Constant drinking only exacerbated her condition, and the house servants would regularly witness Emily tirade through the house without cause.

Although they were no longer slaves, they continued to keep their silence and pay homage to her. Georgy was kept on as the driver and grounds man and lived in Mr. Shannon's former cabin. Maggie stayed on as the cook, to Emily's surprise and delight. When Emily would become violent, Maggie would calm her. Her respect for Maggie was obvious to everyone, but not understood by most who witnessed their interactions. Victoria served as the maid and regularly endured the scorn of Emily, who had grown to despise her.

After learning from the Home Guard about the circumstances surrounding her father's death, Emily had become appalled that Victoria had been engaged in sexual relations with her father. She became livid after hearing the reports, and forced Victoria to work the fields for months, while confining her to be alone at night, punishing her for what Emily deemed a betrayal.

That all changed five months later when the new overseer reported that Victoria was with child. Emily was bewildered at the news but realized the implications. She had Victoria brought back into the house to resume her duties during the remainder of her pregnancy. The slave midwives had delivered the baby, and after washing and wrapping the newborn, they presented Victoria her son. He was a very fair skinned and healthy baby, having a full head of straight black hair. The women all smiled and carried on about him while Emily looked on. She had been sitting through the entire delivery and sipping on a glass of brandy. She walked over to look at the him and named him.

"His name is going to be Jefferson. There was a president named Thomas Jefferson once. Papa told me that Mr. Jefferson liked to frequent his slaves and make babies. I think that is a fair name, since he left me a bastard baby brother." She took another drink and walked out of the room. This was part of Victoria's torment. Being twice bitten by misfortune, with the consolation of a child left by Shay.

After Emily left the room, Maggie patted her on the shoulder, and spoke the words which Victoria would always remember.

"The good Lord sawed fit for the seed to take hold and done blessed this here baby. Now you be a momma, and no matter what, you never be alone."

Victoria looked at her baby and saw only Shay. She kissed his forehead and cried while holding him close. After the war and the change of time, little Jefferson became his mother's shadow and followed her everywhere. He brought life to the old house, and Emily allowed him to roam free. Privately, Emily cared for Jefferson and wanted to let go of her bitterness and love him, but she couldn't. Her intolerance for race mixing had been deeply instilled in her by the late Colonel and Mrs. Walters.

Emily believed that the indiscretions committed by her father after her mother's passing were due to extreme grief and drunkenness. She forgave him for that but could never forgive him for allowing Nathan to be put to death. Emily became a walking quandary, as she loved and hated her deceased father, Victoria, and even herself.

As for Victoria, she was alive but consumed with guilt. She blamed herself for Shay's death and the death of Colonel Walters. She believed that everything could have been different if she never had asked him to steal her away. Victoria was enveloped in misery, and baby Jefferson was her only attachment to sanity. If it hadn't been for him, she didn't know what would have become of her. She visited Shay's grave the following two years, but had to stop altogether, due to becoming physically ill from her grief. This December would mark three years since he had left her, and she tried to keep her mind from the thought.

Although Emily was abusive to Victoria, she treated Jefferson differently, and allowed him to sleep in the guest bedroom on the first floor. Victoria and Maggie continued to sleep in the basement, but now with better mattresses and bedding. The work they performed was paid in room and boarding, with the addition of a few dollars a week. Victoria was unconcerned with her meager earnings. She was happy that her son was sleeping in a more comfortable place than herself.

Before baby Jefferson would go to sleep, he would sit on Victoria's bed and play with a stray kitten, now made a pet. He would sing with his mother and Mama Maggie. One day Victoria decided to take the amulet from her neck and allow Jefferson to play with it. When she asked him for it back, he grinned and playfully put it around his neck, as he saw his mother do. She let him keep it and whispered to him.

"This belonged to your father." She tucked it in his shirt as he smiled. Despite the volatility of his surroundings, he was indeed a very happy child. For the rest of the inhabitants of the plantation, life became no easier and no harder, just different.

Emily finished filling the chamber pot and opened her room door, setting it on the floor.

"Victoria! Empty my pot!" she yelled, her voice ringing down the stairs from above.

"Yes, Miss Elizabeth!" Victoria called back.

———————————

There remained only a few hours before dawn. Caleb Price was sleeping restlessly, on the verge of waking. Just before opening his eyes, he felt himself slipping away from consciousness as he began to dream vividly.

He was walking through a forest looking for something, or someone. He began to panic as he searched through the foggy mist. A figure appeared in the distance, and as he approached it, he saw that it was Shay.

Captain Price was overjoyed at the sight of his son and called out to him in earnest. Shay was dressed in his military uniform and unarmed as he looked back and smiled. As Price walked closer, Shay turned and walked into the mist. The captain ran toward the spot where Shay had stood, feverishly searching for him, but he was gone. Captain Price began to sob from losing Shay a second time, spiraling from joy to sorrow. He stopped sobbing when he heard a faint voice calling.

"Father," the voice whispered.

Captain Price turned around to see Shay once again smiling and standing off in the distance. Overwhelming joy washed over Price as he ran to Shay. As Price approached, the forest became brighter and the mist disappeared.

Shay was so close, but as Price reached out to embrace him, he was awakened from the dream with a sound.

The front door of store had closed shut and Gus was coming in to start his day of work. Price woke up sweating, his eyes wide open and breathing rapidly. He sat up in bed and coughed up the mucus from his lungs while his mind raced.

"Gus!" he shouted.

Gus walked to the back of the store to Price's room and opened the door.

"Good morning, Mr. Price. What's wrong?" Gus asked with concern as Price looked at him with eyes weeping from the dream. Price was at a loss for words as he attempted to bridle in his thoughts and emotions.

Gus walked closer and laid his hand on Price's shoulder.

"Captain Price, are you all right?" Price took a deep breath.

"I'm not all right, Gus. I've been a stubborn old fool. I lost my son, then I lost myself!" Gus rubbed is shoulder in support as Price continued. "I'm a damn drunk. That is what I've become, there is no doubt. Still, where is my son? I haven't even recovered his body!"

Gus stepped back. "Sir, from the letter the man sent we know he lays somewhere in Alabama. I figured you would try to find him after the war, but you have been grieving. I understand why."

"No, there is no excuse for it. I'm an old man. I don't know how much longer I will walk this earth, or even want to walk it. So I have made up my mind."

Gus raised his eyebrows in surprise. "What are you saying, Captain?"

Price stood up from his bed and hobbled over to Gus. "I'm going to find my Shay and bring him home." He spoke with conviction as they stood faced each other. "I will need your help to do it. Will you help me?" Price asked, as he placed his hands upon Gus's shoulders.

Gus's eyes began to water for many reasons. He smiled and nodded his head. "Aye, Captain," he responded, remembering the days when he and Shay were young chaps.

"Thank you, Gus. Thank you."

The next day, each went their separate ways to make the proper inquiries to the official sources to find the exact location of Shay's remains and bring him home.

A few months later, spring was coming into full bloom and ushering in a potpourri of new scents which blanketed New England. Gus was running from the telegraph office to meet Captain Price at the store. They had been in correspondence with a Miss Clarissa Barton of the Missing Soldiers Office. Prior to this, they had written to her and sent the details which were contained in Mr. Levi Naron's letter.

Captain Price was sitting at the counter and reading the news. He stopped to remove and clean his smudged spectacles, when Gus came rushing into the store.

"Here it is, Captain!"

He laid the telegram down on the counter in front of Price, who immediately opened it. He breathed deeply before donning his spectacles.

"If you don't mind, Gus, let me first read it to myself. If nothing comes of this, I'd rather not have spoken aloud the disappointment."

"Take your time, sir."

Price was expressionless as he read the telegram in silence. Miss Barton notified him of a possible match pertaining to his recent inquiry. A Missing Soldier volunteer who was located in northern Alabama had received and filed a request from particular land owners. A new family in the area had purchased twenty acres of property and discovered a grave on it. The land was once part of either the Johnston or Walters Plantations. She also stated that if the remains were claimed, the claimant would be solely responsible for any expenses associated with retrieval. The telegram listed the names and addresses of the property owners along with a waiting for reply statement.

Price took of his specs and smiled as he handed Gus the telegram.

"Good news then?" Gus asked excitedly.

"Indeed!"

Price stood up and leaned over the counter, looking out the window while Gus read the letter quickly, but carefully. He turned to Price.

"So, what are we going to do now?"

Price broke his distant gaze to look at Gus. "I need to go down there alone. I would that you go with me, but you have a wife and child to look after."

Gus frowned. "No sir! We are in this together and will see it to the end." He was firm, and Price took notice. "It's just plain dangerous down there. In many places, there is pure lawlessness and even the random killing of the freed folk! Listen to me, man!" Price yelled as Gus began fidgeting, never breaking his stare. Price lowered his tone. "You survived hell and made it home. I won't have you tempt the fates a second time on my account." Price was calm, but stern.

There was a pensive silence. Gus took a moment and then spoke. "I'm a free man, and I fought to stay that way. I can go anywhere in this country I choose, and I'll still be free. Mr. Price, if they want to take my life, then they can try. It doesn't matter, because whether I stand or fall, I'm still going to be a free man. I'm not just going with you on your account, but on mine, too. The truth is that both of us are doing this on account of our love for Shay. I'm going with you. Now, I have said my piece."

Price looked at him and nodded as he extended his hand and they shook. "Very well, Mr. Morris. Let us plan our trip, carefully and wisely. Mind you, our route, provisions, and weapons will be of the utmost importance. We will have to shut down the store upon our departure, but I will ensure your wages will be paid in advance beforehand. All other expenses will be satisfied by me, along with any other necessities you may incur."

Price removed his jacket from its hook on the wall as Gus nodded. "Yes, sir. I wasn't worried about any of wages, but I thank you."

Price opened the front door and turned to him. "That's why your wife is your better half, she has the sense to worry about such things! You are welcome."

Price smiled and left as Gus chuckled to himself. The humor was lost in a moment as Gus began to mentally prepare himself for the journey back beyond the Mason-Dixon Line. It was the land where he swore an oath during the war, making a solemn promise to himself to never return.

Twelve

THE BUTTERFLY

After a week of thorough planning and making arrangements, Captain Price and Gus began their journey. Price chose not to take the route through the Carolinas, but rather a route to the west of the Appalachians. They carried provisions for three months, calculated to last them until they could resupply in Nashville.

He owned two horses which were quartered in the livery until his return, but he also purchased four more. Over a million horses had been killed during the war, but like Gus, these valiant steeds had survived and were pulled from a team that formerly transported heavy artillery. He had inspected each horse meticulously and stared into their eyes. He counted them as honorable war veterans and worthy of the same respect as any man that ever walked on two feet. The weapons and ammunition had also been prepared and remained at the ready. Both men were willing to take a life, if needed, in defense of their own.

Gus bid farewell to his distraught wife and carefree young daughter, promising a safe return before the end of the year. The captain also had sent a telegram ahead to the attention of a Mr. Stanley Clarke of Alabama, informing him that Mr. Caleb Price and party had left Connecticut en route to his location. Mr. Clarke would also receive a telegram of their progress on the first day of each subsequent month until their arrival. As Gus sat holding the reins, he looked over at Price.

"Are we ready, Captain?"

"Indeed, we are. Take us out."

Gus hesitated for a moment.

"Captain, I meant to ask, don't you think a prayer for our journey is in order?"

"By all means. Please, do as you will."

Gus closed his eyes and bowed his head.

"Dear Lord, we thank you for giving us life, health, and strength. We thank you Master for food, shelter, and clothing. We ask you to protect our loved ones while we are away from home. We ask that you protect us from hurt, harm, or danger along the way. Please help us to accomplish our purpose and bring our loved one home. Please, give us the victory. We humbly ask this in the name of Jesus. Amen."

"Amen," Captain Price acknowledged.

They began the long and arduous journey into the Deep South, planning to cover nearly twelve hundred miles within ninety days. Although they were determined in their endeavor, the future remained unknown to them both. Even still, they took heart.

———————————

Victoria, Maggie, and Georgy were sitting on the back porch, while little Jefferson was playing with the cat in the grass. The late afternoon shade was now covering the porch, while they all enjoyed a time of rest from their daily duties.

"He sho does move fast to be so little," Maggie said, as she sat in her rocking chair on the back porch. Georgy was leaning back on a step with his eyes closed, enjoying the air and light breeze.

"Yes, ma'am. I can't believe he is going on three years and trying to run already!" Victoria replied, as she looked on her child.

Jefferson chased after the juvenile cat, who only allowed himself to be caught in order to receive a stroking.

Miss Emily called Victoria from inside the house.

"Yes, Miss Emily. I'm coming!" she shouted from the stoop.

"What she want now?" Maggie asked, as she rocked back and forth.

"Let me go see." She tapped Georgy to follow her, went inside, and met Emily in the dining room.

"Yes, ma'am?" Victoria asked.

"I saw Mrs. Clarke on a carriage. Evidently, she's coming to visit. Make the tea ready to serve when I call. Make it sweet, too," she said with a sense of urgency.

"Miss Emily, we don't have any honey, and we are very low on our sugar."

"Well, just use the rest of the sugar and make it sweet! We will worry about the damn sugar later," Emily chided.

"Yes, ma'am."

Emily walked into the kitchen with Georgy following behind. She directed him to go out the back of the house and then around to the front porch. Emily walked briskly to the foyer and stopped in front of the mirror, pausing to ensure she was presentable for company. She walked out the front door and stood atop the porch to wait.

Mrs. Clarke was traveling alone in a one-horse buggy and waved to Emily from afar as she approached the house. Emily smiled and waved back, happy to have a female visitor. It was long overdue. The buggy stopped, and Georgy ran out to secure the team while Mrs. Clarke stepped down and walked up the steps.

"It has been such a long time, Miss Emily! How have you been?" Mrs. Clarke asked happily, as she arrived at the top.

"I have been doing very well, thank you!" Emily replied cheerfully, as the two embraced briefly. "Let's go inside and sit," Emily said, as she began to lead her visitor inside.

"Why don't we just sit out here? I can only stay briefly. Mr. Clarke is expecting me back soon. Besides, the air outside is just lovely!" she exclaimed.

"Yes, that is a better idea. Let's sit out here." She motioned her guest to a chair and sat down beside her.

"Victoria!" Emily called out. After a few moments Victoria came to the door.

"Yes, Miss Emily?"

"Victoria, would you bring Mrs. Clarke some tea?" Emily asked.

"Yes, ma'am." She walked back into the house and returned with a prepared serving tray. They both took glasses, while Victoria went back inside.

Mrs. Clarke began the discussion. "I came over here to let you know the land we purchased from you two years ago had a grave on it. We asked some of the sharecroppers who used to slave for your plantation, and they told us that the man buried there was involved in the death of your father during the war."

"I see. Go on," Emily replied with interest.

"Yes, well, I did an inquiry and found a young lady in town, she is a volunteer for the Missing Soldiers Office which is located up North. She informed me that their mission is to locate the bodies of fallen soldiers and return them to their families. Well, after a few months we received word from a claimant who is coming down here to exhume the body and take it up North. I thought it was a wonderful thing to do, getting all the bodies of the soldiers back to their families. Not just our boys mind you, but the Yanks as well," Mrs. Clarke expounded while Emily nodded in approval.

"I agree. That's a good thing, but I'm a bit puzzled about the grave on your property."

"Oh? Tell me, how so?" Mrs. Clarke asked.

"Firstly, I want to apologize for not informing you of that man's grave on your land prior to the purchase. To be completely honest, I didn't know exactly where he was buried and had purposed myself to strike all remembrance of him from my memory. To my knowledge that man was not a Union soldier. He was nothing more than a savage Indian."

"A savage?" Mrs. Clarke replied with surprise.

"Yes, I believe they called him a renegade Indian. He killed my father while trying to steal off with my maid Victoria!"

Mrs. Clarke's eyes widened.

"Oh, my Lord! That is truly terrifying!" she replied while shaking her head. "I definitely want it off my land! Well, I'm so glad I spoke with you. I'm going to tell my husband about this, and we will just let this man come and take the remains back North. I believe his name is Mr. Price. My husband estimates his arrival sometime during the month of June, perhaps even July. He can take the body back with satisfaction and won't know any different."

Emily nodded in agreement. "I agree. If you would please let me know when he arrives," Emily said, smiling.

"I most certainly will. Well, I need to be going. It was a pleasure to see you again," Mrs. Clarke said, as they both stood.

"Likewise."

"Victoria!" Emily shouted.

Victoria returned with the serving tray to take their glasses, and went back to the kitchen. Mrs. Clarke climbed back into her buggy and set off, as Georgy released his hold.

The buggy traveled toward the road, while Georgy looked at Emily for any further instruction. She stared at him for a moment, and then rolled her eyes while dismissing him with a wave of her hand. He smiled and made his way quickly to the back of the house and walked into the kitchen.

Victoria was sitting down at their table across from Maggie, who was finishing her glass of tea. Georgy stood smiling in their midst as Victoria handed him the other remaining glass. He nodded to her in thanks, before taking a large gulp. Jefferson came out of the pantry and looked at the three of them. He scurried toward Maggie's lap, reaching up toward the glass at her mouth. She looked at him and smiled.

"You want some? C'mon take a sip." She held the glass for him to drink. He drank what she allowed but wanted more as she pulled back. "That's enough now." He shuffled to his mother's chair and bent over her lap. Victoria tenderly ran her fingers through his straight black hair.

"He needs to nap," she declared. "Come on, little man." She picked him up and strolled to the basement, placing him on her bed. He turned over groggily and looked at her.

"All right, I'll be right back." She walked upstairs and outside to find their cat. She brought it back to her room where they all lay together, until the cat eventually climbed down and curled up on the floor.

It was high noon in the month of July, and the afternoon sun beat down upon the Alabama countryside. Captain Price took out his handkerchief and wiped the sweat from his forehead, after which he rung it out over the side of the wagon.

"I think I see the town up ahead," Gus said as he drove.

"Thank God," Captain Price replied.

The sun was unrelenting and scorching everything without shelter. They had finally arrived at their final destination without incident and were ready to rest.

The journey had taken its toll on them physically and mentally, and both witnessed firsthand the aftermath of the war. Impoverished towns, displaced folk, and freed slaves constituted the bulk of their encounters. The destruction was nearly incomprehensible to Price. Having been to the farthest corners of the globe, he had never witnessed such sights before. In comparison, the devastation below the Mason-Dixon was of epic proportions. Gus was visibly affected himself, realizing the magnitude of the war and witnessing its legacy first hand.

They stopped at a hotel and Price went inside to secure a room, while Gus watered the horses. A few hours after eating and resting, Price went downstairs to the front desk to ascertain directions to the property of Mr. Clarke. It was half past four o'clock, when Price and Gus left town to head for the Clarke farm.

As they drew closer, Captain Price started to become anxious. He knew Shay had been killed in this land, probably not far off. The anger began to rise within him. There was no object of his fury, or any focus of his blame, just his silent vexation. They turned onto the road which led to a large farmhouse, where they saw a man sitting on the front porch. Price stepped down from the wagon, while Gus remained holding the reins.

"Good evening, sir. My name is Caleb Price and I am looking for Mr. Stanley Clark."

Mr. Clarke nodded. "Yes, sir, I'm Stanley Clarke. I got your telegram from Nashville a few days ago. I been expecting you any day now."

He got up and walked down the steps, where he and Price shook hands.

Price motioned toward Gus and introduced him. "This is my associate, Mr. Augustus Morris."

Gus tipped his hat to Mr. Clarke, who in turn reciprocated a nod of his head. After completing the formalities, Clarke got to business promptly.

"We might as well get right down to it. I can walk you over to the grave and show you where it is. It's getting close to supper and too late to start digging, but if you wait until tomorrow morning, I can procure three or four men to do the dirty work. Also, while they are doing that, I can make the coffin for you. It'll be sturdy and square, so no worries. The men will put the remains in there for you as well."

Price looked at Gus for a moment. "Very well. What is your proposal for the cost of labor and materials?"

"Let's see, I'll take ten dollars for the coffin, including my labor. The men will take a dollar a piece. I think that's fair since they got to fill the hole back in. It shouldn't be more than fourteen dollars. That should do it."

Price nodded, and they shook hands. "Fair deal, I agree."

Mr. Clarke led them through a field heading east and into the forest. He stopped a few yards inside the tree line and pointed. "There it is."

Price and Gus walked around him. There was a small clearing covered with fallen pine needles and a clear oblong depression in the ground. They approached the grave side-by-side and stood over it in silence. Suddenly, Price's grief became unrestrained as he collapsed to one knee and began to sob. Gus continued to look at the grave but was unable to constrain himself any longer and also broke into tears. They both were overwhelmed. Both had prepared for every imaginable situation yet had not considered the arrival of this moment.

Mr. Clarke was taken aback by their reaction. Likewise, he hadn't thought about this moment before and began to feel the guilt rise from his conscience. Yet, it was not enough guilt to cause him to divulge his wife's secret.

"My condolences for your loss. The both of you," Clarke said, as his eyes started to water. "I lost my brother, my uncle, and two cousins. They all hurt in different ways, and my heart goes out to you. Losing your child? Mercy." He wiped his eyes. "I will leave you all to mourn."

He walked back to his house while Captain Price and Gus remained. They had no knowledge of time and no coherence of thought. Unexpectedly, in unison their grief was swept away as abruptly as it had arrived. Price struggled to stand on his own, so Gus helped him. Price took a few deep breaths and pulled out his handkerchief to blow his nose, as Gus did likewise.

"Are you ready to go, Captain?" Gus asked.

Price nodded and the two met Mr. Clarke back at his house and finalized the time to begin the exhumation. They returned to the hotel in town in silence, numb from the emotional upheaval of their hearts. Both men were exhausted, and as Price turned over to sleep, Gus extinguished the lamp.

The room was dark and quiet. Gus rolled on his side and as he began drifting off, he heard Captain Price mumble.

"I love you, Shay."

Price and Gus left town the next morning at nine o'clock and headed to the gravesite. The trip seemed to go faster to them, even though their pace was the same. Unknown to each other, they each purposed to stand strong during the grizzly process.

They made their way past Mr. Clarke's house and then continued on to the forest. They saw Mr. Clarke, along with four men hard at work, digging. A newly fashioned coffin lay nearby on the ground. Mr. Clarke greeted them as they stopped and disembarked.

Mr. Clark saluted and said, "Good morning."

They both responded back in kind and walked into the woods. The men wasted no time doing the work and removed the soil in silence. They were sharecroppers who were once the slaves that worked that very land. Two of the men had dug this grave three years prior to lay Shay in it, but dared not speak of it out of fear. One of the men called out to the group with his hand raised.

"Hold!" The men crowded around for a brief discussion as they inspected the bottom of the hole. One of the men climbed out of the hole and walked to a wagon, before returning with a folded bundle of thick material, which he set on the ground. They continued digging, and after a short time one of them reached out, grabbed the bundle, and pulled it down inside.

Price turned around to face away, as did Gus. Within a half hour, Shay's remains had been recovered and wrapped multiple times. Twine was used the secure the material and bind the bones together so it could be raised without compromising its shape and form. The men lifted the remains and carefully placed it in the coffin. They waited beside the coffin and wiped their sweat off their faces while passing around a canteen.

Mr. Clarke walked up to Captain Price. "I believe the body is a fit. Make sure everything is to your liking," he said.

Price and Gus walked over to the coffin and saw that the body inside was neatly wrapped and secured. Their eyes began to water as they both looked on in reverence. Price issued an order to the men before another emotional scene could transpire.

"Seal it."

The men put the cover on and nailed it shut, sealing it thoroughly. They loaded it onto Price's wagon and stood back, waiting for further instructions. Mr. Clarke looked at the men.

"You all go back to the house and wait for me on the back porch. After me and Mr. Price settle up, I'll be back right directly to take care of y'all." The men nodded and walked back to house, when Price called out.

"Wait!" he shouted at them.

They stopped and turned around as he walked up to them.

"Thank you for your help," he told each man as he shook their hand.

Price and Mr. Clarke settled their business and shook hands. Mr. Clarke appeared agitated.

"Mr. Price, before you go I have something for you." He produced an envelope and handed it to him. "My wife gave this to me for you. I believe it's an invitation of sorts for dinner, from Miss Emily Walters." Price opened the envelope and read the contents to himself. Gus looked on with curiosity.

"What does it say, Mr. Price?" Gus asked.

"It's an invitation from the Walters Estate, for supper. It says today at six o'clock and is signed by Miss Emily Walters," Price replied as he turned his attention to Mr. Clarke. "I thank you for everything you have done, good sir."

"Glad to be of help, and thank you, too. I wish you safe travels back up North."

They walked back to the wagon, while Clarke met the men on his back porch to settle their wages. Price and Gus headed back to the hotel. The pain of Shay's passing was still present, but having his remains in their possession eased Captain Price's angst. They arrived at their room, kicked off their boots, and rested. By two o'clock, they realized they were famished. Gus rolled over and looked over to Price on the next bed.

"Mr. Price, I'm powerful hungry. When are we going to eat?" Price looked over at him.

"You can eat anytime Gus. What do you fancy today?"

"Right now? I could eat my boots. It doesn't matter to me what we eat. What about that invitation? It sounds like rich folks and plenty of fine food."

Price sighed and looked up at the ceiling.

"I don't know Gus. Hell, the woman could be planning to poison us for all we know. No matter how friendly these folks appear to be, we are still considered Yankees down here and not well-liked."

Gus rolled his eyes. "Now Captain, you don't really believe the lady would poison us, do you?"

Price lay with his hands behind his head, deep in thought. "I don't know, although it is possible."

Gus sat up on his bed. "Well, I want to go," Gus stated resolutely.

Price looked over at him. "Very well. We will go visit, but I don't want to stay long. We have the most important leg of our journey to come, and that's to get back home safely. Meanwhile, you might want to eat the last of those peanuts to hold your hunger at bay. We will resupply in Nashville, so be prepared to eat your fill tonight."

Gus hooted with satisfaction and his imagination ran wild, anticipating the home cooked meal to come.

The two napped for an hour before washing up and changing into fresher clothes. They left out of town having separate thoughts on their mind. Gus was thinking about the food, and Price about the trip back North.

As the wagon rolled east, the sun began to set in the west, and they chased their shadows along the dirt road.

———————————

They arrived at the Walters Mansion just before six o'clock, and all was quiet as they stopped the wagon and set the brake. As they dismounted, Emily walked out the front door and stood at the top of the steps. They both saw her and were immediately awestruck by her striking beauty and figure. Her outward appearance proved that the tales of the beautiful Southern Belle were true.

"Mr. Price, I presume?" she asked politely.

"Yes, my lady. Caleb Price. This is my associate Mr. Morris," he said while touching Gus's shoulder. "We thank you for your invitation," Price smiled.

She grinned in return and walked to the door.

"Follow me, please. The food is ready to be served."

The men started toward the stairs, as she opened the door and turned around.

"He can't come inside my house, Mr. Price. He needs to go around back and eat in the kitchen with my servants," she said politely.

Price stopped walking, as did Gus. Gus saw Captain Price turning red and becoming furious.

Gus turned to Price and whispered, "Mr. Price, it's all right. I'll go around back. It's just the way it is down here, my feelings aren't hurt."

He smiled as Price broke his stare from Emily and looked at him.

"Are you sure?" Price asked.

"I don't mind eating with the servants. They are my folk; in fact I long for it."

"Very well, then, enjoy," Price replied.

He then followed Emily into the house, while Gus walked around to the back. She led Price to the dining room, where the table was set immaculately. He followed her to the head of the table, where he pulled back her chair and seated her, after which he took his seat. He looked around the room to absorb the atmosphere of it. Farther away in the great room, he observed two enormous portraits mounted on the wall.

"Are those portraits of your parents?" He asked.

"Yes, they are. They were commissioned nearly twenty years ago," she replied while looking at them.

"Even from this distance, I can see a strong resemblance between you and your father. Indeed, you certainly share his likeness."

She looked at him and smiled. "They have both passed on, but to some degree, the portraits console me."

Victoria walked out of the kitchen and began serving the food. Price looked at her and smiled, causing her to smile back.

Emily spoke up. "Would you care for any spirits? Bourbon, or brandy perhaps?" she asked.

"Thank you, but I must say no. I no longer indulge myself. It does not agree with me in my old age," he chuckled.

She feigned disappointment and frowned. "Well, you will have to excuse me. I will have to partake without you."

"By all means, please do," he replied.

They began to eat, drink, and talk, with Emily focusing the conversation around the cities of the North. She wanted to know, in detail, how life was above the Mason-Dixon. Captain Price inundated her with ample information until she was well full of it.

Suddenly, little Jefferson ran out of the kitchen and through to the dining room.

"Jefferson!" Victoria barked and apologized, before chasing after him into the great room.

Captain Price's eyes followed the child as he scampered across the floor. "Look at the little chap go!" Price remarked with a grin, while Emily stared at Victoria in embarrassment. She refrained from issuing a verbal lashing, and instead took pause, along with another drink of brandy.

Price looked at her. "Whose child is that?" he asked as Emily kept glaring at Victoria.

"My maid's," she responded to him. "That will be all for the time being, Victoria. I have a private affair to discuss with Mr. Price."

Victoria caught Jefferson and picked him up. "Yes, Miss Emily."

She walked out of the room with Jefferson looking back over her shoulder at the Captain.

"He sure does have his eyes fastened on you," Emily said as she watched them walk out.

"It's the bale of white wool on my face. Some call it a beard," he laughed, but she did not.

"Mr. Price, I have something very important to tell you."

Gus and Georgy sat at the table in the kitchen, devouring Maggie's southern cuisine. Maggie sat in the corner and watched them eat, Gus in particular. Victoria was standing near the back door, also watching them, while Jefferson sat on the floor quietly, recovering from a recent spanking. Gus couldn't eat enough, or fast enough to satisfy his appetite, while the women looked on in amazement. Even Georgy watched in wonderment, as he looked across the table at Gus.

"Do you like it?" Victoria asked him.

Gus briefly paused, arching his back to stretch. "Ma'am, this food is so good I'm gone pray once more when I'm done!"

Laughter erupted in the room as Maggie smiled and mumbled.

"I know that's right. Maggie knows what she's doing." She sat rocking with her arms folded.

Victoria turned to Gus.

"Do you mind me asking what you all come down here for? Miss Emily said you all were Yankees."

Gus pulled back from the table for a moment to wipe his mouth and hands. He was trying to belch and relieve his stomach pangs but couldn't.

"Mr. Price and I came down here to get the body of his son. We have him on the wagon now and are about to make our way back to Connecticut. He was a soldier and fought for the North, the same as me. He was my best friend."

"Oh, I'm sorry. I hope you all have a safe journey back," she replied sympathetically.

"Thank you," he replied, and then turned to Maggie. "And thank you, mother!"

She smiled and nodded her head.

"When I found out at that you were coming to claim the remains of your son, I was intrigued. Then I learned of where the grave was located, and I became concerned."

Price became curious. "How so, Miss Emily? Please, make yourself plainly understood."

"Well, I must say that I am truly sorry that you came all this way with the intention of discovering your son's remains. The man you recovered cannot be your son, and I know this to be a fact."

Price sat back in his chair. "Tell me young lady, how do you know this?"

"The man who was buried there killed my father. He was caught in the act, chased down, and killed. They discovered that he was a savage Indian. I'm very sorry for you and the way this must make you feel. But I needed to tell you this."

Price thought for a moment. "I must admit, I was not aware of any of this. Mr. Clarke didn't mention anything at all. Perhaps he wasn't aware himself."

Price stood up from his chair, and walked a few paces away in contemplation, as Emily keenly watched him.

"Miss Walters, I'm sincerely sorry for your loss, but I must disagree with you. I believe I have my son, but I thank you for informing me, nonetheless. I'd also like to thank you for your hospitality. It's getting late and we need to set off."

She stood, a blank expression on her face. Her face contorted as she walked closer to him. "Is that all you have to say? You disagree with me? I just told you the man killed my father! Unarmed and without reason!" She shook her head. "Damn you!" She shouted, with her fists clenched by her side.

Captain Price was both surprised and offended but controlled himself. "Gus! We are leaving! Now!" He waited for a reply.

Gus opened the door from the kitchen and stepped into the room. "Yes, sir."

Price turned to leave, and Gus began to follow him as Emily shouted at him.

"You better not dare walk through my house! Go out the back!" She screamed and pointed to the kitchen door. Gus looked at Captain Price as he exited back through the kitchen. Price looked at her and lowered his tone.

"Just so you know. He was no savage, he was my son. He was a good man with a good heart. That's what I know."

She stepped closer to him with her hands on her hips. Maggie rushed out the kitchen door followed by Victoria and Georgy, to see what trouble Emily was kindling now. They were familiar with this behavior but hoped that this day would be different.

Jefferson scooted into the room past them, and then into the great room.

Emily became increasingly emboldened by her growing audience. "I know that you look like a fool. I just told you! You don't have your son!"

Price was about to respond but halted. He wanted no part of this argument. "Miss Emily, thank you again for your hospitality." He looked past her to Maggie and Victoria. "Ladies, thank you, too. Good evening to you all." He turned to leave, but nearly stumbled over Jefferson, who had been standing directly behind him. Price steadied himself on Jefferson and apologized. "Excuse me, little one," he said as he looked down.

Jefferson looked up at him, smiling. That was when Captain Price caught a glimpse of it.

He bent down and saw the cord hanging around Jefferson's neck and slowly pulled it out of his shirt, exposing what was attached. He had entirely forgotten about it, but now was breathless as he looked on it again. Jefferson pulled away from him and ran to his mother. Captain Price was in a daze and stared blankly, as he stood upright.

"Are you well?" Emily asked sarcastically. "You said your goodbyes. Or is there something else you're itching to say?"

Captain Price's demeanor had changed drastically. With his hands folded, he walked closer to her. "Miss Emily, the child has something around his neck which belonged to my son. Of this I am sure of. I need to know how he acquired it. Please," Price asked humbly, while Emily looked surprised.

"That green thing? I don't know! Why don't you ask his momma?" She turned to Victoria. "Well, where did he get it?" Victoria was speechless, as the events were moving so quickly that she couldn't grasp all of it. She was thinking to herself, *How could this be Shay's father? He was a white man!*

"I asked you a question, Victoria! What's wrong with you?" Emily yelled.

Victoria started to tremble as she picked up Jefferson in her arms.

"I found it," she said, while looking at the floor.

"There! Are you satisfied?" Emily barked.

Price looked at Victoria. "Miss Victoria, I will pay you whatever you deem fit to take back my son's possession."

She looked at him and Emily as her eyes began to water.

He took a step closer. "Please," he pleaded.

Emily interrupted him as she walked to Victoria. "We don't need your Yankee money! You can take it to hell!" She looked at Victoria. "Give him the damn trinket so we can be rid of him!"

Victoria remained motionless while still holding Jefferson in her arms and looking at Emily out of the corner of her eyes.

Emily became enraged. "I said give it to him!" She yelled, while seizing the amulet from around Jefferson's neck. She walked over to Price as Jefferson began screaming and reaching out after her. Emily walked up to Price and threw it down at his feet. "Now get the hell out of my house!" she hollered, as she walked back to the table.

Jefferson was undone. He was crying and screaming for what belonged to him. He attempted to wiggle out of Victoria's arms, but she lifted him up and held him tighter.

"Stop, Jefferson, please!"

She was wracked with guilt for allowing Emily to take her only reminder of Shay, but fearful of Emily's reprise if she resisted.

Captain Price picked up the amulet and looked at it. It was as remarkable as the day he first saw it around Shay's neck, glowing next to the light of the lantern. He was ever thankful and vowed that it would never leave his possession. He clutched it tightly and began to exit the house, which had become filled with the child's screams.

Price arrived at the front door and opened it but stopped as he was about to step through. He waited and listened. Amid the screams and cries, he faintly heard the word again and, *How could this be possible?* He became frantic and returned to the dining room and stared at Jefferson. Captain Price held the amulet by its cord. Jefferson cried out even more, fervently trying to break his mother's hold while reaching toward it.

"Say it again," Price said calmly amidst the tantrum.

Victoria became angry and scolded Price. "Stop teasing him! Just leave!"

Emily walked over to his other side. "You're insane! Get out now!" She yelled.

The house was in an uproar, but Price never broke his gaze with Jefferson and pressed him further. "Say it!" he yelled.

Emily hurried toward her deceased father's study. "I'm getting the shotgun! You're getting the hell out of here! One way or another!"

Price closed his eyes for a moment and calmly repeated the word which he had heard. *"Hu-di-eh."* Suddenly, Jefferson went silent. Emily halted, and there was absolute stillness in the room. Jefferson looked at Price curiously as Victoria looked at them both.

Price walked up to Jefferson and placed the amulet around his neck. Jefferson's disposition changed as he took hold of it and smiled. He looked into Captain Price's eyes and exclaimed, *"Hu-di-eh!"*

Maggie raised her head and arms to the ceiling while uttering praises, before bowing her head down and clasping her hands together.

Jefferson was fixated on Captain Price's beard and reached out and touched the bushy white mass of hair. Captain Price smiled, as a tear rolled down his cheek. He stood up and stepped back, looking around the room. He reached inside his jacket and produced a folded piece of paper.

"I have carried this letter with me everywhere since my son's death. I want you all to listen as I read it."

Emily marched over to him. "I want you to get out now! I swear I will shoot you if you don't leave!"

Maggie looked at her. "Emily, let the man say his piece."

Emily glared at her as if to say something, but just turned away.

Captain Price read aloud:

"Dear Father, I'm sorry that so much time has passed without you receiving word from me. I have been unable to write you, until this very hour. I miss you dearly, and hope all is well with you. I regret that I am not able to disclose my exact whereabouts or my present assignment, but you may be assured that I am doing my very best and serving with honor.

"I have learned much since leaving Connecticut, and I now fully understand many of the lessons of life that you taught me. I have witnessed war firsthand and learned that it brings more than death and destruction. It brings out the best, and the worst, in the people who are trapped under its dark cloud. I hope you can understand what I mean to say.

"However, not all my experiences have been bad. As surprising as it may be, I must tell you that I have met a lady. Through all the chaos and confusion, she brings me peace, as I do her. So much so, that when the war is over, I intend to ask her to come home with me to Connecticut. She is trapped in a wretched place where she does not belong. I know when you meet her that you will approve. Her beautiful eyes seem to speak a language that only my heart truly understands. You know that I've never been in love before, but this I must confess. I love her dearly!

"That is all for now. I will try to write again soon.

"P.S. I hope Gus is doing well, wherever he is. Please send my regards to his mother and father. With all my love, your son Shay."

As his name was spoken, Victoria collapsed to her knees while holding Jefferson. Maggie walked over and helped her to stand while she lowered Jefferson to the floor.

Captain Price looked at Emily. "*Hu-di-eh*. It means butterfly in the Chinese tongue. The child spoke the language of his father, my adopted son," he pointed toward Victoria. "Victoria is the woman in this letter, the love of his life," he spoke boldly as Emily listened, and then turned to her.

"Is it true?" she asked. Victoria was still crying and wouldn't answer.

"I asked you a question. Is it *true*?" Emily shouted.

Victoria wiped her eyes. "Yes. Yes, it's the truth."

Emily lost control of herself. "You are a lying whore! A no-good lying whore!" She screamed, as Victoria stood up to face her.

"No, I am not! I've only been with one man, and your Papa wasn't him! You want to know the truth? He tried to force himself on me that night, and that's when Shay killed him! I am not a whore!" Victoria screamed back at her.

Emily was speechless, but only for a moment. "I want you to get your rags, take that little bastard, and get out now!"

Victoria picked up Jefferson and walked toward the kitchen.

"Miss Victoria!" Price called out. She stopped and turned to him. "Take whatever you can carry and meet me out front. I want you and my grandson to come home with me."

She was in disbelief, but tearfully nodded and walked out, followed by Maggie and Georgy. Captain Price didn't bother looking in Emily's direction, there was no need to. He walked out the front door, where he met Gus, who was nervously pacing beside the wagon.

"Captain Price! Excuse my language, but what the hell is going on in there?"

Price grabbed him by his shoulders. "I would have never believed it, but it's a miracle."

He embraced Gus, who remained puzzled, but who also trusted Price's word. Gus patted him on the back, and Price began to explain the events which had just unfolded.

In the basement, Victoria rapidly gathered her belongings together. They didn't have much; in fact, they had next to nothing. Maggie came down the stairs to help her, and together they wrapped everything up into one large satchel. Georgy appeared, waving his arms in confusion, not understanding what was happening. He grabbed Victoria's arm as she looked at him. She patted her chest and pointed away. He shook his head in disagreement, while she nodded hers and hugged him tightly. She pulled back and put her hand on his cheek.

"You take care of yourself, Georgy," she sobbed. He began to cry himself, while groaning and pacing. Victoria turned to Maggie. "Mama Maggie, everything is happening so fast and I'm afraid!" Victoria remained still, looking to Maggie for guidance.

Maggie held Victoria's face in her hands. "I know you lost your mama a long-time past. But I been your mama and always gonna be your mama! You been shut up way too long child. Now, I declare it's time for you to spread your wings." She pulled Victoria closer, until their noses nearly touched. "Spread your wings and fly away! Far, far away!" she whispered. They embraced, as tears streamed down both of their faces. Maggie drew back. "You needs to go," Maggie said.

Victoria thought for a moment. "Mama Maggie, come with us! Mr. Price will surely take you. You're my mama. I'm going to ask him."

Maggie stopped her. "No. I won't go," she replied.

Victoria looked dismayed. "But why not? I need you!"

"True. But Emily needs me more." Maggie solemnly stepped back, and Victoria seemed dumbfounded. "Go on now, girl. When you get put, you make sure to get word back to me. Let me know all is well."

"Yes, ma'am." Victoria stood stoic for a moment. "I love you, mama!" she cried out, as they embraced again.

Maggie reached down and hugged Jefferson. "I knowed you was special, all along." She stood back up. "Y'all get now!"

Everyone walked upstairs and out the back door. Emily followed behind, harassing Victoria as she walked.

"Finally! Got rid of the rubbish! Oh, happy day!" Emily exclaimed provocatively. Victoria stopped walking, set the satchel down and faced her while holding Jefferson.

"Emily, we always been best friends. No matter how wrong you treated me, I still love you. I can't even stay mad at you. I'm sorry about everything bad that happened to you and everything bad that happened to me. But I'm not going to be afraid anymore, and you don't need to be either. We both don't deserve to be."

"Just get off my property!" Emily screamed.

Victoria sighed, picked up the satchel and walked toward the front of the house.

Emily watched her walk off and then went back inside.

Captain Price and Gus noticed Victoria with her arms full. Gus ran over to her and took the satchel and stowed it in the wagon. She walked up to Captain Price, still holding Jefferson. He smiled at them both.

"Are you ready to leave, Miss Victoria?"

"Yes, sir."

As he began helping her up onto the wagon, she stopped suddenly.

"My kitty! Mr. Price I need to find him. I'm sorry!" Victoria seemed nervous of his response.

"Don't fret, Gus will help you look for it. We will wait." Price helped her seat Jefferson, and then she began walking around the house with Gus following.

Emily poured a glass of whiskey as she watched Price through the front window sitting on the wagon next to Jefferson. She seethed with anger, as she felt her self-control slip away. She desperately wanted to get her father's shotgun and shoot Captain Price. She continued to drink until she saw Victoria walk past the window, holding her cat. Maggie walked into the room to watch them as well.

They all mounted the wagon, with Captain Price at the reins, Victoria sitting in the middle with Jefferson on her lap, and Gus riding shotgun. The wagon slowly began to move.

Anger and sadness enveloped Emily, as she stood watching the wagon travel toward the main road. Suddenly, she noticed a man running across the yard towards the road. It was Georgy with a satchel over his shoulder. He made it to the road and followed behind the wagon.

Emily chuckled. "Dumb fool! Where do you think you are going?" Emily said laughingly. "Nobody wants you."

The wagon continued on its way unhindered, but then stopped. It remained stopped long enough for Georgy to catch up to it and climb into the back. The wagon started to roll again onward down the road.

Emily threw her glass across the room at a mirror, breaking both, and fell back into her chair and began to cry. Maggie watched it all transpire and hobbled over to her. She rubbed her back gently as the tears fell from Emily's eyes.

Maggie whispered to her, "It's gone be all right. Let it go."

Emily looked up while crying.

"Let what go?" she snapped.

Maggie looked down at her with a piercing stare.

"Everything! Every bad thing inside hurting you! Just let it all go and start afresh!"

Emily collapsed against Maggie's chest and wept louder.

"That's it, child. Let it go. Momma is right here with you."

Maggie laid her hand on Emily's head and whispered a prayer for her sake, as Victoria and her family melted into the night.

THE END

Author's Notes

As stated within the preface, this book was inspired by true historical events and the people who participated in them during the American Civil War, while illuminating the lives of lesser known individuals. The acknowledgement of these particular people and events within the book was done with the intention of shedding light on certain myths and stereotypes many people hold to be true as it pertains to the African slave trade to the Americas, and the American Civil War in general.

Not many people imagine that there was a Chinese Union Army soldier like Shay, who was formally adopted by a merchant ship captain in China. Actually, there was not one, there were two, and very well documented. Edward Day Cohota and Joseph Pierce. As their real-life stories are mirrored in this book, so are the men who adopted them.

Captain Price is one such character. In exploring the dynamics of their lives, the reader has an opportunity to ponder the implications of such an adoption, specifically the stereotypes of Caucasian males living during the 1800s. It seems improbable to some, that the selfless and charitable act of adopting an orphan of a socially non-inclusive race would be socially acceptable and occur, but it did at least twice. It is a prime example of an individual who chooses to be obligated to, and driven by, compassion rather than conform to the social prejudicial norms of his society.

Victoria was inspired by my 4th great-grandmother, known as Mary Clark, who allegedly was the second generation of my African ancestors who endured slavery, lived and worked on a plantation in Alabama, and bore three sons from a renowned colonel and surgeon of the Confederate States Army.

Little Jefferson was inspired by my 3rd great-grandfather, Jefferson Clark, the bi-racial son of Mary. I display photographs of them both at my residence, taken during their elder years. They were a great inspiration in the development and the acknowledgement of the vision which compelled me to undertake this literary work.

Levi Holloway Naron or "Chickasaw" is a lesser known historical figure, but one who's life story is remarkable on many levels. Civil War historians who read this book will note that the fictitious "Chickasaw" and his timeline near the end of the war, fits perfectly with the entries of his biography, including him checking on one of his scouts and learning the fate of another. That particular scout inspired the character of Hardy.

These are only a few examples of lesser-known historical facts in the book, which unpretentiously incorporates many other such uncommon or lesser-known details of the time period. I have attempted to explore a variety of topics within various subplots, such as racism, prejudice, religion, belief, class, sexual assault, and nationalism. I was determined to examine the intangibles of the human heart through situational character interactions, such as love, hate, forgiveness, empathy, resentment, guilt, and pride.

Lastly, I have written one climactic ending which can be interpreted and justifiably argued by a reader as several possible endings, regardless of that reader's current belief system and perspective. Whether it be atheism, agnosticism, Christianity, Islam, Judaism, Hinduism, Buddhism, science, or metaphysics, the reader's belief system is not challenged, and no supposition is precluded from possibility. My desire is that this work will be received in the spirit in which it was written, that being love.

C.J. Heigelmann

ABOUT THE AUTHOR

Strongly influenced by the works of Homer, Hemingway, Tolkien, Twain, Emerson, Alice Walker, and Whitman, C.J. Heigelmann fluently expresses his work through a unique style in the classic form of innocence and eloquence, balanced by raw truth and grit without pretention. In 2011, he made the decision to write his first novel and embarked on two years of historical and cultural research for the foundation of his epic work.

The first of his novels, *An Uncommon Folk Rhapsody* is an example of C.J. Heigelmann's pursuit of perfecting the "Written Art of Storytelling," by using strong visuals, emotions, and narrations to substitute for the absence of a human "Storyteller." He is currently an aspiring novelist, media content creator, and is employed on the managerial staff with a major university in South Carolina. His creative passion and impetus derive from his belief that, "Amor Vincit Omnia," or more simply put, "Love conquers all."

For more information on C.J. Heigelmann visit
www.cjheigelmann.com

Made in United States
North Haven, CT
18 April 2023

35544267R10202